SWITCHBLADE

What Reviewers Say About Carsen Taite's Work

It Should be a Crime

"Taite also practices criminal law and she weaves her insider knowledge of the criminal justice system into the love story seamlessly and with excellent timing."—*Curve Magazine*

"This [*It Should be a Crime*] is just Taite's second novel…, but it's as if she has bookshelves full of bestsellers under her belt." —*Gay List Daily*

Do Not Disturb

"Taite's tale of sexual tension is entertaining in itself, but a number of secondary characters…add substantial color to romantic inevitability"—Richard Labonte, *Book Marks*

Nothing but the Truth

"Author Taite is really a Dallas defense attorney herself, and it's obvious her viewpoint adds considerable realism to her story, making it especially riveting as a mystery. I give it four stars out of five."—Bob Lind, *Echo Magazine*

"As a criminal defense attorney in Dallas, Texas, Carsen Taite knows her way around the court house. …*Nothing But the Truth* is an enjoyable mystery with some hot romance thrown in."—*Just About Write*

"Taite has written an excellent courtroom drama with two interesting women leading the cast of characters. Taite herself is a practicing defense attorney, and her courtroom scenes are clearly based on real knowledge. This should be another winner for Taite."—*Lambda Literary*

The Best Defense

"Real Life defense attorney Carsen Taite polishes her fifth work of lesbian fiction, *The Best Defense*, with the realism she daily encounters in the office and in the courts. And that polish is something that makes *The Best Defense* shine as an excellent read."—*Out & About Newspaper*

Slingshot

"The mean streets of lesbian literature finally have the hard boiled bounty hunter they deserve. It's a slingshot of a ride, bad guys and hot women rolled into one page turning package. I'm looking forward to Luca Bennett's next adventure."—J. M. Redmann, author of the Micky Knight mystery series

Battle Axe

"This second book is satisfying, substantial, and slick. Plus, it has heart and love coupled with Luca's array of weapons and a bad-ass verbal repertoire...I cannot imagine anyone not having a great time riding shotgun through all of Luca's escapades. I recommend hopping on Luca's band wagon and having a blast."—*Rainbow Book Reviews*

Beyond Innocence

"Taite keeps you guessing with delicious delay until the very last minute...Taite's time in the courtroom lends *Beyond Innocence*, a terrific verisimilitude someone not in the profession couldn't impart. And damned if she doesn't make practicing law interesting."—*Out in Print*

"As you would expect, sparks and legal writs fly. What I liked about this book were the shades of grey (no, not the smutty Shades of Grey)—both in the relationship as well as the cases."—*C-spot Reviews*

Rush

"A simply beautiful interplay of police procedural magic, murder, FBI presence, misguided protective cover-ups, and a superheated love affair...a Gold Star from me and major encouragement for all readers to dive right in and consume this story with gusto!" —*Rainbow Book Reviews*

By the Author

Truelesbianlove.com

It Should be a Crime

Do Not Disturb

Nothing but the Truth

The Best Defense

Beyond Innocence

Rush

The Luca Bennett Mystery Series:

Slingshot

Battle Axe

Switchblade

SWITCHBLADE

by
Carsen Taite

2014

SWITCHBLADE
© 2014 BY CARSEN TAITE. ALL RIGHTS RESERVED.

ISBN 13: 978-1-62639-058-4

THIS TRADE PAPERBACK ORIGINAL IS PUBLISHED BY
BOLD STROKES BOOKS, INC.
P.O. BOX 249
VALLEY FALLS, NY 12185

FIRST EDITION: MAY 2014

CREDITS
EDITOR: CINDY CRESAP
PRODUCTION DESIGN: SUSAN RAMUNDO
COVER DESIGN BY SHERI (GRAPHICARTIST2020@HOTMAIL.COM)

Acknowledgments

This journey with Luca has been a fun ride and, while I can't pick a favorite out of my book children, I have a special fondness for scruffy Luca and her carefree ways. Thanks to everyone who helped me along the way. Fellow authors VK Powell, Ashley Bartlett, and my wife, Lainey—your careful eyes and valuable insights kept me on track, and these stories are better because of you.

Special thanks to Cindy Cresap, a fabulous editor with a wicked sense of humor.

Sheri, thanks for another excellent cover. Thanks to Len Barot and everyone else at Bold Strokes Books—you all make the business of writing fun.

Thanks to all the readers who buy my books, show up at events, and write to encourage me to keep telling stories. These books are for you.

Dedication

To Lainey, with all my love.
Couldn't do this without you. Wouldn't want to.

CHAPTER ONE

*D**early beloved, we are gathered here today...*
     I started to itch the minute the words left the preacher's lips. Stupid suit, stupid tie, and all the other suffocating layers. The beauty of being a bounty hunter meant I spent most of my days sporting T-shirts, jeans, and boots. Standing in front of all these people in a stiff tuxedo was definitely one of the most uncomfortable situations of my life.

...take her to be your constant friend, your faithful partner, your love, from this day forward...
     The words started to sink in, and suddenly, the suit was the least of my worries. This was really final shit. When that profound thought sunk in, I realized the itch didn't have anything to do with how many clothes I was wearing. I glanced at Jess, but her eyes were locked on the preacher. She'd always been a stickler for authority, even now when she was showing leg instead of sporting a badge and a gun. No way was she wearing a gun under that dress. The idea almost made me forget my current distress. Jess didn't look distressed at all. Was she buying into this shit? Forever, love, fidelity? Did I really know her?

...in sickness and in health, good times and bad, in joy as well as sorrow...
     Well, now he was just piling it on. No one was living up to this litany of virtue. Why does anyone put themselves through this? Why was I the only one not smiling?

...for all the days of your lives.

The itch was powerful now. More powerful than my promise to stand up here and do my part. I started looking for exits. Big crowd, but I was sure I could beat a path to the door. I took one step to the side, but a soft voice and two simple words froze me in my tracks.

I do.

Jess wasn't looking at the preacher now. The invincible Jessica Chance, who'd stepped in front of a bullet meant for me just a few weeks ago, now had tears in her eyes, and my knees buckled at the sight of her vulnerability. I wasn't going anywhere.

What happened next was inevitable and expected, and I struggled to keep my own eyes from welling up as I watched my little brother kiss his bride.

❖

A dozen fake posed family pictures later, I finally found Jess at the bar. If my brother, Mark, had told me about the Olan Mills part of the festivities, I never would've signed on. Tall women in tuxes are the photographer's nightmare. Where should she stand to keep from blocking the shorter guys? Why isn't she with the bridal party instead of with the groom's contingent? I heard the silent questions with every tsk from the guy behind the camera.

Being best man was a hard job. Thankfully, I only had one more task, but I'd need a stiff drink to get through it. I slid up behind Jess. "Buy you a drink?"

"It's an open bar."

You'd have to know her as well as I did to catch the annoyance in her tone, but it was there, and I knew why. I couldn't think about that right now. Not before the toast. I'd practiced what I planned to say about a dozen times, but what had seemed difficult in jeans and a T-shirt, loomed insurmountable now that I was wearing a penguin suit. And then there was the thing Jess was mad about. Hell, I wasn't happy about it either, but what was I supposed to do? A beautiful woman shows up on my porch asking for favors and I'm supposed to turn her away?

Except this wasn't just any beautiful woman. It was Ronnie Moreno, a hot Latina lawyer with whom I'd spent most of last summer. Naked. Our time together had been marred by lies, crime, and a shooting, but I'd survived and, when she took a job at a big deal law firm in D.C., I'd filed away the memories in the "that was fun, but it's time to move on" drawer of my mind.

Now she was back, stressed and needy. The last woman who'd shown up on my doorstep looking for favors had led me down a rabbit hole. I wasn't eager for a repeat performance. But whatever it was that interested me in Ronnie in the first place hadn't totally vanished. All it took was her face at my door to flood my head with indecision, which should be a clue for me to run in the opposite direction.

Seconds before she'd knocked, Jess had her arms around me, and I had words I'd never spoken out loud on the verge of falling from my lips. Talk about saved by the bell, but I wasn't sure which of us had been saved by Ronnie's timing. I'd told Ronnie to bug off for the night, and she had, but not before pressing a card in my hand. On the back she'd written her number and a hotel address in flowing script. I hadn't thrown it away.

"Want to hear my toast?" I asked Jess, trying to keep my tone nonchalant, but knowing she would hear the fear.

"Save your energy for the big moment." She ordered us a couple of beers and handed me one. "Don't drink all of this before it's time." She stared at me for a moment and then softened her tone. "And I'm sure it's great."

She was the only one. "Have you seen my dad?"

She glanced around the room and nodded. "He's over at the other bar with Maggie. Don't worry so much. It looks like she's got him well in hand."

As worried as I was about ruining my brother's big day with a flop of a toast, I was more worried about Dad drinking himself into a frenzy or a stupor. Wasn't sure which would be worse. My mother had already filled the role of monster-in-law with her over-the-top micromanaging ways. Mark didn't need more trouble before he and his lovely bride were able to escape to a resort where no family could find them.

I realized some of my jitters had to do with the air between Jess and me, but I didn't really know what to do about it. Talking about feelings was so not my thing, but I waded in anyway in the hope it might clear the air. "Jess, about earlier—"

She flashed a big, bright smile, and I assumed she was going to wave it off. I couldn't have been more wrong. "Earlier? When the skank from your past showed up at your door? What, Luca? What about earlier?"

Her tone was even, cool, and simple, but I read volumes beneath the words. She was pissed. Real pissed. Wish I knew what that meant. Was she jealous or just annoyed? Could she possibly have been feeling what I had? Had we both been teetering on the edge of something more? If so, what were we going to do about it?

"And now for the toast from the best man, er, woman!"

If I were closer to the DJ, I would've kicked him in the groin. Wasn't sure which was worse: giving a toast in front of several hundred strangers or analyzing my relationship with Jessica Chance. As the guy in the maroon tux shoved a mike in front of my face, I resigned myself to the fate of having to do both.

CHAPTER TWO

Y ou coming in?" I tried not to slur my words, but I knew it was pointless. Post toast, I'd indulged in the open bar like the guest they always warn you about. Champagne, beer, shots of tequila. They'd all tasted great at the time, but right now, they were churning in my belly like an angry wave. Jess had parked her car in front of my apartment several minutes ago, but neither one of us had made a move. I wasn't sure if I could. I wanted to. I had lots of moves I wanted to make. I might be a mess, but Jess looked as hot now in her low-cut dress as she had when she'd picked me up for the wedding hours ago.

"You're wasted."

"I've been wasted before." It was the solid truth, but no matter how wasted I was, I got her point. I may not be the expert when it comes to relationships, but I knew ours had taken a turn that afternoon, and dealing with it had to be done in a sober moment. This wasn't it.

"Go inside, Luca. If you can't make it on your own, I'll help you to the door."

I heard the soft undercurrent, but it didn't contain any promises beyond the assistance she'd offered. I wanted her to help me inside, help me undress, and then make love to me like always, as if the words I'd almost spoken hours earlier were nothing between us. But like a petulant child, I chose to engage with anger instead of asking for what I wanted. "I don't need your help."

"Okay, are you planning to sit in the car all night?"

Seemed like a good alternative since she wasn't offering up anything more, and I'd be damned if I was going to ask. No, she had to make the first move. I made a show of reaching for the door handle and cracking the door. "Don't worry. I'm leaving. Sorry you had to endure a whole evening with me." I turned away as I spoke the words, not wanting to witness their effect fall short.

I sighed as I felt her hand on my shoulder, but my relief was short-lived when she spoke. "You need to get your shit together or you're going to be alone for the rest of your life."

She wasn't coming upstairs. Not tonight anyway. Time to stop deluding myself and move on. Dad, Mark, even my mother had coupled up, and I'd fallen into the trap of thinking I should too. Well, that was a mistake easily remedied. I shrugged off her hand and stepped out of the car, grabbing onto the roof for balance as I fired back a retort worthy of a five-year-old. "Maybe being alone is exactly what I had in mind."

I caught a glimpse of her face as I stumbled away, but I didn't let the hurt I saw stop me from leaving.

❖

I woke the next day to light pouring into my bedroom window. I felt like I'd been tied to the bed, and when I glanced down at the beer-stained tuxedo shirt still covering my long frame, I realized I wasn't getting my deposit back. One more reason to hate this day. I comforted myself with thoughts about all the others who were feeling the aftereffects of last night. My dad was probably nursing his own hangover. My mother was likely still bitching to the man I knew only as husband number four about all the things she thought went wrong with the ceremony. Mark and Linda were probably well on their way to the resort in Belize not caring in the least about the trail of debris they'd left in their wake. Weddings suck for those who are left behind.

I reached over to my cell phone to check the time. Noon. That wasn't too bad. Wasn't like I had anything to do. I'd just finished rounding up a slew of jumpers for my go-to bondsman, Hardin Jones, and I wouldn't get any new work from him until Monday at the earliest. I scrolled through the missed calls and counted half a dozen from the number I now knew was Ronnie. The lady was nothing if not persistent. I tossed the phone back onto the nightstand and rolled over, pulling the covers over my head. Not like I could do any more damage to the tux at this point.

I'd just drifted back to sleep when a loud pounding at the door woke me. I wasn't expecting company, but Jess had a tendency to show up whenever she wanted. Despite my feigned nonchalance the night before, I regretted the way we parted company. I strode, barefoot, to the door in my untucked, crumpled shirt and tuxedo pants. Sometime between the ceremony and this morning, I'd lost my cufflinks and a few buttons, but I cared more about seeing her than how I looked. I swung the door wide.

Ronnie Moreno wore a red dress, low-cut neckline, and high, high heels. She looked better than she ever had. I blinked, mostly at the bright light, but partly to make sure my eyes weren't messing with me. When she spoke, the bubble burst.

"You get a job as a butler?"

She was real all right, and she was the last person I wanted to see. "Very funny. I'm just getting my money's worth out of this rag before I have to return it."

She wrinkled her nose. "You'll probably have to pay them to take it back. Why don't you go change into something more comfortable and then we can talk?" She didn't wait for a response before she pushed her way into my apartment and started toward the kitchen. I reached for her arm to stop her, but when I saw the steaming cup of coffee in her hand, I let her pass.

"Give me that and we can talk about anything you want."

"Hot and dark. It's all yours."

I took the coffee from her hand but ignored the remark. She didn't own me off just one cup, but I took a sip and groaned. When she settled onto my couch, I was unable to protest. She'd earned a few minutes of my time. "Tell me what you want."

"Sit down. It's complicated."

I sat, not because she told me to, but because I wasn't awake enough to stand. "Spill."

"You remember my brother, Jorge?"

"The cop?"

"That's the one."

"Nice guy." I let my tone say it all. I didn't care for the guy. He'd been an ass when I'd gone out with his sister, and I didn't expect much had changed since I'd last seen him. "What's up?"

"He's in trouble."

"Boys will be boys."

"Serious trouble." Ronnie leaned in as she delivered her words, her expression fierce, like she could frown her way into making me care about the douche she was related to.

"Okay, so he's in serious trouble. Why aren't you tapping one of his cop buddies to help him out?" I was only mildly curious, but her reaction to my suggestion provoked a visceral reaction.

"No fucking way. Those so-called buddies are what got him into trouble in the first place."

And that explained why she'd shown up on my doorstep. I'd never told her my story, but it wasn't a secret. She must've heard something—probably from her brother—that made her think I'd be sympathetic to an outsider on the force. Well, she was wrong. The closest connection to the Dallas Police Department I had was when Jess wound up naked in my bed. "Sounds like he needs a lawyer. Know any good ones?"

"Funny. We need some help."

"You need to go elsewhere. Unless your brother's on the lam and someone's going to pay me to hunt him down, there's nothing I can do for you." I stood up. Time to change out of these clothes and wash away the memory of last night's train wreck.

Ronnie didn't get the hint, so I urged her along. "I have stuff to do. You should go."

"Luca." Her voice shook. "I need you."

Her words were the perfect trigger to shut me down. "No, babe. Nobody needs me." I wasn't even curious enough to ask questions.

All I wanted was for her to leave. Now. I'd had my coffee, and there was nothing else she could do for me.

I walked to the door and waited with my hand on the knob. An uncomfortable amount of silence later, she rummaged in her purse, pulled out a bundle of papers, and stood. As she walked toward me, I smelled a whiff of her familiar perfume, a memory I thought I'd banished from my brain. When she drew closer, I saw the tiny beauty mark near her ear. I'd kissed that sensitive spot more times than I could count. When she placed a hand on my chest, I struggled not to gasp. I remembered all the times she'd climbed on top and ridden me to orgasm, and I gave in to a small shudder as she whispered in my ear, "I'm not nobody."

The light heat of her breath had barely dissipated when I felt her gently push the papers into my hands. Within seconds, she was gone. I stared at the open door. Torn. I don't have much willpower when it comes to beautiful women, no matter how much crap they send my way. A few long strides and I could catch her, pull her back, and wrest back the control she'd just robbed.

I waited out my resistance and then shut the door. Speaking of crap, I had an armful of papers I assumed Ronnie had left to rev my curiosity. I tossed them on the kitchen counter and walked away. She didn't have any right to assume she could jet back to Dallas and get me to do her bidding. Last time I'd done a favor for her, she'd lied every step of the way and nearly gotten us both killed. She could find someone else to do her dirty work. I wasn't buying.

CHAPTER THREE

Monday morning came too soon. When the first rays of sunlight poked past my closed eyelids, I covered my face with a pillow and tried to fall back asleep. Lasted a little while, but then the memory of basic life necessities like food, beer, and gas for my Bronco invaded my rest. I'd spent the better part of my last chunk of earnings on stuff for Mark's wedding, and I needed to earn some more cash if I was going to fund my personal pyramid of needs.

I pulled on sweats and running shoes, grabbed a five from the last of my stash, and headed out the door for a pseudo run to the corner store for a cup of black coffee to start my day. I must be getting old because it usually only took me a day to recover from a massive drinking binge, but two days out and I still felt the ache of alcohol struggling to run its course. Once Ronnie had left yesterday, I returned to bed and spent the rest of the day there. Now I was starving and caffeine deprived. Luckily, I had enough cash to net a cup of coffee, two glazed donuts, and a hot dog.

So much for the run. I stood outside the store, wolfed down my purchases, and started to feel human.

Home again, I showered and then dug through my closet until I found a lone clean T-shirt and an only worn once pair of jeans. After stuffing the smelly tux in the bag it came in, I headed for the door. As I was leaving, I spied the papers Ronnie had left yesterday morning. Tempted to throw them in the trash, I decided against the effort and headed out to my aging Bronco, hoping it had more gas in the tank than I remembered.

Hardin Jones Bail Bond Agency was down the street from the Dallas County Jail and criminal courthouse, perfectly situated for friends and relatives as they looked for a friendly face when their loved ones ran afoul of the law. For a percentage of the bond amount set by the judge, Hardin would spring the loved one out of jail and guarantee their appearance for court dates. In exchange, the accused would have to check in with him on a regular basis, but invariably, some went missing because they couldn't obey Hardin's rules any better than they could obey the law. That's where I came in. If Hardin turned in the fugitive, he wouldn't owe the court any money, so he paid me a percentage of what he stood to lose and I tracked these deadbeats down. I got occasional work from other agencies, and even some lawyers who wrote their bonds—that was how I'd met Ronnie—but Hardin's agency was my main source of business. I was hoping he had some work this morning.

I pushed through the door of the only slightly remodeled former gas station and waved at the chain-smoking gatekeeper. Sally Jesse ran the front office, dealing with all the sureties who came in waving cash, begging for bonds to get their loved ones out of jail. Right now, she had an entire family, including three drooling toddlers, sitting in front of her desk. The presumed mother of the brood was bawling while her stern-looking man friend filled out forms on a clipboard. I raised my eyebrows at Sally, and she pointed to the back.

Hardin was in his office, scuffed boots propped on his massive desk. He wore a John Deere cap even though he was inside. Come to think of it, I'd never seen him without it. He spit into a cup and cleared his throat. "Hey, Luca, whatcha up to?"

"Nothing, which is kind of a problem. Got any work?" I hadn't been by in a few weeks. Between nursing Jess back to health and all the wedding craziness, I hadn't had the energy to take on any cases. But now that I was out of food, beer, and gasoline, I didn't have a choice.

He reached into one of the desk drawers and pulled out a couple of files. "Got a couple. Nothing big. Been a little slow lately. Holidays."

He didn't have to say more. Law enforcement generally came to a screeching halt this time of year. Cops, prosecutors, and judges, all loaded up with lots of vacation time they needed to use by the end of the year, tended to take off work in droves, leaving the courthouse a dead zone between Thanksgiving and New Year's. Less court dates meant less bond jumpers. Perfect.

If I found both these deadbeats, I wouldn't come out much ahead, but I might be able to leverage my pay into bigger winnings. I shook off the idea. Normally, I'd take a small payout like this and buy in to a card game to try for something bigger, but my regular gaming house had recently experienced a bout of bad luck and had shut down for the season. Driving to Oklahoma to the casino would require more gas than I wanted to spend. If I caught both these jumpers, I could eat or pay rent, but not both. I already knew which thing would go by the wayside. Hopefully, my landlord, Old Man Withers, would go visit his daughter in Florida again this year, and I could avoid him until crime season picked back up.

As I left his office, a nagging thought turned me back. "Hey, Hardin, you heard any scoop about a cop getting into trouble? Jorge Moreno, Miguel Moreno's nephew?"

He cocked his head and worked the wad in his mouth over to one jaw. "Can't say that I have, but Miguel's doing time with the feds, so probably the apple doesn't fall far from the tree. Why are you interested?"

"Just heard a rumor. No big deal."

"I'll keep an ear out. Let you know if I hear anything."

If there was anything to hear, he'd let me know. I left Hardin to his chew and headed back to my ride. My nineteen ninety Bronco still served me well, thank God. I didn't need a lot of newfangled equipment for my job, but wheels were essential. In deference to progress, I carried an iPhone and owned a laptop, for which I snagged Internet service from my next-door neighbor's not well protected Wi-Fi, but most of what I do involves tracking down folks the old-fashioned way—knocking on doors, spying in windows, and the occasional breaking and entering. My only other equipment is a small arsenal of weapons, including a long Colt forty-five I'd carried since I left the force.

I steered the Bronco back toward home and considered my next move. The hot dog and donuts from this morning had long since stopped fueling my day. Instead of pulling into my apartment complex, I opted to turn into the bar a few blocks down. Maggie's had been my go-to place for beer and food for years, mostly because Maggie let me run a tab. Now that she was dating my father, I occasionally suffered pangs of guilt for accepting food and drink I might never be able to pay off, but I got over it every time I thought about other things I could spend my well-earned funds on.

It was kind of early for lunch, and the place was deserted. I took a seat at the bar and spread out the files Hardin had given me while I waited for someone to appear and notice they had a new customer. The first case was Jerry Etheridge. Jerry's crime was driving while intoxicated, first offense. I was surprised he'd jumped bond since the worst thing that usually happens on DWI cases is probation. Since the judge could hold him without bond for missing his court date, he'd do more time for avoiding court than he would if he'd been found guilty of the crime. Of course, folks in trouble don't always think rationally, a fact I could attest to from my own experience.

Jerry should be fairly easy to catch. The file listed his employer as a local bank, and his wife signed for his bond. Likely they had a little three bedroom, two bath in the suburbs. Maybe even a dog and child. I'd eat lunch and head on over to pick him up.

"You still set on eating food that's bad for you?"

I looked up from the file into Maggie Flynn's frowning face. She was dressed fairly tame for her, in a solid purple dress and big gold earrings that flounced through her wavy red hair. I was used to seeing her in crazy, mismatched patterns that hurt my eyes. She'd probably worn out her varsity wardrobe with all the wedding activities over the last week. Her pointed question was an attempt to goad me into the same healthy eating she'd bullied my father to take on since they'd started dating. What she didn't know was he snuck beer and grease at every given opportunity. Unlike my father, I wasn't much into hiding my vices. "Cheeseburger and fries. You can put lettuce and tomato on the burger if that makes you feel any better."

She slid a draft beer my way, shouted my order to the kitchen, and then slid onto the stool next to me. "You back at work?"

"Gotta eat."

"True. How's your gal?"

"Gal?" I knew she was talking about Jess, but I didn't feel like telling her I didn't have a clue. It kinda gnawed at me that Jess hadn't called since she'd dumped me at my place after the wedding. What if I'd died from alcohol poisoning? What if I'd tripped trying to get into my apartment and was wasting away on the stoop? Guess she didn't give a shit, and if she didn't, neither should I. I knew my reaction was less than adult. I was the one who'd gotten sloshed and ruined any chance we had at making up after Ronnie showed up on my doorstep.

Jess didn't like Ronnie, and I couldn't say I blamed her. There was the whole cops don't like criminal defense attorneys thing. Throw in the fact Ronnie skated real close to the edge of the law, and Jess had quickly decided Ronnie wasn't right for me. What I didn't know was whether her reaction was that of a jealous lover or a patronizing friend. If Jess wasn't speaking to me, guess I'd never find out. I thought about the stack of papers Ronnie had left on my kitchen counter, papers I'd intended to ignore, and I realized it wasn't just curiosity that had prompted me to ask Hardin about them. Maybe I would poke around to find out what was going on with Jorge Moreno. When Jess found out I was looking into a fellow cop, a Moreno no less, that would get a rise out of her. In the meantime, my casual response to Maggie's question had gotten a rise of its own.

"Luca, you need to settle down. Look at your brother. Mark's a nice boy and he's found a nice girl. Nice wedding, nice honeymoon, nice life. You could have all that."

I almost spit my beer across the bar as I snorted with laughter. Nice wasn't a word anyone would use to describe me, and I liked it that way, but trying to convince Maggie otherwise was a wasted enterprise. "Do you think my burger might be ready?"

She huffed off, and I knew I hadn't heard the last of her nagging. Any day now I expected her to announce she and my father were getting married. Once the bug hits, it doesn't let go. All the more reason for me to steer clear of Jess. After all, she'd practically sobbed like a baby at Mark's wedding. Jess was the last person I expected to be all sentimental over some stupid vows. Her reaction shook my confidence in the universe. Yeah, I'd gotten a little choked up too, but I wrote it off more to fear than mush.

File number two was another small-time crime. The unimaginative Susie Kemper was on probation for shoplifting when she'd picked up a new case for the exact same thing. Her attorney had talked the judge into setting a bond on the new case, but when the probation officer loaded her up with conditions on the first one, she decided to skip out. Another case of dumb judgment. If I was facing hard time, I might skip out on court dates, but it looked like all she had to do was toe the line and she would've been right back on probation. I shook my head, but didn't spend a lot of time mourning Susie's thick skull. Stupid people kept me fed.

Maggie dropped a plate of grease and comfort in front of me and pointed at my empty beer mug. I nodded, but vowed that would be my last for the day. As tempting as it was to drink away the afternoon, I decided to be a productive citizen. I'd round up these two, collect my fee, and be home in time to celebrate with a six-pack in front of the Mavericks game if my TV antenna was working. I live the high life.

CHAPTER FOUR

Jerry Etheridge's house was exactly as I suspected. Moderate, in a decent neighborhood, and dead quiet. The whole neighborhood was quiet, too quiet for me to take a stroll down the street and sneak a look into his garage to see if his car was there. Even if his car was there, didn't mean he was. He wasn't supposed to be driving without an ignition interlock device, a not as fancy as it sounds thingie that you have to blow into before you can start the car to prove you haven't been drinking. The device then beeps at you during your drive to remind you to keep blowing, as if blowing into a tube while driving a moving vehicle is less dangerous than the DWI you got arrested for in the first place. Court records showed he either hadn't gotten the device installed, or hadn't bothered to turn in the paperwork if he had. I was betting on the former. His wife drove a Smart car, but I'd already swung by her job at a local insurance agency, and the bright yellow go-cart was parked out front. Didn't look like two regular-sized folks could've fit in that tiny ride. I'd lay all the money I didn't have that Jerry was in the house.

I wasn't supposed to break into people's homes, and I sure wasn't supposed to be carrying a gun if I did. Bounty hunters are licensed private investigators. Key word: licensed. If I got caught breaking the rules I could lose my license and then most bonding companies wouldn't want to work with me. It had happened before, more times than I could count, but breaking the rules was kind of a necessity in my line of business. I rarely had to fire my gun since flashing the big piece was usually enough to tame any desire to fight back, but no way was I going to approach some of these idiots without one. The possible payout from Jerry's little case didn't seem worth risking a show of force. Yet.

An hour later, I called it. There hadn't been a single sign of life from the Etheridge house, and the beers I'd had at lunch were taking their toll. I drove back home and considered my options, finally deciding to try Jerry again in the morning before his wife left for work. I still had a couple of hours of daylight so I resisted the pull of my couch and drove to jumper number two, Susie Kemper's neck of the woods, which couldn't have been more different from Jerry's neighborhood. The minute I pulled up in front of the ratty apartment complex, I understood why she skipped out. Poor people weren't cut out for probation. Probation sounds easy and all, but for a lot of folks it's way harder than a couple of weeks in jail, which is the most a shoplifter can usually expect, even for the second offense. After you enter your plea, you get a long list of conditions. Take this class, do this community service, pay this fine, pay this fee. And you have to pay for the privilege of the classes and community service, not to mention court costs. Judges will tell you they'll never violate you for not making payments, but every time you turn around, someone's holding out their hand and you start to feel the pressure. When you don't have enough money to buy groceries, you make a hard choice. In Susie's case, it was a dumb choice, since instead of talking to someone about her problem, she just lit out. I almost felt sorry for her, but then I thought about all the bills I had to pay and how she was my best chance at a paycheck.

I found apartment 204 easily and figured I'd play this one straight. I'd seen her picture, and no way was she going to outrun or outfight me. What I hadn't considered was the wild fit of barking I heard when I knocked on the door. Ferocious, kill you now, eat you later kind of barking. I'm not scared of much, but after I'd seen a junkyard dog eat his way through a guy's leg years ago, big, burly dogs commanded all my respect. I looked over my shoulder to see if anyone would notice if I slunk quietly away. Not a soul in sight, but before I could make my getaway, the door creaked open and a pixie face poked out.

"Not buyin'," Susie announced.

I scoured the door opening for signs of the beast. Nothing. No way could I leave now. "Not selling." I placed a hand on the door to keep her from closing it in response to my next words. "I work for Hardin—"

Barely got the words out before we were both struggling for control of the door. "Get out," she yelled.

"You'll have to come with me to get things sorted out. I'm not leaving until you do."

Her size completely fooled me. She wasn't budging, and Fido the Terrible was cheering her on in his best "I'm going to tear you to shreds" voice. For a second, I considered letting go of the door and taking off. Only thoughts of my next meal and a few shards of self-respect kept me from running. I shouldered into the door and finally managed to make some headway by grabbing her hair. She yelped and let go of the door. I pushed it open cautiously. Still no sign of the dog, but as insurance, I tightened my hold on her scalp.

"Let go of me, bitch!"

"Call off your dog and I will."

I watched her expression change from defiance to resignation as she considered her options. Finally, she said, "Jellybean, down."

Good thing I hadn't run. I'd never in a million years respect myself for running from a dog named Jellybean. I pushed farther into the apartment and finally laid eyes on the beast. A gorgeous Husky with brilliant blue eyes rolled around on the floor making odd noises that sounded suspiciously like words. In person, Jellybean inspired absolutely no fear in me. "What's wrong with him?"

"He wants you to rub his belly."

I wasn't falling for that. If I put my hand within reach, he would surely tear it off. "He's your dog. You rub his belly."

She responded by pointing at my hand, which still clutched her hair. I let go and she bent to the floor and began petting the monster. He responded with more of his special language. All signs of aggression were gone, and he was probably laughing at my fear. I didn't know jack about dogs, but this one seemed like an expensive breed, not the kind owned by a two-bit criminal who could barely make ends meet. "Where'd you get him?"

"Found him. Last week. He was eating out of the trash. Someone must've let him go. He just followed me home. Asked around, but no one knew where he was from, so I let him stay. That's why I missed court. I was taking care of him."

A likely story. No doubt she was softening me up to keep me from bringing her in. Sorry, Judge, I can't come to court because the dog *is* my homework. Not likely. I looked around the place. The inside was as unkempt as the outside. She couldn't afford to keep a dog, and what the hell was she going to do with it when she wound up finishing out her time in jail? Jellybean—stupid name—would be better off in a shelter. Dog that good-looking would get adopted in no time.

"How did you know his name?"

"He didn't come with a name, so I had to make one up."

Of course you did. "I have to take you in." Better to say it up front.

To her credit, she took it like a champ. "I know. But what about Jellybean? Can you take him?"

I looked between her and the dog and tried not to fall under the spell of their pleading eyes. I supposed I could say I would take the dog in. She didn't have to know that "in" meant a shelter. With luck, I could get Susie booked in and Cujo to the shelter down the street from the courthouse before they closed. I nodded and she practically burst out crying. Steeled against her tears, I said, "Let's go. I'm in a hurry."

"I need one minute." She took off to the kitchen before I realized she was in motion. I followed, and Jellybean trotted along beside us, like he owned the place. Just as I was about to grab Susie and drag her from the apartment, she turned around with her hands full.

"Here's his favorite toy and some food. I didn't have time to get him a leash, but he's real good about sticking with you when he goes outside."

I took the stuffed pink dinosaur and the bag of dry food and watched as she patiently explained to the dog how the nice lady was going to take him home. He answered with a few short sentences of his own and a glance in my direction to let me know he'd understood every word. I was pretty sure whatever pay I earned from this job would not be enough.

❖

"You can't bring that mutt in here."

Jellybean yawned and Susie protested, "He's not a mutt."

The three of us were standing in the hallway outside the holding cells of the Lew Sterrett Justice Center aka the Dallas County Jail. All I wanted to do was turn Susie in, turn the dog in, collect my fee, and find some dinner, but Susie's insistence that I not leave the dog in the car and the deputy sheriff's insistence that I not bring the dog into the jail combined to put a damper on my day. I squared off with the officer. I didn't know this guy, but I could tell he wasn't cutting me any slack. Deputy trumps fugitive. I threw up my hands. "Fine, I'll take him outside, but can we hurry this one along? I have somewhere I need to be."

Deputy No Dogs shot me a withering glance. I'd probably just doomed any chance of making it to the shelter before they closed. I took Jellybean outside and tied his rope leash to a bike rack. Most action that rack had ever seen. Nobody rides a bike to the jail.

Back inside, I waited while they processed Susie into the jail and gave me the paperwork I'd need to present to Hardin in order to collect my fee. I started to dash back outside, when I saw Jess waving me down. I glanced at the door, half hoping Jellybean had chewed through his rope, and waited for her to approach. I knew I'd been a supreme jerk last time I'd seen her, but I couldn't get over the fact she hadn't called even once to check in.

"Hey, Bennett. Earning your keep?"

"Every little bit helps. You slumming it over here?" Jess was a homicide detective. More time spent investigating bigger crimes, which meant less arrest volume.

"Had to talk to a guy about another guy. You know."

I nodded. I did know. My time on the force hadn't lasted long, but it had been long enough to get a good feel for the job. Good enough to know I wasn't cut out for all the rules that came with working for someone else.

"You headed out?"

I looked into her eyes, trying to figure out if the question was an invitation. Maybe we could fall back into our usual routine of casual sex, pretend the night of the wedding had never happened. I was willing to try if she was. I flashed a long, slow smile to let her know I was game. "Yep."

"Great, let's grab dinner. My treat."

Not at all what I had in mind. Should've sorted that out before I implied I was free. But I was hungry. We could grab food at Maggie's and be steps from my bed. I started to say as much, but she beat me.

"Not Maggie's. A real meal where we actually sit at a table and people actually wait on us."

Uh oh. All the signs were familiar. She wanted to talk. Again, not what I had in mind. Jess had never been much of a talker, and I liked that, but I could sense lately that had changed. I scrambled for a way out. "I'm not really dressed for someplace nice."

She cast a look from my boots up to my T-shirt and leather jacket. "You look nice enough. Come on." She turned around and started out the door. I had no choice but to follow and be a little angry that she knew I would.

She was moving really fast, but then pulled up short a few yards out the door. "What the hell!" she snarled.

I looked around her and immediately knew what was wrong. Jellybean. She knelt beside the dog and felt around his neck, muttering the entire time. "No collar and a rope for a leash? Typical. What if he got loose and ran off? Bet the jerk who left him here would be sorry then."

I was the first to admit I was a jerk a lot of the time, but at least I hadn't left the dog to subsist in a locked apartment when I arrested his owner. *But you're going to take him to the shelter.* I knew I couldn't tell Jess that as surely as I knew I had to tell her I was the one who'd tied the dog out here. I tapped Jess on the shoulder. "I'm the jerk. I tied him out here."

She shook her head as if my words had fuzzied her brain. "Why? What are you of all people doing with a dog?"

"What do you mean, me 'of all people'?"

"Face it, Luca, you're like the last person on earth I'd trust with a pet. Look how you live."

Wow. Talk about laying it all out. If this was a foreshadowing of what our dinner conversation would be like, I was ready to bow out now. I looked at Jellybean who stared up at me with his soulful blues, and I swore I detected a trace of sympathy. I'd rather spend a few hours with him than getting lectured about how my wild ways weren't good enough for the perfect Jessica Chance. As the thoughts churned, a plan formed. I could keep the dog at my place one night if it meant avoiding whatever Jess wanted to discuss. Half-baked though it was, it inspired me to blurt out, "I live just fine. I'm taking my dog and going home."

I nudged her aside and reached for the rope. She held it firmly and just out of my grasp. "If this is really your dog, what's his name?"

My plans hadn't included actually naming the beast, and no way was I going to tell Jess I owned a dog named Jellybean. I stared at his shiny coat, his pearly white teeth, and his big blue eyes, but none of that inspired me. My thoughts flicked to his recent, although brief, relationship with Susie and how we'd come to meet. Within seconds, I had it. A name. And it was a good one.

"His name is Cash."

CHAPTER FIVE

An hour later, I pushed through the door of my apartment with a pizza box and a six-pack in my hands and Jess and Cash on my heels. Jess carried a huge bag of dog food in one arm, and a bag of chew toys and accessories dangled from her hand. I'd tried to talk her out of buying so much stuff, but she'd insisted. I decided I could take it to the shelter when I turned him in.

I set the pizza on the only table I had, an ancient, chipped coffee table, and peeled two beers off the pack and handed one to Jess.

"Do you have a bowl?"

"Drinking out of the can not good enough for you?"

"For the dog. He needs water."

I looked down at him. He was reclining on the floor with one paw draped over my boot in an I-own-you kind of way. He looked comfortable and entitled. How in the hell Jess divined he might be thirsty, I have no idea, but I wasn't in the mood to argue. I reached in the cabinet and pulled down a red plastic bowl, filled it with water, and then watched the dog drink a quarter of it down. "Great, now he's going to have to pee."

"Dogs do that, you know."

I started to fire back, but when I looked at Jess, I caught the slight grin and realized she was kidding. Her smile made me remember the start of last Friday evening, made me wish we could have a do-over. It'd only been a few days with no contact, but I missed what we'd had, whatever it was. I knew one part of us I really missed, and suddenly, I was hungry for something more than dinner. "I know, I just wanted…" I didn't really want to have to ask for what I wanted, so I gestured vaguely in the direction of the pizza.

"He'll be fine while we eat. When we're done we can walk him together."

"You think he can last a little longer than that?"

Jess stepped into my arms and slid her arms around my waist. Her breath on my neck was warm, her lips insistent. I had my answer. Good thing we both liked cold pizza.

I would've undressed her right there, but the dog was watching, so I led the way to the bedroom. Over the years we'd been friends, our dance had been choreographed into a familiar routine, but this was the first time we'd been together since I'd allowed my mind to think those three little words I hadn't dared to speak out loud. As we stood facing each other in the dim light of my room, I was seized by a quick and powerful fear that I'd forgotten the steps, that whatever we'd had was gone, replaced by the void of my unspoken words. For a second, I considered telling her I'd changed my mind, that I was hungry for actual food, that I wanted to walk the dog. Anything at all to keep from having to feel whatever I was feeling.

Before I could act, she kissed me. Soft at first. Her lips pressed into mine and tugged them open, teasing and light. I remembered this. This was good. The months we'd gone without faded away. Could it be this easy for us to slip back into what we'd had?

I ran my hands through her short blond hair and drank in the spicy, fresh smell of her. Every pass of her tongue sent sparks through my entire body, and I arched against her, craving more. More than we'd had before, more than I'd ever thought we could. We were well on our way. Maybe it *was* this easy, but we were definitely not slipping back into what we'd had. No, we were moving toward something, something worth holding on to. I fought back the fear that threatened to freeze me up and gave in to whatever this was, tearing her shirt over her head, ripping off my own clothes to speed things along.

We moved more quickly now. Down on the bed. Skin on skin. Her legs between mine, my hands on her arms over her head, my tongue circled her breast. She arched against me, and I met her cry for cry. With each touch, I was grounded, I was home. We'd done this a million times before, but this was different and the same all at once. Unlike the other women who'd paraded in and out of my life, I cared about Jess sticking around. I didn't know what to call it. I wasn't sure I wanted to name it, but it felt good. It felt right. I didn't want to lose it.

❖

"You hungry?"

"Definitely." I shook my head to clear away all the complicated thoughts cluttering our good time. Jess was propped on her elbows and I reached out to touch the spot on her shoulder where she'd taken a bullet for me just a few weeks ago, a tangible reminder she was different from the rest. I was hungry again, but I'd settle for pizza and the domestic bliss it represented. Didn't sound so bad. At least we got to eat.

We both sat on the couch and dove in. Thank God she didn't ask me to get plates. We devoured the pizza right out of the box while the dog watched from a respectable distance. I didn't care how well behaved he was, I could tell he wanted pizza bones. He wanted them bad.

"You start feeding him your food, he's never going to settle for his."

I swear she could read my mind. I looked from the pizza in my hand to the giant bag of dry food sitting on my kitchen floor. No matter what Jess said, I respected the dog for wanting the good stuff. "Come here, doggie."

He trotted over, laid his head on my knee, and gave me the soulful look before gently taking the piece of pizza I'd torn for him. Who was I to deny him a little pleasure? He wasn't going to eat like this at the SPCA. I'm all about living in the moment. As I offered him another piece, Jess stood, gathered our trash, and took it to the kitchen.

"What's this?"

I looked up from the hungry beast and stared at the sheaf of papers in her hand. Took me a second to click, but I quickly realized she was holding the information Ronnie had dropped off yesterday. I'd planned to toss it, but I'm not big on cleaning house. It could've sat there for days before I would've gotten around to throwing it out. I shrugged at Jess, hoping she wouldn't dig any deeper.

Didn't work.

"Jorge Moreno? Is that what she wanted? She wanted you to help her crooked brother?"

"Tell me how you really feel."

She smacked the papers on the counter. "Tell me you're not helping him. That you're not helping her."

I opened my mouth to say the no she wanted to hear, but I stopped short. I hadn't planned on helping Ronnie. Hell, I hadn't even planned to call her to tell her as much, but the way Jess let her name spoil whatever it was we'd shared for the past hour shook me a little. She'd always given me a hard time about Ronnie, especially when her suspicions that she was up to no good were confirmed. In her view, Ronnie had helped her crooked uncle cover up a sex ring and a murder. It was more complicated than that, but cops are prone to absolutes. What I didn't get was why Jess was still so judgmental. It'd been months since Ronnie and I were a thing, and in the meantime, Jess had gotten hung up over a chick who was pretty crooked herself. Where did she get off scolding me for something I hadn't even done yet?

I stared her down and she let the papers fall to the floor. We'd known each other long enough for her to get that pushing me into a corner wasn't good for either of us. There were a ton of things I could've said to stop her before she walked out the door, but I stayed buttoned up. She could come around first for once. I was tired of always being the one in the wrong.

❖

The next morning, I woke up to a cold nose against my neck. His stare was penetrating. I knew that look. Jellybean, I mean Cash, was hungry.

I climbed out of bed and poured him a big bowl of food while wishing I could send him to the corner grocery with a note around his neck asking for a cup of coffee.

I've never really understood pets. Seems like they mostly just sleep and eat, on your dime. I was all for one that was utilitarian, like a seeing eye dog or a search and rescue hound, but those were rare. Despite his display of ferocious barking at Susie's place, Cash seemed a little too friendly to protect me from anything. Besides, I didn't need much in the way of protecting. I could run real fast and I was a crack shot. He was a beautiful dog, but I'm not big into keeping things just because they're pretty. He'd make someone a fine pet, if he didn't eat them into poverty first.

I tossed through a pile of clothes and found sweats that weren't standing on their own yet. I dressed for a run that would work the dual benefits of clearing my head and putting me in good proximity to coffee. I opened the door to leave, but stopped when I heard Cash speaking in his strange dog tongue. When he was done, I cocked my head to let him know I didn't understand a word he'd said. He cocked his head back at me. Guess we were at an impasse. I had one foot out the door when suddenly he was at my side, his brand new leash hanging from the sides of his mouth.

"Oh, I get it. Why didn't you just say so?" He barked in response, the sound muffled by the mouthful of leather. I'd told Jess to buy the cheap leash, knowing the folks at the shelter wouldn't care about him having top of the line accessories, but she'd insisted on going all out. The food she'd bought had been some organic, all natural shit that probably wasn't good for him. Pesticides and preservatives build immunities. At least that's how I justify eating so many. Besides, he wouldn't eat like that at the shelter or, chances were, at his new home. I should get him used to real world food, and I had just the thing in mind.

Cash was a faster runner than me, which I attributed to his extra legs rather than my sluggish morning self. When we arrived at the convenience store, I walked him in and waved down the protests of the cashier. The place was a dive. Wasn't like a dog was going to bring it down a notch. One cup of coffee, three donuts, and two hot dogs later, Cash and I left. I could tell by the way he drooled over his half of the food that the organic crap hadn't done much to fill his belly.

The excursion left me tired. I curled up on the couch with the sheaf of papers Jess had found so objectionable. I hadn't really wanted to know more than I did about Ronnie's brother—that he was a cop and a jerk—but I'm not impervious to the call of curiosity.

The case against him looked simple. He'd been caught working with a confidential informant to set up fake drug busts. The department had tagged him with two possible motives: beefing up his arrest record, and kickbacks from the CI. I'd heard the story on the radio when it first broke. It was a big deal around town. Apparently, the scheme had been going on for several months before Jorge got caught, and in the meantime, he'd racked up a nomination for officer of the year because of his role in one of the largest busts in DPD history, which of course, turned out to be all fake. DPD had a practice of doing field tests on drug busts but not actually sending the drugs to the lab for additional testing unless the accused decided to fight the charges.

Lots of Mexican nationals had pled guilty rather than rot in jail for the months it took to have the drugs tested by the lab. Since everyone assumed no one would plead guilty for something they didn't do, the scheme hadn't been exposed until one of the deportees hired a hotshot civil rights lawyer to investigate. The lawyer had gotten the court to order a test on the drugs and exposed the whole scheme. The civil cases were pending in federal court, and if they went the way the pundits predicted, the Dallas Police Department was going to owe a boatload of bucks to the wronged individuals who'd been smart enough to sign on to the suit. As a result, the DA's office had changed the way they processed all drug arrests, and now they waited months until lab results came back before pursuing cases. That cost the county lots of cash and caused a load of friction between prosecutors and law enforcement. Faced with paying out a ton of settlements, the police department had set their sights on finding, firing, and prosecuting whoever put them in this position in the first place.

Didn't surprise me that Jorge had cut corners. Didn't surprise me that anyone would. But he hadn't been in vice very long. In fact, he'd barely been promoted to detective. Seems like he wouldn't have had time to foster the kind of connections necessary to make the deals he'd been accused of. I flipped through the papers. The investigation into his behavior had started with a tip. Internal affairs had poked around and then brought him in for questioning. Cops aren't allowed to refuse to answer internal affairs questions about allegations of criminal activity—not if they want to keep their jobs. The investigators had read him the required Garrity warning and taped a long and arduous interrogation. No copy of it here, but the summary said he denied any wrongdoing. Not surprising. When the investigators showed pictures of Jorge's CI, Roberto Garcia, to some of the arrestees, they had no trouble picking him out and, faced with trouble of his own, the CI sang like a bird. Jorge was indicted, and he had a trial date set for February of next year.

That was the sum of it. Pretty open and shut. I didn't know what Ronnie expected me or anyone else to do. I glanced through the pages one more time to make certain I hadn't missed anything. And I had. There it was, right in the middle. The name of the person who'd tipped off internal affairs. Now I knew why Ronnie thought she could hook me into helping her brother. I knew the tipster well: Detective Teresa Perez.

Teresa and I had big bad history that started when I was a rookie cop, a level I hadn't gotten beyond. I'd never had anything against her, but she hated my guts because she thought I'd gotten her partner killed. Maybe I was partly at fault, maybe not. I'd bypassed all the departmental psych crap designed to get me to process the whole mess by quitting the minute I got out of the hospital. Yeah, I'd gotten shot for my troubles, a tiny fact that Teresa didn't bother to credit in my favor. She'd held a grudge for years, and her anger had bubbled up again just last year when she was all too happy to try to pin a murder on me just because I happened to stumble across a dead body or two while looking for Maggie's worthless brother who'd gone missing. Perez wasn't big on letting things go.

I tossed the papers back onto the counter and began an internal debate. I'd had no intention of working on Jorge's case, but Perez's involvement piqued my interest. Part of me said she probably had very little to do with it, but another part of me remembered how it felt to be the focus of her vitriol. Didn't make me feel sorry for Jorge, but my curiosity was up. I picked up the phone and dialed Ronnie's number.

CHAPTER SIX

"Just to be clear, I'm not saying I'm going to help."

Ronnie looked at me with the wolfish smile I'd fallen for in the first place, and we both knew I was lying.

I told Ronnie on the phone only that I wanted to meet her for lunch. I'd picked Maggie's because I didn't want her in my place, and I didn't want to be at hers. Maggie's was the best place I knew to avoid a confrontation with someone other than Maggie. A few minutes in it became clear that meeting here had been a mistake.

The first clue was the off-brand draft beer that sloshed over the top of the warm mugs when she slammed them on the table. Maggie pulled out an order pad—I'd never seen her use one before—and waited for our order as if she didn't know I would want a big plate of the greasiest thing she could fix.

"Is your girlfriend working tonight?" She rapped her pen on the pad and tapped her foot. Maggie didn't need to add on all the extra signs. I could tell she was pissed. I'd be lucky to get anything other than a salad or broccoli tonight. I shot a glance at Ronnie who pretended to ignore this exchange. I followed her lead and dove in with my order.

"Can we get a couple of cheeseburgers and fries? Put bacon on mine if you have it." I saw both Ronnie and Maggie flinch slightly at my order. Well, they could both suck it up. If I was going to have to sit here with a beautiful woman I wasn't going to sleep with, then I'd soothe my soul with another of my favorite vices. Ronnie could eat or not. I didn't care.

Another lie. I did care. I don't know why the woman got under my skin, but she did. From the second I'd met her in the courthouse halls, she'd captivated me with her dark good looks and fresh from the pages of a fashion magazine beauty. Not that I read fashion magazines, but I'd heard that expression on one of the two channels my TV managed to receive on an intermittent basis. That day in the courthouse, I'd known she was way too classy for Dallas criminal defense work. Jess had been with me, and she'd predicted trouble. She'd been right on. Ronnie had caused me all kinds of problems, including a trip to the hospital I still hadn't paid off. Every nasty letter I got from the collection agency should've made me hate her more, but it didn't. I thought I was done with her after putting her on a plane to D.C., to her mid six-figure job, but seeing her now, I wasn't so sure.

Jess would kick my ass if I got caught up with her again. And she should. I waited for Maggie to wander off before I launched back into my ground rules. "I'll hear what you have to say, and then I'll make up my mind, but if I do get involved, I call the shots. I'll let you know what's going on, but I don't report to you or Jorge. Understood?"

She smiled. My tough veneer was having absolutely no effect on her. "Anything else?" she asked in a syrupy sweet voice.

"Yes." I paused and did some mental math. Food, beer, rent, gas, phone bill times three, plus a cushion. "I'll need five grand down. Nonrefundable. I'll let you know when I need more." That was a lot of money—to me anyway—and it wasn't how it was done, but I'm not a private investigator who charges by the hour and produces neat little bills for my very important clients. I rounded up fugitive lawbreakers and got paid a cut of the money I saved the bondsman. If I was going to do this, then I wanted enough money up front that I wouldn't care if she walked when she found out her brother really was a dirty cop. I'd heard defense attorneys make the same gripe. Their guilty clients wanted their money back because you couldn't get them off, and their innocent ones wanted a refund since how hard could it be to free an innocent man? Money up front removes the risk.

"Assuming the money isn't an issue, which it isn't, you have any other terms?"

The only ones I could think of were for her to stop wearing low-cut blouses and stop talking to me in suggestive tones. I wisely decided not to name those requirements. Instead, I ignored the question. "How do you know Jorge's not involved?"

"Because he told me he's innocent."

"Oh, well then. Let's go see the judge."

"I trust my brother."

"Great, then you can testify on his behalf, but if you think your word is going to go a long way with the jury, you have no idea what you're in for. Who's the prosecutor?"

"Joshua Terrance. Head of Public Integrity. But word is the DA himself is going to try the case."

"Guess your brother's made it to the big time. Now, do you have any factual basis for believing your brother?"

Ronnie leaned across the table, and I caught a whiff of familiar perfume. Don't count on me to analyze what it smelled like, flowers, fruit, hell, I don't know, but it drew me in, and I caught myself leaning forward to hear what she had to say.

"Sure. Jorge had barely been promoted to detective and hadn't been in vice long enough to make the kind of connections he would need to pull something like this off."

My thoughts exactly. "Okay. Anything else?"

"Did you happen to notice who turned him in?"

Perez. "Yeah, I noticed."

"And you don't find that a little bit suspicious? She's not even in vice."

I found it very suspicious, but I feigned nonchalance. "It's a little unusual."

"It's very unusual," Ronnie persisted. "And you know she hates me."

"And you think because she hates you, she set up the department in a huge civil class action lawsuit and pointed the finger at your brother for causing all the problems? No offense, but I doubt she even remembers you."

"Oh, she remembers all right. Jorge said she told everyone she knew about his crooked uncle and sister. Caused him a lot of problems. But you're right. I don't think she pointed the finger at him for that reason. I think she's covering for something bigger."

I recognized the tone. Not specific to her, but my memory of any conversation I've ever had with a conspiracy junkie. They all started the same. The junkie's voice got lower, they hunched forward, and they made pronouncements designed to evoke gasps. She was about to tell me the cover-up went as high as the police chief, maybe even the DA himself. Five grand wasn't nearly enough. I pushed away from the table and started to stand up, but Maggie's sharp tone stopped me in my tracks.

"Where do you think you're going?"

I glanced up into Maggie's angry eyes. She was shoving a full plate of greasy goodness my way, and the gesture took the sting out of her words.

"If I'm going to make this death food for you, you're damn well going to eat it. Now sit down." She dropped both plates on the table and stormed off. Ronnie frowned when I stole a fry from her plate and blew on it before wolfing it down. She was into froufrou food. Cheese and fruit plates, wine, caviar. One time I'd shared dinner with her family, and her embarrassment over the homemade enchiladas and tacos was palpable. A burger and fries might kill her. I hoped mustard ran down her perfect chin.

"I'm not going to listen to your theory if you don't eat, so dig in."

She glanced from me to her plate, her expression almost desperate. Finally, she pushed back her sleeves, hefted the giant burger, and took a huge bite. As mustard indeed dribbled down her chin, I roared with laughter and kept my word. "All right, all right. Tell me what you think happened."

She swallowed and wiped her chin. "Look, I don't know. I only know that nothing about this feels right. I've talked to some of the individuals who were arrested, and none of them remember ever meeting Jorge. Something is completely off about all of this. If I could explain it, I wouldn't be here trying to get your help. Miguel's contacts won't talk to me, and I don't know anyone else here who can do the work. "

She wasn't bullshitting. Her only real connection to Dallas County criminal law had been her uncle, attorney Miguel Moreno, and his practice was shuttered since he was doing time. The Moreno name was not one to open doors in the local legal community. I tried not to take it personally that I was a last resort. "I was serious about the five grand."

"I left my checkbook at my hotel. Want to follow me over and get it? I'll buy you a drink."

"No, thanks." I wasn't falling for her charms. She probably thought she could talk me into the sack and talk me out of getting paid. "Besides, I don't take checks. My coffee can bank has problems processing them."

She raised her eyebrows. Not sure if it was the reference to where I kept my money or the fact I'd turned her down. Either way, she recovered quickly. "I'll get you the cash."

I stood and threw my last twenty on the table. I didn't have a clue if she was serious or not, but I wanted her to know that just because I kept my money in a coffee can didn't mean I wasn't flush. "Great. As soon as you do, I'll get started."

I walked out, hoping I hadn't made a huge mistake.

❖

True to my word, I wasn't going to do any real work on Jorge's case until I saw some money, but I decided gathering a little background information would satisfy my curiosity and give me a head start if she actually came through. There are at least two sides to every story. Usually more. While I'd promised Ronnie I'd look into Jorge's situation, I hadn't made any promises about the outcome. And I wouldn't. If Jorge was a bad cop, he was on his own. Best way to find out if he was really crooked was to talk to the people he worked with.

It had been a while since I'd been on the force, but I still had a few friends outside of Jess. No way was I going to hit her up for information even though she was usually my most reliable source. Whatever was going on between us was rocky, and I wasn't about to complicate it more by appearing to do favors for Ronnie. I considered trying to talk to John, her partner, but partners are like spouses. If you talk to one, you may as well be talking to the other.

I settled on Nancy Walters. She wasn't my first choice because she was a notorious gossip and there was a huge risk that whatever I told her would get back to Jess and a dozen other people. On the other hand, she was the most likely person to have the kind of information I was looking for.

Nancy had been in our class at the academy, and we kept in touch only because she was a regular on Jess's softball team where I'm occasionally called up to play due to my one skill, the ability to run really fast. I picked up the phone to call her, but decided it would be better to catch her unaware. She'd never been shy about having a thing for me, and setting a time to talk might be mistaken for a date. I checked the time. If I hurried, I might be able to catch Jerry Etheridge's wife coming home from work. If I could catch her as she pulled into the garage, I was certain I could talk my way into the house where I was certain Jerry was holed up. Ronnie hadn't paid yet—I should focus on earning a real wage until she did.

When I pulled up outside the insurance office, the bright yellow Smart car was still parked in the drive. Minutes later, at five on the dot, Jerry's wife skipped out the door and headed to her car. But she wasn't alone. No, she was likely skipping because of Mr. Tall and Handsome who held her hand all the way to her car and opened the door for her. I was transfixed. Mostly because I figured he was about to get in the driver's seat, and I wanted to see the pretzel maneuvers he was going to have to execute in order to fit behind the wheel.

He ducked his head and managed to accordion his way into the car in an amazing show of athletic feat. Before I could recover from the sight, they sped away. I shot a look at my fuel gauge and weighed my options. I had a feeling Alice Etheridge wasn't headed directly home, but I wanted to follow even if it was likely to be a big fat waste of time. I stepped on the gas and peeled out of the parking lot.

They were easy to tail since they were completely engrossed with each other. I hate driving behind people I know are paying absolutely no attention to the road, but I was a little fascinated by their interaction. When she wasn't leaning over to kiss him, her head disappeared out of sight. I had a pretty good idea of what was going on, and I purposely stayed a good distance behind in case her affections caused him to lose control of the car.

About ten minutes later, they pulled up to one of those motels where everyone assumes you're renting a room for an hour even if you aren't. I parked so I had a good view of the whole place and waited. Alice's head was still out of sight, and the tin can they were in started to rock back and forth. Just when I was certain the yellow car was going to roll over on its side, she popped up and checked her lipstick in the rearview mirror. Seconds later, they were out of the car, headed to the motel office.

Instinct led me to pull out my phone and snap a few pictures. After that burst of activity, I waited about fifteen minutes before becoming monumentally bored. Time to poke around. The main office was deserted, so I pounded on the counter bell until a pimply high-schooler showed up to ask if I needed a room.

"No, I don't need a room. Especially if you're renting to fugitives." I flashed my private investigator's license and put it away before he could tell I wasn't a cop. These situations were about the only time my license got to see the light of day. In this case, it did the trick.

The kid's voice was all stuttering when he said, "I don't know what you're talking about."

"Oh, I think you do." I waited a few beats to ramp up his angst. "That couple you just rented to?"

"Uh huh."

"Modern day Bonnie and Clyde. You wouldn't believe the trouble they've been in. I'd take them in myself, but I'm working undercover. I need you to call the local cops and say you noticed some suspicious activity in their room." I leaned against the counter and pulled back one side of my jacket, just enough to reveal a glint of metal from the long Colt tucked into my shoulder holster. I wanted him scared, and I didn't care if it was because of me or the couple who'd just checked in.

"You think they're dangerous?"

I shook my head. "No telling. I just know you need to get them turned in quickly or you risk getting yourself and the owner of this place in big trouble for aiding and abetting."

He picked up the phone and I hightailed it to my Bronco. I drove to the next parking lot, making sure I still had a good view of the room that was about to be the scene of trouble. It took a while for the cops to arrive. No surprise, since the motel clerk didn't have anything specific to tell them, they probably thought it was a dumb call. Which it was as far as they were concerned. I only wanted one thing out of it. Maybe two, if I was lucky.

When the DPD cruiser pulled up, I got out my phone and zoomed in. A few minutes later, I had several shots of Alice and Mr. Handsome waving their arms while talking to the cops in the doorway of a motel room. Perfect.

I left them to their explanations and sped back to the Etheridge residence. I went straight to the front door and knocked loudly. Jerry didn't answer, but I saw a curtain move, and I knew he had to be inside. I yelled, "Mr. Etheridge, I need to talk to you about your wife's affair and criminal activity. Can you please open the door?"

I, of all people, know that curiosity makes people do dumb things. And Jerry was no different. The door creaked open and an indignant voice said, "I don't know what you're talking about."

I pushed my way into the open door and shoved my phone under his chin. "That's your wife, Alice, right?" It was the picture of Alice and Mr. Handsome practically running to the Chateau Rendezvous. He stiffened, and I started scrolling through the shots, ending with the one where the police were questioning his wife and her paramour in the doorway of their love nest.

I put the phone away and shrugged. "Maybe I got it all wrong. Maybe they're working. Off-site. And they called the police to help with a big insurance problem."

His shoulders slumped. There was no good explanation for why Alice was at a cheesy motel instead of back home with her needy, fugitive husband. He knew it and I knew it. Now I was just waiting for him to wonder why I was here.

"What do you want?"

Not the question I was expecting, but it worked for my purposes. "We need you to come in and talk to some folks about what you know. It might help you in the long run." Nothing I said was a lie, just vague. Not that I'm averse to lying. It's just that the more specific the story, the more chance you'd hang yourself on the details later.

Jerry nodded, resigned to his cheating wife and realizing she was more focused on getting laid than helping him hide from the law. I didn't bother cuffing him. He was too beat down to make a getaway. Wasn't until I turned him in at the station that he started to click that something was off. I almost felt sorry for the guy, but then I remembered how much I needed the money and I stopped feeling bad.

An hour later, Hardin handed me a stack of bills, small, but better than nothing, and I headed home. When I reached my front door, I heard a sharp cry, followed by soft whimpers. What the hell? No one had a key to my place but the super, and I'd warned him, with the Colt, about entering without permission. Jess had a habit of using her badge to get him to cough up the key. Could she be in there? Hurt?

I drew my gun and turned the handle. It was still locked. I eased the key into the lock, turned it and, with one fluid motion, turned the handle and threw open the door. Nothing. I saw nothing. I kept my gun trained as I moved through the living room and into the bedroom. Wasn't until I came back through that I saw the culprit. Cash was prone on the kitchen floor in front of his dog bowls. Empty dog bowls. Shit. I'd completely forgotten about the damn dog. I poured a healthy dose of dog chow into his bowl and filled his water dish. I hated to admit it, but Jess was right. I wasn't cut out for taking care of anyone but myself.

CHAPTER SEVEN

I rolled out of bed the next morning and nearly tripped over the furry beast sleeping on the floor. I had two things to do today. Take the dog to the SPCA and avoid my landlord. I had the rent, but giving it up would take a large portion of my stash, and I had better ways to spend my funds. I'd take care of the easy part first. I gathered the dog's things.

Cash knew I was up to something, and he hung back while I scoured the place for his stuff. He had more belongings than I did, and he'd made himself completely at home by leaving his stuff in every corner of the place. I should drop him at Jess's door to pay her back for loading him up on personal belongings. But then I'd have to see Jess, and she'd know I was full of shit when I'd acted like I could take care of another living thing.

I'd have to see her eventually. We were best friends. Spring would come and she'd want me to fill in on her softball team. I'd need to bug her for information on one of my cases. We'd give in to the simple pulls of physical craving that usually brought us together because that was the one thing we could count on.

Had I been fooling myself to think there was something more?

A rap on the door jarred me out of my thoughts. I glanced down at the dog and hoped it wasn't my landlord. I was prepared to deny him the rent, but I wasn't prepared to explain the dog while doing so. "Who's there?" I called out.

"Delivery for Miss Luca Bennett."

Words I rarely hear. I'm a naturally suspicious person. Unordered and unexpected delivery made my antennae go up. "Leave it."

"I'm sorry, ma'am, but you have to sign for it."

I hesitated. Last thing I had to sign for had come from my brother. He'd sent new cufflinks for me to wear at his wedding. He should still be on his honeymoon, but what if whatever was at the door was from him? I weighed that against the other possibility it might be something bad, like a constable waving a subpoena. I hadn't been bad lately, at least not that kind of bad, so I opened the door.

The guy on the other side could use a good meal. I needn't have worried about trouble since a light breeze would land him on the other side of the complex. He shoved an electronic clipboard my way, and once I signed, he produced an envelope. I took a step back. Good news never comes in letters you have to sign for.

"Who's it from?"

He consulted his gadget. "Someone named Moreno. Said it was an urgent delivery. I tried yesterday afternoon, but you weren't here."

Okay, so it wasn't bad news. Not necessarily anyway. Once he left, I tore open the envelope. It wasn't the cash I'd demanded, but it was the next best thing. I held the five thousand dollar cashier's check with both hands. Don't get me wrong—the money was great, but like most other great things, it came with strings. Strings to Ronnie, strings to my past with the DPD, and strings that were likely to tangle up whatever I had with Jess.

I felt something nudge against my back and turned to see the dog, nosing his way through the crook in my arm. I widened the space to let him in, and once he set his head on my leg, I stroked his head. I may not have liked the responsibility that came from having a living thing rely on me for food and shelter, but I actually kind of liked this odd comfort. I hadn't asked for it, but it felt pretty good.

"All right, Cash, we have some errands to run." I stood and dumped the bag with all his belongings onto the floor. He romped around and nosed at his toys until I waved him to the door. I held the leash, and he immediately sat down, waiting for me to snap it on his collar. I started to, but then decided he'd earned the chance to walk without it. Besides, if he ran off, that was his problem. How many other homes was he going to find that had just had five Gs delivered to the door?

I rarely went to the bank, but I kept an account there just in case. When I paid my rent and my phone bill, I did so with cash, in person, but I couldn't just stick Ronnie's check in my coffee can. It was cold enough that I left Cash in the car while I was inside. I took my money in large bills except for a few random twenties. The crisp cash felt good in my hands, made me feel flush. I considered paying my overdue rent after all.

When I climbed back in the car, Cash left my seat and positioned himself in the front passenger seat, upright and alert. We looked pretty silly—human chauffeuring canine. For fun, I drove through a Whataburger and bought us each two biscuits with egg, cheese, and bacon. Cash waited more patiently than most humans as I unwrapped his share and tore it into pieces. If Jess could see me now, she'd realize she was wrong. I was perfectly capable of taking care of this dog.

I called Ronnie on the way home and she answered, breathless, on the first ring. "I thought you would've called by now. What have you found out?"

"Take a breath. I just got the check and I had to take it to the bank to make sure it was legit. You and me don't have the best track record when it comes to trust."

"And you have no track record when it comes to forgiving and forgetting. When are you going to meet with Jorge? Maybe you could come to my parents' for dinner tonight. We're all going to be there. I'm sure they'll be relieved to know we have help."

I flashed back to the one time I'd been at Ronnie's parents' house. Her mom had spoiled me with extra helpings of homemade enchiladas. As tempting as it was to indulge in another such meal, I wasn't being paid enough to glad-hand with the family. "I'm busy tonight. Besides, I'd like to do a little legwork first. Tell Jorge to meet me tomorrow morning at the boat dock at the lake. He can get his morning run in and talk to me at the same time."

"You mean so you can get your morning run in and talk to him at the same time. Luca, I'm paying you good money. I expect you to give him the benefit of the doubt."

"Pretty sure you know paying good money doesn't guarantee results, especially not with me." She should remember from our last working encounter that it wasn't in my blood to ignore where the facts led just because I was getting paid. "The lake at eight a.m."

"Fine."

When I hung up, I turned to Cash who'd listened to the entire call with his head cocked. "She thinks she owns me, but she doesn't."

He muttered a few words in Husky and then did a couple of circles on the seat before settling in. I considered my next move. I didn't really have any legwork planned. I'd told Ronnie that because I'd wanted a full day to enjoy my newfound riches before I had to work for them, but now that I had the freedom, I was antsy. Maybe I should actually find out what I could before meeting with Jorge so he couldn't taint it with his version of the facts. I pointed the car in the direction of DPD headquarters and went in search of Nancy Walters.

❖

Nancy had recently been promoted to detective, and she was doing a stint in vice, making it likely that she knew some of the players, including Jorge Moreno. That, coupled with her finely honed gossiping skills, made it worth the risk that she would let Jess know I'd been pumping her for information immediately after we talked. I parked on a street adjacent to the Jack Evans building and glanced over at Cash who sported a stray crumb from his morning biscuit on his jaw. I picked it off and offered it to him and he gave me a look of gratitude and a few yips that sounded oddly like "thank you." I made a snap determination that his charm might be useful and decided not to leave him in the car.

Entering police headquarters always filled me with a sense of dread. It'd been years since I'd been a young cadet, graduating from the academy. I'd never been bright-eyed enough to be a true believer, but I had thought maybe I could make a decent living and do something good in the world. Too soon into my life as a patrol cop, I'd been schooled in the realities of police politics. I'd been teamed up with a senior officer, Teresa Perez's partner, Larry Brewster, and we'd taken a domestic call. After Brewster got shot by the perp, I'd said to hell with protocol and went after the bad guy instead of waiting for backup. I wound up catching him, although I got shot in the process, and Perez's partner bled out before the ambulance arrived.

His death hadn't been my fault, but Perez blamed me anyway and threatened to blackball me as a maverick. I wasn't scared of her, but I decided to quit the force and do my own thing. Sometimes you have to break the rules, and I can't work with folks who don't get that. Perez had never forgiven me for what she perceived as my carelessness and we'd had a few other run-ins over the years, most recently when I'd first met Ronnie and done some work for her and her uncle. When Perez found out I was poking around into Ronnie's brother's case, she was going to come unglued.

I approached the security desk and told the uniformed gatekeeper I had an appointment with Detective Walters. He ignored my request and pointed at the dog. "Can't bring the mutt in here."

This guy was never going to be promoted to detective. I may not be a dog person, but I knew Cash wasn't a mutt. He was a purebred Husky, and any moron could tell that. Instead of getting into useless argument about dog breeds, I came up with a solid lie. "Service dog. He goes everywhere with me."

"Where's his vest?"

"I spilled a Slurpee on it. Got all sticky. You ever tried to clean sticky frozen mess out of a dog's hair? Call Walters. She'll vouch for me." I punctuated my lies with a hard stare to convince him I could pass a polygraph on this subject. He finally shook his head and picked up the phone. About five minutes later, Nancy showed up.

"Luca Bennett! I knew you'd eventually be in a relationship, just didn't think you'd wind up with such a hairy one." She bent down to pet the dog. Cash backed up a few steps and sniffed the air.

I was relieved to see he wasn't going to cuddle with every chick he met.

Nancy ignored Cash's snub and motioned me over to the side. "When did you get him?"

I didn't bother sticking with the service dog story. "More like he got me. A jumper I picked up the other day had found him. I was meaning to turn him in, but he kind of got attached. Figured maybe he could be useful."

"Sure. Strays can come in handy." She jerked her chin at the guard on duty. "He's not going to let you bring him in unless he's got a vest."

"That's cool. What I want to talk to you about, well, I'd rather do it somewhere else anyway. You got time?"

She glanced at her watch. "It's a little early for lunch, but if you're buying, I could probably get away."

Guess I was buying. I gestured at the dog. "Sure, but somewhere we can eat outside. I don't want to leave him in the car for too long." When she raised her eyebrows, I responded, "I don't want him to tear up my car. We haven't known each other long enough to establish trust."

"Right. Let me go sign out and I'll meet you on the corner."

I knew what the real deal was. Nancy didn't mind being seen with me out on the street, at the bar, or at a softball game, but her fledgling career as a detective didn't need the burden of being seen helping me. The slight rejection stung a tiny bit, but I shrugged it off and led Cash to the Bronco.

A few minutes later, Nancy opened the passenger side door and waited for Cash to climb into the backseat. "You should get a harness for him in the car. So he doesn't go flying through the window if you have to stop suddenly."

I looked between her and the dog. "You sound like you know a lot about pets. You want him?" Her eyes lit up, and I was instantly sorry I'd made the offer even if it was a perfect solution. I may be able to cart the dog around for a few days, but long-term, he'd want things I couldn't deliver. Regular meals, a comfortable bed, a routine. Maybe giving him to someone like Nancy, who had a steady job and demonstrated responsible behavior was the perfect solution.

She cocked her head and clucked at him, and he cocked his head and spoke a few words of his doggy language back. "OMG, what's that sound?"

"He talks. At first I thought I was crazy, but I looked it up online. Apparently, it's a Husky thing." I mimicked his speech and he replied in kind.

"Wow, that's pretty amazing. I wish I could take him, but I just refurnished my house and it's not exactly pet-proofed."

I acted disappointed, but I changed the subject before she could come up with a bunch of places I could take the dog to find him a new home. "Hunky's okay with you?"

"Yeah, that's good."

We made small talk in the car. Well, she did, talking about who was dating whom and who was cheating on whose girlfriend. I nodded my head and murmured grunts every now and then to let her know I hadn't nodded off. I barely knew half the people she mentioned since I didn't spend a lot of time hanging out with the party crowd. Drinks in bars cost too much money, and I wasn't interested in dressing in anything other than jeans and T-shirts. This trip to lunch at the local gay hamburger spot and a few random drinking outings at Sue Ellen's after winning softball tournaments was the most time I spent even close to the bars.

As we pulled up in front of the restaurant, she dropped her biggest piece of gossip. "I hear Chance dumped the doctor she was dating and now she's seeing someone else."

I slammed into the curb and cussed. "Fucking street parking." It was more diplomatic than saying fucking Jess or fucking Nancy.

Nancy cocked her head. "It's called a curb. Every city has them. You pull up to it, not on it."

I bit back a retort and shook my head. "Whatever. You hungry or not?" I started to open my door, but she tugged on my arm.

"Did you hear what I said about Jess?"

She wasn't going to let this go, and that's all I wanted to do. "She's seeing someone, right?"

"Right."

"You know who it is?" I braced for her answer.

"I was hoping you would fill in that tidbit."

I stared at her eyes for a long few seconds, trying to decide if she was baiting me. Last thing I needed was for Jess to find out I'd been gossiping about her, but what if she was the one going around saying she was seeing someone. Could that someone be me? She couldn't have had time to start seeing someone else, could she?

The idea burned a hole in my stomach. I wanted answers, but I wasn't giving any. I dropped my stare and shook my head. "Don't have a clue." If Nancy already knew something, she'd have to up the info first. I wasn't talking.

We ordered from the counter and found a seat on the patio outside. Cash settled in beside my chair, sitting at attention, and several women stopped to admire him, even casting curious glances my way. Nancy's cop stare burned a hole in each of them, and they scattered. I'd never considered the dog could be a chick magnet. "You want to borrow him?" I offered, more to get Nancy to lighten up than anything else. She'd always had a thing for me, although we never discussed it. "You could take him to the park and pick up chicks."

"I don't need a dog to get laid."

There was no mistaking the angry undertone. Was she jealous of the dog or jealous of me? Whatever the case, I needed to move things along before she got pissed at me, so I launched into the real reason for my visit. "Ronnie Moreno is back in town."

Her eyes flashed steel, but she made kissing noises. "Bet that's keeping you busy."

"It's not like that."

"Why else would you hang around her? Although, I can't believe you'd sleep with that woman after what she did to you."

"Like I said, it's not like that. You know her brother, Jorge?"

"I know of him. He was promoted not long before I was, but just like his sister, he's into wasting opportunities."

I ignored her innuendo. No one had understood when I spent last summer fucking Ronnie after she'd lied, broken the law, and almost gotten me killed on a case. Like I'm the only person with bad judgment when it comes to women. Hell, when the bad parts were over, I'd figured she'd already done all the harm she could. Why shouldn't I get some kind of bonus out of it? And sex with Ronnie was a big bonus. The memory of it made me question why I wasn't collecting this time.

Nancy waved her hand in front of my face. "Earth to Luca. You want to tell me what you want?"

The list of things I wanted was longer than it had ever been, but I narrowed it down to only what was related to this case. "I want to know everything you know or can find out about Jorge and the charges against him."

The burgers came at that moment. The twink waiter set down all four baskets and then tsked his disapproval. He'd probably never eaten an entire burger in his life, and he clearly thought we were gluttons. I let Nancy stew over my request while I tore up one of the burgers for Cash. I set the basket in front of him and he stared between it and me until I nodded my head and then he scarfed the contents like it was his last meal. I started in on mine while Nancy picked at her food.

"Luca, I'd love to help you."

"I hear a 'but.'"

"Yeah, mine. I just got promoted. The last thing I need is IAD to find out I'm poking around in a pending investigation."

"I think it's past IAD. Public Integrity has it." I referred to the unit at the DA's office that prosecutes cops and other public officials who run afoul of the law. "The case has already been indicted."

"Then it sounds like you already know more than me."

"What I know you can get from the papers. What I want to know is more about Jorge. What kind of a cop was he? Was he respected? Who did he work with? How did he get set up with CIs all on his own so soon after joining vice? That's all stuff you can tell me and no one else can." I waited to see if the flattery would work. Nancy didn't gossip for her health. She did it to be the most popular kid, the one everyone gathered around to find out the juiciest news, the one in the know. I didn't judge her for it—everyone does what they need to—but I wasn't above taking advantage of her ever-hungry ego.

"And you don't want to go to Jess."

It wasn't a question. Sometimes Nancy was smarter than I gave her credit for, although she couldn't possibly understand my real motivation for not asking Jess for help. Better she think I was heartbroken about losing my fuck buddy to some real relationship potential than find out I had come close to being the real relationship potential. Nancy liked me and Jess, but she'd never really liked us together since she had me pegged as a rogue who would never settle down. I wasn't about to dispel her of the notion. Wasn't sure I could.

I assumed what I hoped was a beat down expression. "No, I don't want to go to Jess."

She reached a hand across the table and briefly squeezed mine. "I'll help you, but promise me you won't do anything stupid."

Easy promise since, despite the opinions of others, I didn't usually view my own actions as stupid.

Seemingly satisfied, she said, "Moreno's in deep shit."

"That's what I hear. Anything to it?"

She shrugged. "Your guess is as good as mine. The main evidence against him is from a confidential informant and your best friend Teresa Perez. Whatever you may think about Teresa, she has lots of credibility in the department."

"And she hates Ronnie Moreno."

"Only because she hates all criminal defense attorneys. Oh, and the fact Ronnie's associated with you, probably doesn't help."

"But would she really throw a fellow cop under the bus because he's the brother of a woman who happens to be a defense attorney who dated me?"

She shrugged and took a bite of her burger. While she chewed, I had an epiphany. "You know, I hadn't given this any thought before, but where was Jorge's partner during all this? You'd think if Jorge was making side deals with CIs, his partner would either be in on it or suspect something was up." I started to think I was on to something. I hadn't seen any reference to Jorge's partner in the reports Ronnie had given me. Of course, maybe internal affairs was holding back some info. Wouldn't be the first time. "You wouldn't happen to know who his partner is, would you?"

"Sure. It's Greg Jackson. He's been around vice for a while. You know how it is. They pair up new detectives with old ones. I'm paired up with an eighty-year-old. Bet she was the first female cop. Ever."

"Poor you. Do you know Jackson?"

"I know him well enough."

"You think he would talk to me?"

"Maybe, if you ask him."

I leaned forward and did my best attempt at begging. "I was really, really hoping maybe you would ask him for me."

"I don't know, Luca. I shouldn't get involved."

"You don't have to. Just ask him. If he says no, I'll leave it alone," I lied.

"I'll think about it, but I don't think he's the type to talk out of school."

Unlike you, I thought, but wisely decided not to say out loud. The best and worst thing about Nancy was her big mouth. I took advantage when I could and tried to avoid giving her too many personal details to divulge. Which made me think of Jess and whatever was going on with her personal life. As much as I wanted to pump Nancy for more information about what she knew and how she knew it, I wasn't sure I could handle whatever else she might say.

Stick to the case. When it's over, when Ronnie's back in D.C., you can sort things out with Jess. Or crawl back into your lonely little life.

I looked down at Cash, who lay prone underneath my chair, letting rip some major post-burger snores. Guess my life wasn't as lonely as it could be.

CHAPTER EIGHT

Nancy didn't think about it long. An hour after I dropped her back at the station, she sent me a text. The meet with Jackson was scheduled for eleven p.m. He'd been working solo since Jorge had been suspended, and he agreed to meet Nancy and me at a bar south of town. That he agreed to meet me at all was a big step, and to celebrate the small victory, I decided to take the rest of the afternoon off until Nancy showed up to collect me for the meeting.

I considered a quick trip to the casino, but the small part of my brain that dwells on things responsible told me I'd never make it back in time. Once I got started, I usually kept going until I ran out of money, met a woman who distracted me, or got too drunk to handle either. With a fresh five grand at stake, I had more to lose than usual. Instead, I washed a load of clothes, did the dishes, and then instructed Cash on the finer points of taking a nap.

I was well into my lesson plan, when I heard knocking at the door. Wasn't the fierce pounding of a not-yet-paid landlord, but I considered ignoring it anyway. Until I heard the voice.

"Luca, I know you're in there. Please."

There's something about the pleading tones of a desperate woman I should learn to resist. Ronnie, dressed in sharp blue courtroom drag, stood on my doorstep, hand raised. I tugged her through the doorway and glanced around for signs of Withers before I shut the door. "You should call before coming over."

"What? So you could give me a ton of reasons why I shouldn't come?"

Hands on her hips, she was fiery, a trait I'd come to love and hate. Her passion had been the thing that attracted me to her in the first place. Quick and sure, she inspired arousal and retreat in equal measure.

I contemplated acting on old impulses. And why not? I wasn't tied to anyone. Whatever it was that had sparked into flame between Jess and me had just as quickly burned out. For all I knew I was the only one who'd felt anything anyway.

I raised a hand and brushed my finger along Ronnie's puffed up, angry lips, and her frown fell away. I felt her breath hitch, and I traced a line from her lips to her hairline, pushing her thick waves away from her face. I could lean in and kiss those lips. I should. Shouldn't I? I wanted to. Didn't I?

The desire grew faint with every question mark. And this is why I don't think things through. Thoughts kill action. Happens every time.

I backed away and motioned for her to sit down. She was disappointed, and I could tell she had been hoping for more. She could hope all she wanted. Thankfully, Cash rushed over and took the only free spot on the couch.

"When did you get a dog?"

"His name is Cash." I deliberately avoided her questions. This wasn't a personal call. Not as far as I was concerned. She could answer my questions, but her money didn't buy her the right to ask me a bunch of personal questions. Five grand wasn't nearly enough for that.

"He's handsome."

"Yep. You want to tell me why you stopped by?"

"I thought you might have an update for me."

I picked up my phone from the table between us and glanced at the display. "See this thing? You call it and you can either talk to me or leave a message. If I have something to tell you, I'll use it to make contact."

"And when you decide to ignore me?"

"I need free rein. I told you I'd meet Jorge in the morning."

"You also said you were doing some legwork today."

"And I did."

"Did the cop you had lunch with today tell you anything?"

I'd had enough. As much as I'd hate to do it, I'd march right down to the bank and pull out what was left of the money she'd paid, but no way was I going to be micromanaged, followed, and spied on.

I stood up. "I'll get you your money back tomorrow. We're done."

"I have a right to keep up with what you're doing. You really think talking to cops will help? They're the reason he's in this mess."

I started to defend Nancy's honor, but bit back the words. She'd hired me to do a job, and it was none of her business how I did it. I told her as much.

"Luca, he's my brother. If anything happens to him, my mother will die."

"Don't drag your mother into this."

"Don't make me beg."

"Why not? You're really good at it. What you're not so good at is being grateful. Maybe I've had enough of sticking my neck out for you."

"If that's true, then you wouldn't have agreed to help in the first place. You may like the money, but I know that's not what it's all about for you." She moved closer, her breath warm with whispered promises. "And you know it too."

I backed away. Not because I wanted to, but because I knew if I didn't I was going to fall for her charms one more time. She sensed my fear and played it.

"I've never known you to be scared of anything. Am I really too much for you? Or are you just so hung on up on Jessica Chance that you won't take advantage of what's ripe and ready?" She closed the distance between us again, and before I could sidestep, I was locked in a searing kiss.

I'm not a rock. I kissed her back. For a while, focusing on the physical and ignoring all the warning bells that clanged a symphony in what was left of my brain. When she finally pulled back, I struggled to breathe, but there was no air left in the room.

"She holds back when she kisses you, doesn't she?"

If not for those words, I probably would've remained in a haze, hypnotized by her sexuality. But no way was I going to stand there and let her try to dissect whatever it was Jess and I had. Even if it was nothing, it was our nothing, and I refused to discuss Jess with Ronnie.

I decided against telling her that. She was stubborn. Tell her you don't want to talk about something, that's all she wants to talk about. So I did what I do best, I avoided the issue by changing the subject. "Tell you what. I won't quit until after I talk to Jorge. Tell him to be on time tomorrow. But if you don't leave now, we're done. You understand?"

Her know-it-all smile pissed me off. "I understand. But, Luca, I hope you know we're not even close to done."

Before I could say another word, she was out the door and I was left wondering what she really wanted from me.

❖

Nancy showed up at ten fifteen and I met her at the door. When I motioned to Cash to follow us, she didn't say a thing. She drove a two-seater Corvette. I glanced at Cash and considered our options. "I think I'll take my own car."

"Don't be silly. We'll fit."

I knew we could make it work, but when I'd agreed to let her pick me up, I hadn't considered riding shotgun to an unknown destination, and the thought made me a little edgy.

"Come on. Don't be a baby. You scared of a little speed?"

Whatever. I wasn't scared of anything, and to prove it I opened the door and peered in. "Nice car. You work a lot of overtime to pay for it?"

"I always work a lot of overtime, and not everyone can drive an antique."

"Very funny."

She patted the wide console between our seats. "Cash can sit here."

I motioned for him to take his place. Once she hit the highway, I crossed my fingers he'd live through the ride. The way she drove, he might fly through the windshield if she had to make a sudden stop.

When we finally pulled off the interstate and I could hear myself over the engine, I asked Nancy exactly where we were going.

"Lucky Seven."

"Sounds like a casino, not a bar."

"It's both, but casino is kind of a fancy word for what goes on in the back room. Mostly small-time card games. Nothing big enough to interest us."

Maybe it didn't interest Dallas vice, but I'd been itching for a decent card game since a local mob boss had put my favorite game out of business. Bingo, aka Morris Hubbard, had been running a gambling house in Dallas since I'd been old enough to remember, but just a few weeks ago, local mobster Geno Vedda had left a couple of dead bodies at Bingo's house. Between the cop scrutiny and the blood in the carpet, Bingo had had to shut his place down for a while. Maybe the Lucky Seven would be my new local haunt.

"Careful, Luca. I can see your wheels turning."

"Seriously? Gambling is not a vice. The city would be better off if you guys investigated real crimes instead of consenting adults playing table games. Besides, the state has no problem running its own sanctioned gambling."

I'd had this same conversation with Jess more times than I could count, and she had a tendency to agree with me in the abstract, but she was always quick to point out how quickly I ran through my paydays at the gambling table. What can I say? Other people like to go to the mall and buy useless shit. I like to wager my money. At least sometimes it actually paid off, and I didn't have a closet full of clothes I would never wear.

Nancy just shook her head. "Fine. Do what you want, but don't call me when you run into trouble. These guys don't run a tab, and you'll get your legs broken if you can't pay your debts."

"I thought you said it was a small game."

"Small to us, but to them it's everything."

"Bet they love having vice in here."

"Far as I know, this isn't a regular hangout for Greg. I don't have a clue why he suggested this place, but that's his truck." She pointed at one of the two vehicles in the lot. "You plan on leaving the dog in the car?"

It was cool enough, but I had no idea how he would behave in what I imagined was a pretty expensive ride. Besides, I liked the idea of strolling into a bar with a big dog at my side. "No, I think I'll bring him with."

We entered the dimly lit building, and Nancy pointed to a guy at the bar and whispered, "That's him." Like I wouldn't know since he was the only live body in the place. He looked up as we entered and motioned for us to join him at a booth in the corner. The low light couldn't hide the scattered bits of trash on the sticky floor. When we sat down at the booth, I was careful not to place my hands on the table. Instead of his customary sprawl on the floor, Cash, following my lead, stood beside the booth.

Nancy introduced us, and Jackson said, "Barkeep's in the back. He should be back soon."

"That's cool." I wanted a beer, but I wasn't sure I wanted to risk botulism to drink it. That was saying a lot for me. "I guess Walters told you what I want."

"You want to figure out a way to pin Moreno's crimes on someone else. Am I right?"

I glanced at Nancy who nodded, prompting me to be straight with him. "That's about right."

"And I'm thinking I might be the prime candidate."

"Actually, I hadn't gotten that far, but if the shoe fits."

He took a deep pull from his beer bottle and then wiped his mouth with the back of his hand. "Then I guess I shouldn't be talking to you at all."

"I guess you knew that before you ever agreed to meet with me, so I'm thinking you have something to tell me or we wouldn't be here at all." I waited while he contemplated the inside of his bottle.

I wasn't hopeful. I imagine he'd decided to show up tonight out of some cop solidarity thing or maybe just to size me up, but no way was this guy going to give me anything that would help Jorge. I'd just about decided it was time to take off, when he spoke.

"Walters, you mind waiting for us at the bar?"

Nancy looked between us, clearly puzzled about the request and reluctant to comply, but she did what he asked. Jackson waited until she was settled on a barstool before he started talking.

"Jorge is green. He never should've been promoted to detective so soon."

"Okay."

"He's a nice enough kid, but he doesn't get how things work. You know what I mean?"

I didn't have a clue, but I nodded to keep him talking.

"Some of the guys let him work their CIs, but he didn't really know what he was doing. When I tried to give him advice, he did that rookie thing, acting like he knew more than he did, saying he had it handled. You know what I mean, don't you, Bennett?"

Didn't take a rocket scientist to read an undercurrent there. He knew I'd been a rookie once and had never made it any further. I tried to follow what he was saying, but I really didn't have a clue where he was headed. "Did you know the CI he used, the one that testified before the grand jury?"

"Garcia? I knew him, but he was bad news."

"Why was he still on the books?"

"Other guys used him. He earned his keep."

"Care to give me names?"

"It's your investigation. You figure it out. Me? I've got too much at stake. The boy didn't listen, and that's his fault. I've got my own stuff to take care of."

He glanced around nervously, and I saw him fix on Nancy who was seated at the bar, acting like she wasn't trying to listen in. I lowered my voice to a whisper. "She okay?"

"Who's to say? Jorge didn't set this up on his own, and whoever did has the power to take anyone down."

"Funny. You seem to be immune. You want to tell me why you didn't get swept up by internal affairs?"

He shook his head. "Your guess is as good as mine." He stood up.

Not much of an answer, but Jackson was done. I asked a few more questions, but he waved me off and downed the rest of his beer. I finally gave up and climbed out of the booth. Nancy jumped off her barstool, and the three of us walked out of the bar. I looked down at Cash. He seemed a little twitchy. "Cash, you need to pee?"

Instead of a simple yes or no, I got a long string of whines and yowls. I turned to Nancy and shrugged. She said, "Pretty sure that's a yes. There's a field behind the bar where he can take care of business. I'll wait here. I need to talk to Greg."

Greg didn't look like he wanted to talk, but I figured I'd give her a shot. I whistled to Cash to follow me, and we walked behind the bar where I shooed him into the field. While he did what dogs do, I took stock of the surroundings. From the back, the bar looked like a rundown house with decades-old Christmas lights. The strings of big bulbs were the only outside decoration, although I had noticed a couple of neon beer signs through the window when we'd been standing out front. Hadn't seen a single customer in the place, but maybe they were in the back room playing cards. I doubted this was a place Jackson hung out when he was off duty, which made me wonder why he'd picked the place. The three of us would stick out like a sore thumb. Not only were we the wrong color for this part of town, we looked like we were gathered for something official, and folks who hang out in these kind of bars aren't partial to the official. Guess it was a good thing no one else was here tonight.

I looked across the field. Cash was no longer conducting business, but he was very interested in something moving through the brush, and he'd wandered pretty far off to find it. Probably a rabbit or a possum. Something likely to bite his nose if he caught it. I walked to the edge of the tall grass and whistled. He better come running because I wasn't about to wade in to get him.

Damn dog. He acknowledged my call with a few soft yowls, but he kept his nose to the ground and refused to come. From where

I was standing, I could see a portion of the front parking lot. Nancy was standing next to Jackson's truck and he leaned against the cab. Her arms were moving wildly, but I was too far away to hear what she was saying. I hoped she was almost done because I was ready to leave whether she was or not.

"Cash, get your ass over here right now."

I got a look, a whine, and a yip before he went back to his role as bloodhound. He seemed way too confident that I wasn't going to leave him. What he didn't know was that the chances of that were higher than me going out into that field and getting bit by a rabid raccoon or possum. Freaking dog.

I waved at Nancy to signal I was about done. When I finally caught her attention, she waved back and a loud pop accented the gesture.

That was weird, was the only thought I registered until I saw blood fan out across her chest. Her outstretched arm, the one that had been pointed toward me, was the last thing to hit the ground. Behind her, Jackson yelled something at me, but I couldn't make out the words. He emphasized the point with his own waving arms, but all I could think was don't do that, man, didn't you see what just happened to her when she pointed my way? As if he heard me, he stopped waving, grabbed Nancy's prone body, and started to drag her off behind his truck.

In the midst of continued gunfire, Cash's voice rang loud, and I dropped to the ground and turned, finally registering that whatever was happening in front of me, was coming from behind and over toward where Cash had been exploring. Two guys with guns were running away through the field, in the opposite direction of the bar, but only one was getting anywhere since the other had a Husky attached to his arm. The endearing sounds Cash usually made had turned into ferocious snarls as he gnawed on one of the gunmen's arms. I pulled out my long Colt and fired it once in the air. The noise froze both of them, and before Cash could resume his meal, the guy took off running after his friend. Cash looked at me and barked as if asking whether he should follow.

"Stay, Cash. Stay." I motioned for him to come to me and then fired another shot to encourage the guys to keep going in the direction they were headed. I wanted to go after them, but Nancy was down. Last time I'd left an injured cop to chase a bad guy, the cop had died. I only hesitated a second before running over to Jackson's truck.

Nancy was sitting up against the right rear wheel—definitely a good sign. Jackson was lying flat on his face, blood spreading out on the ground around him—definitely not a good sign. I shot a look at Nancy and she held up her phone. "I already called it in. See if you can turn him over. They got me in the shoulder. I can't move him."

I holstered my gun and used both hands to roll Jackson, nice and easy, while looking for the entry wound. It was in his chest and he was barely breathing. I tore off one of his sleeves and pressed it against the wound. All we could do now was hope the paramedics got here quick. I turned back to Nancy. "You okay?"

"I think it just grazed me. I'll be fine."

She didn't look fine. Her face was pale and her hands were clammy. She looked like she was going to pass out. I'd probably looked that way the first time I'd been shot. A few times later, I knew what to expect. It hurt like hell and I felt like I was going to die, but I never did.

I looked at the doors to the bar. Something was bugging me, and I scanned the porch trying to figure it out. Nothing, no one. Everything looked exactly the same as it had when we'd arrived. Deserted. I had a feeling no one was playing cards in the back room and the bartender who'd served Jackson was nowhere in sight. Yep, only two vehicles remained in the parking lot, Nancy's and Jackson's. I bet the building was empty. This whole thing reeked of a setup.

Before I had time to process the thought, three black and whites roared into the dirt parking lot, sirens and lights full on. I got to my knees and put my hands in the air, bracing for the treatment to follow. Nancy's officer down call would bring the full force of DPD down on whoever had committed this crime, and right now, they were going to focus on the armed civilian who didn't have a gunshot wound as the likely suspect. Thankfully, Nancy was conscious or I would be facing a grueling interrogation. As it was, the questions would come, but at least I wouldn't be the focus. I'd been booked in as a murder suspect before, and it wasn't an experience I wanted to relive. Probably not a coincidence that the time before had been while working a case with Ronnie. Jess was right. The woman was trouble, and I planned to lose her as soon as I got through this.

Just before the officers opened their doors, I leaned over to Cash whose head was stretched across Jackson's thigh and said, "Stay down. No matter what." His yip was muted, and he hunkered down while I turned back to face what I knew would be a very long night.

CHAPTER NINE

"Talk to Detective Walters. She'll tell you what you want to know."

We were on hour three, and I was getting cranky. I couldn't remember my last meal, and I had no idea where they'd taken Cash when they'd escorted me to this interrogation room at police headquarters. Some detective I didn't know with a shiny bald head had asked me to repeat my story about fifty times, and his anger escalated each time I relayed the facts. I didn't have a clue what Nancy or Jackson—if he was alive—would say, so I kept the details to a bare minimum to accommodate variations. And I sure wasn't about to ask about the dog. If they thought I cared about the dog, it would give them a wedge.

I'd expected a grilling, but I hadn't thought it would take this long for them to sort out that I wasn't involved in whatever had gone down. I attributed part of the problem to Nancy being at the hospital getting stitched up and Jackson being in no condition to talk about anything.

"We want to hear your side of the story."

"I don't have a side."

He turned and nodded at an invisible friend. "She doesn't have a side. That's convenient. So you just happened to be at this nightclub where a couple of cops get shot up and you don't have a scratch?"

I wanted to make fun of his calling the dilapidated Lucky Seven a nightclub, but instead I shrugged and then pretended like I was fascinated by something on the floor. I was done talking. If this kept up much longer, I was calling a lawyer. I mentally cycled through my contacts and quickly realized the last time I needed a lawyer Ronnie had filled the bill. She'd be the logical choice this time since she'd gotten me into this mess. She owed me. But if I called her and she helped me out, we'd be back to even. No, I'd call Hardin if things dragged out. He'd know someone who could help me out.

I heard the door open, but I didn't look up. Apathy was my new best friend.

Until I heard her voice.

"Luca Bennett. I knew you'd be back. Couldn't make it as a cop, so you decided to take a few down instead?"

I couldn't help it. I looked up into the eyes of my nemesis, shooting her what I hoped was a strong you don't scare me look. Teresa Perez was a bitch on a good day, and she rarely had good days, especially not when I was around. We hadn't gotten along since the day we'd first met. She'd been Jess's mentor on the force, and I figured she always wondered what Jess saw in me. Last year when Ronnie hired me on a case that placed me at a murder scene with a dead stripper, Teresa had been certain I was up to no good. When she couldn't pin it on me, it only fueled her constantly brewing anger. What had happened tonight was likely to make her explode, especially if she learned why we were at the Lucky Seven to begin with.

"Come on, Luca. I thought you liked Walters. Why'd you go and get her shot? Or do you just like getting all your women shot? Is that it?"

I gripped the edge of my chair with both hands and resisted fighting back. I knew she was referring to Jess. A few weeks ago, she'd taken a bullet meant for me after I stirred a hornet's nest to life. I knew Jess well enough to know she figured she was just doing her job, but if I hadn't gone off half-cocked, she wouldn't have had to race in to save me. Perez probably compared what had happened with Jess to the death of Larry Brewster, and maybe she wasn't far off the mark. I'd left him to go after the shooter, and Perez was convinced that if I'd obeyed orders to stay put and wait for backup, he'd still be alive. The doctors said it wasn't true, but I still felt a trace of doubt. I was the trouble spreading harm to the people around me.

I shook my head to get Perez's venom out. Maybe I was the bad seed, the evil center to a vortex that whirled the unlucky souls around me into harm's way, but I wasn't about to admit it to her. I faced her square and spoke the only words she was going to hear from me tonight. "Book me or let me go."

❖

"Get in."

Jess didn't wait for me to respond before she got behind the wheel of her car. I squinted at the sunlight reflected off the chrome. What a way to spend the morning.

After I'd repeated my mantra of "I'm not talking" to Perez for the fourth time, she and Detective Baldy left me in the interrogation room for another couple of hours. Occasionally, a uniformed officer poked his head in and looked me up and down and then stepped back out. Once, he brought me a cup of water that I stubbornly refused to drink. Finally, Detective Baldy cut me loose without so much as a "take care." When I walked outside and saw Jess waiting, I knew the reason for the curt release.

I stared at Jess's car. I didn't have a lot of options for a ride since my Bronco was back at my apartment. I climbed in the passenger side and barely had the door shut before Jess slammed the gas. Jess shot me a look that said we had some talking to do, but after a night of no sleep and no food, I wasn't in the mood. I leaned back in my seat and shut my eyes, wishing for a nap on the way to wherever she planned to take me.

Before I could count ten sheep, I felt the car slow and then stop. Coffee? Donuts? I opened my eyes and struggled to focus on the building in front of me. We were in the parking lot of the SPCA. "What the hell?"

"They dropped your dog here." Jess didn't wait for a response before getting out of the car, and I finally realized she expected me to follow. As we approached the doors, I pointed to numbers painted on the door. "They're closed."

And that was good, right? I'd planned to take the dog to the shelter, and last night was proof I didn't need complications in my life. If we picked up the dog, I'd have to walk him and feed him before I could do anything I wanted. I turned to walk away, but Jess walked around to the back of the building. A couple of seconds later, she shouted for me to follow. When I found her, she stood next to an open door and a baby butch dressed in scrubs.

"They have a twenty-four hour emergency clinic," Jess offered, as if that would explain why we were here.

My apathy about Cash disappeared, replaced by anger. "Did those assholes hurt him?"

Jess and the butch both wore confused expressions, but I persisted. "He was fine when the cops got there. If they hurt him, I'll…"

I didn't know what I'd do, and I wasn't sure why I cared so much. But I did. I started to push past them, but Jess grabbed my arm.

"Hold up. He's fine. I just meant, we can get in this way. You know, because the clinic's open even though the adoption desk doesn't open until later."

"Okay." I calmed down and tried to breath through the word "adoption." "What's the drill?"

Jess pulled out her badge and showed it to the child dressed like a doctor. "Her dog"—she pointed at me—"was brought in by mistake. We need to pick him up."

Butch junior glanced between us, no doubt wondering why Jess was hanging out with the likes of me. I didn't need a mirror to know that I was wrinkled, dirty, and smelled like a Dumpster. Jess, on the other hand, was fresh, pressed, and wore a touch of that musky cologne that turned me on. Judging by the lingering look, it turned the child on too. I waved a hand in front of her face to break the spell. "Hello, my dog?"

She reluctantly tore her gaze away from Jess and motioned for us to follow her into the building. Jess flashed me a grin, and I knew she had noticed the baby butch salivating. I wanted to punch them both.

A minute later, we were in front of a line of crates all filled with howling canines. Except one. Cash sat up when we walked over, but didn't say a word. I know I hadn't known him long, but his silence was totally out of character. I nodded and he stood up. Still not a word.

"Something's wrong. Have you checked him out? Made sure he's not hurt?" My questions were directed at the baby butch, but I couldn't help but notice the odd expression on Jess's face in response to my interrogation. What? She thought I didn't give a shit about the dog? I may be a jerk, but I wasn't heartless. Did she really think I was heartless?

Maybe she did. Maybe she had good reason. I couldn't process that right now. All I wanted was to go home, crawl in bed, and pretend I'd never met Ronnie Moreno.

"Oh shit." Thinking her name triggered my memory. I was supposed to meet Jorge this morning. At the lake. The clock on the wall told me I had about forty-five minutes to deal with the dog, lose Jess, get my car, and get to the meeting. Likely impossible and I should blow it off, but after what had happened last night, I was personally invested. Nancy was a good person, and even though I hadn't been the direct cause, I felt guilty about her getting shot.

"Do you want the dog or not?"

Jess tapped a finger against the crate and waited for my response. I could tell she'd misinterpreted my cussing to be about the dog, and that was good. She didn't need to know anything more about what else I was up to. That there was any question I was going to take Cash home showed she still didn't think I had it in me to take care of anything other than myself. "Of course. He's my dog."

Fifteen very long minutes later, Cash and I climbed into Jess's car. She turned the key in the ignition. "You want breakfast? We could stop at Fuel City, grab some tacos."

"Actually, if you could just take me home, that would be great. Then you could go on with your day and all..." I left my voice trail off, and I looked out the window to avoid her scrutiny. Didn't work.

"You got somewhere you need to be? Because if it's like the place you had to be last night, you can forget it. We're having breakfast and then you can tell me all about what you were up to that got Nancy and Jackson shot."

"How are they doing?"

"Don't even think you can change the subject. Nancy's fine. Bullet went straight through. Jackson's a whole other story. Got hit in the spinal cord. They did surgery, but he's in a coma and they don't know if he's ever going to wake up."

"Oh." I didn't know what else to say. I didn't know the guy, but I didn't wish him any harm. Someone did though, and I found it hard to believe it had anything to do with me or the questions I wanted to ask him. "Where's Nancy?"

"They're keeping her for the day. She'll probably go home tonight or tomorrow. Why? You want to get in touch with her so you can keep your story straight?"

I didn't bother answering. Why had things between Jess and me gotten so contentious? Was it just the reappearance of Ronnie, or was it something else? Like my inability to say what I was really feeling, thinking? I decided to test the theory and see if things changed. "I want to tell you something, but I need you to promise you're not going to blow up at me."

Jess pulled the car over into a gas station parking lot. Ever law-abiding, she parked in an actual spot, turned off the engine, and turned to me. Cash sat in the backseat, and he moved up a little and placed his head on my shoulder. I couldn't see his face, but I knew the effect his picture-perfect handsomeness would have on Jess. She could barely hide a smile as she answered. "Okay. Spill. I promise not to get mad at you in front of your dog."

"I reviewed the file Moreno left for me about her brother's case. There are a couple of fishy things about it. First off, he'd barely been promoted to vice when he's making all these deals with established CIs. Doesn't seem like he'd be in a position to go off on his own and set up an operation of the size he's accused of."

"Okay, what else?"

I heard a slight grating of teeth, but otherwise, her response was calm and measured. I pushed on. "Do you know who reported him to IAD?"

She shook her head.

I was genuinely surprised she hadn't heard. "It was Perez."

Her turn to be surprised. "How would she know anything about it?"

"She told IAD that a snitch she worked with on a homicide investigation tipped her off. I don't buy it. Especially not when she showed up at the station last night to give me the fifth degree. If no one's dead, then why is a homicide detective taking the lead on last night's shooting?"

"She was at the hospital too." Jess wasn't really talking to me. She was thinking out loud, and I wisely shut up and listened. "Stayed with Jackson like glue until they took him into surgery."

I waited to make sure she was done talking. "Okay, so what do you think that means?"

She shook her head. "Could mean nothing, but I have to admit it is a little strange. I've never seen the two of them hang around together."

She seemed really calm and like she was actually listening to what I had to say, being kind of thoughtful about it, so I plunged ahead. "I'm supposed to meet Jorge this morning. To talk about the case."

"Luca, you need to stay as far away from him and this case as humanly possible." Her voice rose with each word.

I held up a hand and pointed at Cash. "Whatever happened to not getting mad at me in front of the dog?" Cash helped me out with a pleading look.

"Whatever. Go meet him, see if I care. I'll take you to your place. Whatever you do after that is your business."

I looked at the digital readout on her dashboard clock and did a quick calculation. It was seven forty-five. No way could we make it to my apartment and get back to the lake in fifteen minutes. But the getting to the lake in fifteen minutes part was doable if we skipped going by my place. "I kinda need a ride." I talked real fast to squelch her protest. "Take me to the lake and drop me off. I'll find a way home later. I'll even check in later to let you know I made it back okay. Don't you want to find out why Nancy got shot?"

That last bit of play on her naturally curious mind was dirty pool, but it's all I had. She started the engine and drove out of the lot. "I'll take you to the lake, but I'm not dropping you off. I'm staying. I do want to know what happened to Nancy, but based on your inability to keep her out of trouble last night, I think you're going to need some help."

"Wait a minute. This is my case. In case you forgot, you're not a PI. You're duty bound to do what some muckety-muck at DPD tells you to do, and right now, they're trying to hang my client out to dry. Pretty sure you being anywhere near the case is a conflict."

"Then it looks like you're the one who's got a conflict. You want to meet Jorge, you take me along. You want to do this on your own, I can let you out here."

"Here" was a ratty part of town consisting of old warehouses and liquor stores. I wasn't sure why Jess was being so persistent, but I'd figure out how to shake her later, after I got what I wanted. I nodded, and she drove us to the meeting place.

CHAPTER TEN

White Rock Lake was about as yuppie as I ever get. It was a haven for fitness freaks who liked to pretend they were actually in the great outdoors—a myth that was dispelled the minute you saw the downtown Dallas skyline on the horizon. Most mornings, you could find a bunch of chiseled riders on souped-up bicycles, running moms with strollers, and even a few sailboats if the wind was right. I liked it because it made me forget I lived in a crummy apartment, drove a beat-up Bronco, and wasn't likely to ever be anything other than a bum.

Jess pulled into the first parking lot we came to and idled the car. "Where exactly are you supposed to meet him?"

"Tell you what. I'll get out here and I'll meet you at the Bath House."

"I'll tell you what. I'm not leaving you until you tell me where you're meeting him."

Her expression was stern. She wasn't backing down. I resorted to pleading. "Come on, Jess. You know he's not going to talk to me with you around."

"Look at me. Do I look like a cop right now?" She pointed at her jeans and T-shirt. "I don't know the guy and he doesn't know me."

"Sure, not now, but he'll eventually figure it out, and when he does…" I didn't really know how to finish the sentence. What I wanted to say was Ronnie would be super pissed I'd brought a cop, especially Jess, to this meeting. Besides the jealous girl issue, Jorge was under indictment, and Ronnie had probably told him not to talk to law enforcement about his case. But I didn't get the feeling Jess was here as a cop so much as she was here to make sure I didn't get into trouble, a fact that once would have rankled. I was perfectly capable of taking care of myself, but I knew the minute I verbalized that, she'd point out a million examples of times that hadn't been the case. She was way better with specifics than me.

I looked up from the conversation in my head to see her waiting. Either I came up with a good, neutral excuse to ditch her or I could give in.

I gave in. "Come on, but no talking. You're like my bodyguard or something. No talking. Get it?"

She raised her hands. "Got it. You're the boss. I'm in the background." She drew a finger across her lips. "No talking. Got it."

I shot her a withering stare to let her know I knew she was mocking me. "We're meeting him at the boat slip. Hurry, we're running late."

Didn't take long to reach the spot. I spotted Jorge the minute we pulled up, and while Jess fiddled with turning off the car, Cash and I jumped out of the car. I'd resigned myself to the fact she was coming along, but I wanted a two-second head start to keep from spooking him. He was standing at the edge of the water, tossing breadcrumbs to the birds gathered on the shore. Even from a distance, I could tell he was beat down, shoulders slumped, haggard expression. The first time I'd met him, I'd known he was the type who'd be a cop for life. Well, no matter what the outcome of this investigation, he'd never be a cop again, and the realization was obviously taking a toll. Must be hard to want something so badly and lose it.

He looked up and I ducked my head to keep from showing him the pity I felt. He called out, and Cash dashed from my side and ran over to him. Damn dog. I ran over to join them.

"Jorge."

"Luca." He bent down and rubbed Cash's neck. "This your dog?"

"Yeah."

"She's beautiful."

I didn't bother correcting gender or supplying a name. I already didn't like that I had any feelings of pity for him. No sense making small talk. I heard footsteps behind me and remembered we did have one issue to clear up before we talked about his case. "I brought a friend. Her name's Jess."

He looked over my shoulder, then back at me. "Hey, I'm barely comfortable talking to you. If I hadn't promised Ronnie, I wouldn't be here."

You and me both, brother. "Ronnie trusts me and I trust Jess. You want my help, you have to talk to both of us."

"You got your money, right? What's up with setting conditions?"

"Your rich sister can't buy everything." I was ready to leave. I didn't need his help to figure out who'd set us up the night before and gotten Nancy shot, and I really didn't need to be sassed by a loser who'd probably blown a promotion for a few bucks on the side. I whistled at Cash and started to walk away, when Jess spoke up.

"She's the best chance you have. You really going to blow it because you're too proud to trust her?"

He puffed up, but before he could say anything, I pointed to a nearby picnic table. "Let's take it down a notch. I'm here to help you. If you want me to leave, I'm out of here, but I'm thinking you don't have a whole lot of folks on your side right now."

His resistance faded away, and he followed me to the table and we all settled in.

"Tell me about your partner, Greg Jackson." I watched him closely to detect any sign that he knew what had happened last night.

"He's a decent guy, but he wasn't big on me being assigned to him. He'd been with his old partner for years."

"And what happened with that?"

"Don't have a clue. I heard they had some kind of fight, and Davis, the other guy, asked to be transferred."

I resisted exchanging glances with Jess, but I filed away the bit of information for further investigation. So far, Jorge hadn't shown any signs that he knew what had happened to Jackson last night. "You ever talk to Davis?"

Jorge shook his head. "Never even met the guy. I hear he's in homicide now. Went there right after he left vice."

A transfer was one thing, but a step up to a more elite unit was another. Cops don't get to just pick and choose their assignments. Davis could've put in a request, but generally, a bump up would've required time and lots of hoops. I tried not to make too much of it. Could be the move was already in the works and Davis's desire to move to another unit was what caused the friction and not the other way around. I could work all that out later. Right now, it was time to drop the bomb and see what Jorge had to say.

"Jackson was shot last night. He's in a coma."

Jorge sprang up from the table. "Holy hell. You're fucking kidding me!"

I snuck a look at Jess as Jorge paced around, muttering obscenities. She rolled her eyes, and I had to wonder about all the show for a guy who wasn't "big on him."

I motioned for Jorge to sit back down and told him the rest. "Here's the kicker. He got shot right after meeting with me to talk about your case. Any idea if there's a relationship there?"

He shook his head, too quickly in my opinion, and I pressed on. "And a good friend of mine, Nancy Walters, who arranged the meet, was shot too. Just so you know, that's really the only reason I'm still interested in what's going on."

He hung his head. "I'm sorry about your friend and Jackson, but I had nothing to do with them getting shot. Too many people are getting hurt."

I sensed he meant more than folks getting shot. "What's that supposed to mean?"

"Just seems like whoever set me up will do anything to keep the truth from coming out."

"Maybe. Maybe it's not really all about you. If I'm going to figure this out, I need you to be perfectly honest with me, answer whatever I ask, even if you think the details don't matter. Can you do that?"

He nodded and I turned to Jess, hoping she would read my mind. She didn't need to hear the specifics directly from him. When he found out she was a cop, which was likely, she'd be in a weird position, not just with me, but with her buddies on the force. She called out to the dog, "Hey, Cash, let's go for a walk."

I waited until she'd put some distance between us before I motioned for Jorge to start talking.

"Jackson, he's been around a long time. Knows all the CIs. At first, he set up all the deals. It was like he didn't want to share, like I was going to steal his collars. I figured we were a team. An arrest would count for both of us, but it took him a while to come around."

"So, this CI that ratted you out, Garcia, is he one of Jackson's or someone you brought in yourself?"

"He had a record, but nothing recent. I picked him up and saw that he'd been registered with the department a while back. He hadn't done any work for us in a long time though."

CIs had to be on the department's registry in order to be paid. "Who registered him?"

"I don't remember. I was just glad I didn't have to go through the trouble to get him on the books. We talked and he agreed to make some deals for me."

"You mean you and Jackson."

"Yeah. That's what I meant."

That wasn't what he meant at all. I made a mental note to find out more about Garcia. Maybe Jess wouldn't mind a tiny bit of legwork since she'd bullied her way along to this meeting. I looked around and saw her and Cash playing fetch with a stick about a hundred feet away. For some odd reason, I liked seeing them get along so well. I'd never pictured Jess as an animal lover, although I had to confess I'd never really given it much thought. Her house was really neat, which seemed kinda like an animal-free zone. Of course, my place routinely looks like a bomb exploded in it and I never would've pictured me with a furry friend either.

I focused my attention back on Jorge and the CI. "Describe a typical buy with this guy."

I hadn't been on the force long enough to do more than hear about how vice cops did their thing, but I hung out with enough of them to hear war stories and figured I could tell if he was feeding me crap or not.

"I got the cash and recorded the bill numbers. I gave the money to Garcia and then staked out the area while he did the buy. When he was done, he'd come back, describe the perp, give me the drugs, and I'd make an arrest."

"You turned in the drugs and the money?"

"Whenever we made an arrest. You know how it is, sometimes the guy gets away."

"And you field-tested the drugs?" I asked, referring to the procedure where they tested a small amount of the contraband.

"Sure. Either me or Jackson did."

"How did you decide?"

"He did mostly. I mean, what was I supposed to do? He had seniority."

"Let me guess, the false positives were only on the buys that you field-tested."

"You got that right."

"Sounds like Jackson set you up."

"That's what I thought. At first. But it doesn't make any sense. I mean, what does he get out of it?"

I may not have been a cop long, but I'd left the force way more jaded than this guy. Was he really so naive not to see that his partner, who didn't like him in the first place, probably had a side deal with the CI to split the money and had conveniently set him up to take the fall? Maybe Jackson's talk the night before about how he didn't trust this CI was meant to throw me off his trail. "Did IAD talk to Jackson?"

"They talked to everyone."

"He's your partner. I'm pretty surprised he got cleared. Seems like if they thought you were dirty, they would've figured he at least knew something about it."

"Maybe he's not cleared. Maybe they were just waiting to see if they could get me to talk. Maybe he cut a deal with them. How the hell am I supposed to know? Not a single one of my so-called brothers in blue will even talk to me. About anything. And now you say Jackson's in a coma? Well, sounds like we'll never know what happened."

I watched him carefully through his rant, but I saw only fear, not satisfaction that the truth may never come out. Guilty guys have a tell. They protest too much, they can't look you in the eyes, they wave their arms. Something. Jorge didn't show any outward signs he was a bad guy, but I wasn't fully converted to the Jorge Moreno fan club. I looked over my shoulder and caught Jess's eye, willing her to rejoin us. She motioned to Cash and they both trotted over. Cash nuzzled my leg and Jess stood with her hand on his back. It was the most connected I'd felt to her since the afternoon of Mark's wedding. I prayed she'd keep reading my mind for a few minutes longer.

"Okay, Jorge, here's the deal. Not a word from you to anyone about anything to do with the case."

"Ronnie already told me that."

"Yeah, but that was before you knew your former partner got shot up. Don't show up at the hospital with flowers for Jackson or anything stupid like that. Go home, do whatever you family types do when you're not working, and let us handle the rest. I'll call you when I know something or if I have more questions. Got it?"

He nodded. "When will I hear from you?"

"Soon. I've got some ideas."

Jess looked like she wanted to say something else, but she took my lead and we headed back to the car. After Cash and I climbed in, she looked at him first, then me, and said, "Where to?"

I was sleepy, grimy, and hungry, and I could think of only one place I wanted to be.

"Take me home."

CHAPTER ELEVEN

G o take a shower. I'll make us something to eat." Jess strode off toward the kitchen and Cash followed, leaving me standing alone in her living room. When I said I wanted to go home, I'd meant my home. I hadn't thought past Jess dropping us off and Cash and me crawling into my unmade bed and spending the rest of the day snoozing off a night of being in custody. Now that I was here, in her tidy, roomy, comfortable house, my idea of a good day didn't seem so great. When I reached the bathroom, with its gleaming surfaces, cool ceramic tile, and rows of fluffy towels, I considered moving in.

I showered long enough to prune my skin, but I finally felt like I'd managed to soap off the stench of the interrogation room. Now I smelled like Jess. Some kind of spice. I'd spent the night, or at least a few hours in the night, here many times, but I'd never bathed in her house. I held up the bottle of liquid soap. White tea and ginger. Seemed kind of girly, but the smell was fresh. I liked it on her, but I wasn't sure how I felt about smelling it on me.

Cash nudged the door open as I was toweling off. I bent down to pet him.

"He's hungry, but I told him we had to wait for you."

Jess stood in the doorway, staring at my bare chest. The last few months, I'd doubted how she felt about me, but right now I knew that if nothing else, my body still turned her on. I dropped the towel to the floor. "Think he'd mind waiting a bit longer?"

She stepped forward and pulled me to her, raking her fingers over my exposed flesh. I was naked, clean, and hungry—perfect for the taking. I nuzzled my way toward a kiss, but just as I thought I knew where this was headed, she pulled back. "Let's eat, talk, and then we can do whatever you want." She and Cash left me to ponder her decision.

Her priorities were screwed up, but that was nothing new. She paid her bills on time and obeyed traffic laws too. I finished drying off with a new towel, and then pulled on a pair of sweats she'd left on the counter. Too short, but they smelled like her, and since that was as close as I was going to get for a bit, I enjoyed what I could get.

When I walked out of the bedroom, I detected a very different smell. Butter, batter, syrup. When I got to the kitchen, Jess was manning a griddle and she already had a platter stacked high with pancakes. I almost wept with gratitude. I can't remember the last time someone made me breakfast without making me pay for it. Even my mother, who'd played at the role of housewife until I was in high school, thought making breakfast meant lining up cereal boxes and setting out bowls. I leaned against Jess and reached around to grab a pancake off the stack. She swatted me with the spatula. "Hands off."

"I'm more for hands on." I took a huge bite and held up the crescent moon shape it had become. "Oh, sorry, were you talking about these?" I chewed for a few seconds. "These are amazing. Since when do you cook? And isn't it Thursday? Why aren't you at work?"

"Since always. Yes, it's Thursday, and I took the day off. I'm entitled."

She seemed a little touchy about the taking off work part, so I focused on the cooking. "You've never cooked for me before."

"First time for everything." She shot me an uncomfortable smile before turning her focus back to the griddle. Made me wonder if she'd cooked for someone else. Like her last girlfriend, Heather Deveaux, a doctor who'd turned out to be part crook. Heather had spent quite a bit of time here over the past few months, which was exactly why I hadn't. I felt a tiny stab of jealousy that the doctor with the shady past may have merited more personal attention from Jess than I did.

"Where did you learn to cook?"

"Since when are you so interested in my personal life?"

"Guess I'm surprised that after all these years, I can still learn new things about you."

"I've always cooked. My mother was a lousy cook. It was either learn to cook my own meals or starve."

Funny how different our approaches were. My experience with a mother who couldn't or wouldn't cook meant I'd eat pretty much anything, from anyone, anywhere, whereas Jess took it upon herself to get what she felt she deserved. "I never thought of learning. I guess I thought the 'I don't cook' gene was alive and well in my DNA and I shouldn't even bother."

She piled a plate full, added butter and syrup, and pushed it my way. "Here's one more day you can put off learning how to take care of yourself."

I couldn't read her tone. Sounded part wistful, part pissed. I tried to catch her eyes, but she was back at the griddle, dishing up a second plate.

"Jess?"

"Go ahead and start eating. It'll get cold."

I started to say she sounded like my mother, but she didn't. She sounded like someone else's mother. Didn't really matter, I wasn't in the mood to be mothered. The pancakes looked fantastic, but I was looking for something way more satisfying.

"Aren't you going to eat?" She set a plate on the floor and slid into the seat next to me. I glanced down and saw that Cash was already halfway through the two pancakes she'd given him. When I looked back up, she smiled. "Don't tell me you have him on a strict diet."

We both laughed and then dug in. I could barely contain my reaction as the strong flavors burst on my tongue. "Oh my God, these are amazing. What do you put in them? Crack?"

"Yes, I kept some from my days in vice and sprinkle a bit on all the food I make. It's made me quite a hit with the ladies."

I wanted to relive the taste more than I wanted to make a smart remark, so I shoveled another huge bite into my mouth. Jess smiled again like she was glad to give me such a simple pleasure. I glanced down at Cash, who'd wolfed down his take in three solid bites. "Sorry, fella. I'm not sharing. You'll have to suck up to her to get more."

As if on cue, he placed a paw on Jess's leg. "Do all Huskies have eyes this blue?" she asked.

"Like I would know. I don't have a lot of experience with dogs."

"You two seem to fit together."

I caught a hint of wistful in her tone. "You want to tell me why you showed up this morning?"

"And here I thought it was my job to save your ass."

I nodded at the confirmation she'd been the one to get Perez off my back. "Seriously, how did you find out what was going down?"

"John," she referred to her partner, "heard it on the radio. He figured you'd be in a bind. I made a few calls and found out Perez was on the warpath and decided to check it out myself."

"And coming along this morning to meet with Jorge, what's up with that?"

Jess pushed her plate to the side and leaned in on her elbows. I saw the strain in her eyes, the way her lips tightened. She had something serious to say, but she wasn't sure either how to say it or if she wanted to. I urged her along. "Whatever's going on, I'm in the thick of it now. I'm going to sort through it if for no other reason than to find out who shot Nancy. Wouldn't it be easier if we shared information? I trust you. Can you trust me?"

The wait time was pretty prolonged, and I began to wish I hadn't reached out, asked for help. No matter how many times Jess came to my rescue or fed me intel, she was a cop, through and through, and if she ever had to choose between me and the fellowship…Well, I didn't really want to know how that would go down.

"It's not about trust."

"You sure about that?" Should I say how I really felt? The minute Ronnie had charged back in, Jess had backed way off. I could tell she didn't trust whatever feelings we had for each other enough to know they could survive a little interruption from the ex.

Hell, I didn't even trust me. Why should I expect her to? I'd wanted to kiss Ronnie back at my apartment, and I wasn't entirely sure what had stopped me. Until I knew how I felt, how could I expect Jess to trust me?

But Jorge's case was different. It was business, and however much of a slacker I might be, I could be trusted to keep my word to the people I cared about. And I cared about Jess. I even cared about Nancy, for all her annoying flirtatious ways. "Look, I get why you wouldn't trust me, but I promise you all I want to find out is the truth. If it turns out Jorge is a bad cop, I'll back off, but I get the feeling something isn't right here and I think you do too. You can't get caught looking into this on your own, so use me for cover. And I can't find out all I need without someone on the inside. Together, we can figure this out." I walked over to stand behind her chair. Wrapping my arms around her, I leaned down and whispered in her ear. "We're always better when we work together, right?"

She turned into my embrace and kissed me. Soft at first. I tasted sweet syrup, and then hot need as the intensity of the kiss escalated. I pulled her upright, out of the chair, and pressed against her. Hip to hip, chest to chest. I loved the way we fit. Years of intimacy meant there was no awkward jostling, only mindless melding, allowing us to get lost in the rush. All I wanted right now was to feel her skin against mine, the quickening pulse of her heart, the wet between her legs.

She broke the kiss and I waited for her answer.

"I trust you."

Just what I needed to hear.

❖

After a half day in Jess's bed, Cash and I took a cab home to pick up the Bronco. Jess funded the expedition after we both decided that if we were going to work together, we needed to do a better job about hiding that fact. I hadn't wanted to leave at all. Full from pancakes, sated from sex, and content in Jess's bed was much more pleasant than facing my grungy, lonely apartment.

I called Nancy's cell as soon as the taxi dropped me off. Surprisingly, she answered on the first ring.

"Where are you?" she whispered.

"Home. Where are you?"

"Checking out of the hospital."

"Want me to pick you up?"

"Not a great idea. I've got plenty of folks here who can give me a ride."

I got it. She was surrounded by fellow cops, and the last thing she needed was for me to show up and raise questions. "How's Jackson?"

"Same."

"We need to talk."

"I'll call you when I get home. Maybe you can bring dinner over later and we can visit." She clicked off the line. The dinner and visit comment was likely for the benefit of whoever was standing around, but it wasn't a bad idea. I sent Jess a text to let her know I'd heard from Nancy and we might be going over later. I didn't figure Nancy would mind if I brought Jess along, and that way we could save her from having to repeat whatever she had to say.

I wanted to crash, but Cash was restless. I couldn't summon enough energy for a run or a trip back to the park, but I decided a walk to Maggie's for a late lunch might be the perfect solution to both our needs.

Moments after we walked through the door, I was in fear of losing my dog. Cash greeted Maggie like she was his long lost mother. She pulled him into a fierce hug and showered his head with kisses and promises of steak. I tapped on Maggie's shoulder to interrupt the lovefest. "Hey, we're hungry. Can you feed us?"

Big Harry, Maggie's head cook and bottle washer, called out, "Don't think we're supposed to have dogs inside."

Before I could reply, Maggie asked me in a loud voice, "Luca, what's the name of your *service* dog?"

"Cash." I wasn't sure where she was going with this and hoped I wasn't going to have to act like I'd suddenly become blind. It was one thing lying to the guy at the police station, but Maggie's crew was like family.

"Cash is a good name for a hardworking dog. We will feed the *service dog* for free. Harry, make him a steak."

Harry walked away, muttering, "Service dog, my ass."

I waited until he was out of sight and repeated, "Service dog, my ass."

Maggie was quick with a reply. "They have service dogs for all sorts of things: traumatized soldiers, crime victims, you name it. I saw it all on one of those Discovery channel shows." She bent down and snuggled Cash. "None this pretty. He's a looker for sure."

"Quit flirting with my dog."

She ignored my warning. "What're you doing with a dog, anyway?"

"Why can't I have a dog? Why does everyone think I can't have a dog?"

"Settle down. Everyone, huh? Guess I'm not the only one thinks it's weird. That ought to tell you something right there."

I was too hungry to cipher out her cagey response, so I let it go. "What's for lunch?"

"Whatever you want. I've given up trying to get you or your father to eat better. I know he runs around eating junk when I'm not around. No sense fighting it."

She was one up on my mother already. "Great. Burger with fries. Put bacon on it. And cheese. And a beer."

Maggie shook her head and poured me a beer. "Your brother is supposed to get back in town tomorrow night."

I had to think for a moment before I realized she was talking about his honeymoon. "I thought they were going to be gone a whole week."

"Linda could only get so much time off work."

"That sucks." My new sister-in-law—wow, that sounded weird—had just started a pediatric fellowship at Baylor. I didn't know what a fellowship meant other than she was a doctor who had to work all the time.

"I was thinking it would be nice if we decorated their house, had some food waiting for them when they returned."

"You mean like break into their house while they're still gone?"

She smacked me on the arm. "Don't be silly. They left a key. I've been checking their mail, picking up their newspaper, feeding the cat."

"They have a cat?" I had a hard time seeing my brother with any kind of pet, let alone a fuzzy, snobby cat. Of course, I never would've pictured my brother happily married either, but he'd looked pretty pleased on his wedding day.

"Focus. I'm going over there tomorrow with your father. You'll come with us."

It wasn't a question. "Sure." I decided to agree since I was sitting right here in front of her. I could always bow out over the phone at the last minute. Way easier to tell Maggie no when she wasn't in my face.

By the time my food was ready, the place got busy and Maggie didn't have time to harass me anymore. When I finished, I drove over to Hardin's place to see if he had any new business for me. At any moment, I could discover the smoking gun that proved Jorge was guilty as hell, and when that happened, Ronnie was likely to let me go. Better plan for the inevitable, even if planning wasn't my strong suit. Something about spending the morning in Jess's put together fairyland made me want to be a better person. I wasn't going to over think it, but it might feel good to fill up my coffee can and pay the rent too.

Hardin kept a lean staff on Saturdays, and Sally was on her own dealing with a client. She called out that she'd only be a minute, so I sat and pretended to read an ancient magazine in the waiting area. Before her client's ass hit the door, she called out, "Hey, Luca, next time you get caught in a shootout why don't you give us a call to spring you?"

"Very funny."

"That your dog?" She pointed at Cash and I nodded. "Handsome devil." She walked to the back door. I knew enough to follow her outside, and I held her purse while she dug around for a cigarette. Between puffs, she barraged me with questions.

"Heard one of your pals got shot up last night and the other guy's down for the count."

"Nancy's okay. The other guy's still alive as far as I know. His name's Greg Jackson. Vice cop. You heard of him?"

She answered with a long stream of smoke punctuated with a bobbing head. I looked down at Cash and had the random thought that smoke might not be good for him. Like it was good for me either. I shook off the odd sensation of worrying about the welfare of another being and focused on Sally. "Tell me what you know."

"If there was gunfire, you can bet Jackson was the cause of it. That guy's bad news. I've heard about him from lots of our clients." She lowered her voice to a whisper. "And it's not like he's never been in trouble himself."

I looked around to see if there was anyone else in the vicinity who could overhear our conversation, but no one else was anywhere in sight. Still, I matched her tone. "He's been arrested? Here in Dallas?"

"Yep. But it all got covered up."

"And you know this because…" It wasn't that I doubted her. Sally was in a position to hear and see all kinds of stuff, but a lot of it was rumor and speculation. Everything wasn't always what it seemed, and I didn't want to get my hopes up. That Jorge's partner had a record might be nothing more than a coincidence.

"I know you think I'm a party girl," she said, probably referencing the time I'd seen her out at the bar, half-dressed, dividing her attention between several women, "but I spend most nights listening to the police scanner. It was around a year ago, but I remember the call."

She took another puff. She knew I was hanging on her words, and I knew she was drawing out the story for maximum effect. It was working.

"Nine one one call on a domestic disturbance. I hate when we get those guys. They always have a ton of bond conditions and a protective order they're sure to violate."

"Sally!" I waved my hands to keep her on track. "Tell me what you know."

"I'm getting to it." Puff, puff. "The call was to Jackson's place. Wife said they got in an argument over how well done she'd cooked his steak, and he cleared the table with a baseball bat before coming for her. Broke her arm. Officers on the scene called for detectives from family violence. A detective showed up. Ambulance took the missus to the hospital."

"And Jackson?"

"Left the house. His wife divorced him, but no charges were ever filed."

"How do you know?"

"Because I kept tabs on it."

"Why were you so interested in his case?" I was beginning to think Sally's penchant for gossip had caused her to blow the importance of this event out of proportion.

"Because I'm nosy, that's why. Everything about the call was off. From the way the dispatcher acted when the call came in to the detective who responded to the scene."

I perked up. "Spill."

"Well, they only sent one detective even though protocol calls for two. And they sent the wrong kind. You have any idea why they would send a homicide detective to the scene of a domestic disturbance?"

The minute she said homicide detective I had a feeling I knew who had shown up, but I had to ask anyway. She took a long pull off the cigarette before answering, and it took every ounce of self-control I had not to strangle her.

"Teresa Perez. You know Perez, don't you?"

I hadn't known Sally or even Hardin at the time of my first run-in with Perez, but the story of the shooting that led to me leaving the department had made the papers. Because both our names had been mentioned in the various articles written on the subject, we'd forever be linked. That, and the fact that Perez played on Jess's softball team. And she kept showing up whenever I got in trouble. But the latest links defied coincidence. Teresa Perez, a homicide detective, just happened to show up to interrogate me about a cop shooting—no homicide involved. Teresa Perez also just happened to have been on the scene of a domestic disturbance with the same cop who'd gotten shot last night, and who now didn't have a record when he probably should've. I was pretty sure I hadn't even begun to scratch the surface. I needed to get away from the haze of smoke and back to my place to sort this out.

"How do you remember this?" I asked her. "Didn't you say it was a year ago?"

"I'm telling you, it's my hobby." She pulled her iPhone out of her purse and scrolled through the screens. "Look, there's even an app you can use to listen to the police scanner."

I stared as she pressed the button and brought the app to life. Suddenly, we were listening to a dispatcher at the Dallas Police Department sending officers to get rid of a panhandler blocking a busy intersection. Before the officers responded, a loud ring interrupted the transmission. Sally checked her phone. "Not me."

I pulled my phone out of my pocket and looked at the screen. It was Jess's partner, John. We were acquainted through Jess, but he hadn't ever called me just to chat. I punched "answer." "John, what is it?"

"Have you heard from Jess?"

"Not since this morning. Why? What's up?"

"I just got word Perez is on her way over there. She's not happy about Jess getting you sprung this morning, and there's no telling what she's up to now. I strongly suggest you stay far, far away."

"Why didn't you call her?"

"Her phone's off. She called me this morning and told me she was taking the day off to get you out of a mess, so I just figured you two were together." His tone implied he didn't think springing me out of police custody was the only reason Jess had taken the day off.

"I left there a while ago. Perez is a piece of shit. So help me, if she does anything to Jess, I'll—"

"I mean it, Luca," John interrupted me. "Don't get in the middle of this. Jess can handle herself. You'll just make it worse."

I hung up before he could finish warning me off. He knew me well enough to know he was wasting his breath. I signaled to Cash we were leaving, and shouted "thanks for the scoop" over my shoulder at Sally. A strong suggestion not to do something was a strong signal I should do exactly the opposite.

CHAPTER TWELVE

D idn't get enough pancakes?"
Jess stood in her doorway, wearing faded jeans and a tight black T-shirt. She was barefoot and her hair was as mussy as when I'd crawled out of her bed hours earlier. She looked sexy as hell, but all I could think about was who else was about to show up. I walked in with Cash and tugged Jess back into the house, slamming the door behind us. I walked over to the window and peered outside.

"Luca, what's going on?"

"Perez is on her way over."

"And?"

"And I think she plans on causing trouble. She's pissed you got me cut loose this morning."

"Where'd you hear that?"

"John just called me."

Jess shrugged as if she didn't have a care in the world. "What kind of trouble can she cause?"

I gave her my best "are you fucking kidding me" look, but she didn't give in.

"Seriously, Luca, I can handle her, but it's probably best if you're not here when she shows up."

"I'm not leaving, and there's another thing—"

The doorbell interrupted me, and I glanced through the window while Jess went to answer the door, and then braced for the fallout.

"What the hell?" Jess looked up from the peephole and shot me a withering look. "Why is Ronnie Moreno standing on my doorstep?"

I hadn't figured out how to tell her I'd called Ronnie, so I'd done what I usually do when something's uncomfortable. I put off dealing with it until absolutely necessary. I thought I'd have more time to think of a good explanation. "I called her."

"What the hell for?" She shook her head. "You gave her my address?" Her voice rose. "You gave your ex-girlfriend my address?"

I knew it would be silly to shoot back that Ronnie had never been my girlfriend. Kinda made me look pathetic, and Jess already knew I'd never had a girlfriend before. I'd called her because she was the only lawyer I knew who owed me enough to drop whatever she was doing on a Saturday afternoon and show up to help out. Jess may not think she needed an attorney, but I didn't trust Perez. And now that I knew she was twisted up in Jackson's mess, I suspected her capable of all kinds of evil. I grabbed Jess by the shoulders and forced her to look at me.

"Here's the deal. Perez is up to something. I can either beat her up or Moreno can get in the middle with her lawyer mojo and ward her off, but I'm not letting her do anything to fuck up your career. Are we clear?"

Jess shot daggers for a few seconds before cutting her eyes. "Okay, but I do the talking. Tell your girlfriend not to butt in unless I tell her too."

Girlfriend. Right. I ignored her goading and answered the door. Ronnie swept into the room, brimming with questions.

"Luca, what's going on? Did you find out something about Jorge's case? Is it bad? I was at my mother's and I had to make up some excuse about leaving. They are worried sick about Jorge, but I didn't want to tell them it was you that called, well, because my mother loves you and I didn't want them to get their hopes up." She stopped for a quick breath and then turned to Jess. "Jorge says you're helping him. Well, he didn't know who you were, but I do and I can't tell you how much I appreciate you taking a chance like this."

"Helping him?"

Jess's voice was strangled. I rushed over to her side and grabbed her hand in an effort to defuse the explosion I knew was coming. Once I was certain Jess wasn't going to blow, I turned to Ronnie. "Jess went with me to meet Jorge this morning because my car was…" I wasn't about to tell her about my involvement in the shootout last night. "It wouldn't start and she gave me a ride. That's it. She's not involved. But now Teresa Perez thinks she is, and she's on her way over here. I don't know what she wants, but I can guarantee she's not coming over here to offer her assistance. I need you to keep Jess out of this, or I'm off the case. Can you do that?"

Ronnie looked back and forth between me and Jess while I prayed she would keep things professional. "How do you want to play this?" she asked.

The doorbell rang again and Jess took over. She pointed at me. "You. Get lost. She doesn't need to know you're here." She jabbed a finger in Ronnie's direction. "You stay quiet unless I specifically ask you to talk."

I considered arguing with Jess. After all, my car was parked out front, and Perez was an ass, but she wasn't stupid. But since the goal of getting Ronnie here was to keep Jess out of trouble, I decided to do my part and I strode into the bedroom and listened through the cracked door.

Their voices were somewhat muffled, but there was no mistaking the tone. Perez was pissed.

"Where is she and what is she doing here?" Perez demanded. Pretty clear she was talking about both me she and Ronnie she.

"Neither one of those things is any of your business. Does your captain know you're investigating somebody else's case? Don't you have enough to do without sticking your nose into things that don't concern you?"

"Careful, Chance. A cop gets shot, it's everyone's business. Unless you're working for the other side. Is that your problem?"

"I'm as much a cop as you are. Don't you dare imply differently."

"Then you won't mind if I look around. Make sure you're not trying to hide anything."

Ronnie interjected. "She would mind, and unless you have a warrant, you need to leave, Detective Perez."

Uh-oh. Should've known any woman I'd been with wouldn't be able to follow instructions. I listened for the fallout, but instead, I heard Jess say, with steely calm, "Yeah, what she said."

Teresa Perez was anything but calm. "Oh, so that's how it's going to be? You going to listen to the advice of this piece of shit lawyer over your fellow police officers? How far you've fallen, and all because of that Bennett trash. When are you going to figure out she's bad news and you're never going to save her from herself?"

Silence.

I listened hard, but nothing. Apparently, neither Ronnie nor Jess had a single word to offer in my defense. I was on the verge of mounting a protest, when Jess spoke.

"Detective Perez, you need to leave my house now and you better not be back here without a warrant. And stay away from Bennett. Do you hear me?"

"I hear you loud and clear. Finally showing your true colors, hey, Chance? Well, I hope she's great in the sack because your career is finished." Seconds later, I heard the door slam.

I sat on Jess's bed. We'd spent a lot of time here in this room, but hardly any of it had been about anything other than physical satisfaction. How satisfying was it if it ruined Jess's life? I may not have understood what she found so fulfilling about being a cop, but I didn't want her to lose the central thing that had defined her existence for as long as I'd known her. I especially didn't want to be the cause of that loss.

"Luca, you coming out here or what?" Jess's voice boomed.

I wanted to crawl out the window. Now that the adrenaline had worn off, I couldn't believe I'd called Ronnie and that she'd actually shown up at Jess's place. The last thing I wanted to do was face them both, in the same room, but there were limited places to hide.

When I entered the living room, they were both sitting on the couch, talking. To each other. No raised voices, no frowns. If I didn't know better I'd think they were old friends.

"Am I interrupting?"

Ronnie looked up, an elusive expression in her eyes. "Not at all. Jessica was telling me how you two met."

"Nice. Next we can call my mom and she can tell you stories about my childhood."

Jess pointed at the chair next to the couch. "Sit."

I didn't want to, but I did. It was one small thing I could do for her.

"Now," she said, "Tell me what you meant when you said Perez is all twisted up with Jackson."

I'd given Ronnie a thumbnail sketch over the phone, but now I told both of them what I'd learned from Sally. By the time I finished, Ronnie was on the edge of her chair, practically frothing at the mouth.

"So you're telling me that Teresa Perez covered up the fact that Jackson beat his wife? That he broke her arm and put her in the hospital?"

"I don't really know what happened, but it sure sounds that way. And then she ratted out your brother, who just happened to be Jackson's partner for stuff Jackson himself may have done. And then she shows up when Jackson gets shot to try to manage the investigation and pin the shooting on me, or at least get people to think it was caused by my investigation into your brother." When I said it all out loud, it was obvious we were talking about more than a string of odd coincidences.

Ronnie obviously agreed. "Sounds like a little Freedom of Information Act request is in order. I'll serve them with a subpoena too just to cover our bases." Ronnie pulled out her phone, but before she could start dialing, I reached over and grabbed it out of her hand.

"Give that back to me," she said.

"Slow down, Atticus Finch. There are complications." I gave a slight nod in Jess's direction, hoping Ronnie wouldn't make me spell out the conflict. I shouldn't have sweated it. She knew exactly what I meant, and she didn't hold back telling me exactly what she thought.

"Hold on a minute. Are you telling me I shouldn't use information you obtained while you were working for me because it might get your cop buddies in trouble? Hey, Luca, you think maybe you shouldn't have taken my money if you weren't willing to do the job I hired you for?"

Before I could answer, Jess spoke up. "She's right, you know. You need to figure out where you stand."

"What's that supposed to mean?"

"It's time to stop living your life like there are no consequences. You can keep working on this case, get to the truth, but people are going to get hurt along the way—some of them good people. Your choice."

I looked back and forth between them, but neither one of them was going to save me from the decision. I could stick with Ronnie and find out the truth about Jorge's case, discover why Nancy got shot, and how Perez was involved. I'd earn my five grand, maybe more. I could pay my rent, feed me and my dog, all while doing a job way more meaningful than chasing bail jumpers. How was what Jess did so different from this? If I followed through, I'd be doing exactly the same thing she did on a daily basis. I might hurt Jess in the process, but it was beginning to sound like she was choosing Perez and all the silence among cop shit over me, so there was that.

"Ronnie, give us the room. I'll call you later."

She looked surprised. Of course she did. She thought she'd won this round. There weren't going to be any winners, but I needed a second with Jess before I could even say what side I was on. I stared her down until she stood up, brushed off her skirt, and walked over to my side.

"I'll call you later." Her words sure, confident. Wish I felt that certain.

I waited until she'd driven away before taking the spot she'd occupied on the couch. Next to Jess, but closer. Didn't matter how close I got, we were a million miles apart.

"I've got a job. I made a promise."

"Like that's ever meant anything to you." Jess didn't face me as she spoke, but instead of biting, her tone was neutral, like the words didn't matter. We'd had this discussion endless times. She did the work of the righteous; I caught the dregs who got away. If I didn't feel like working, I stayed in bed. Even when I did work, I didn't have any of the badges of a respectable position: a regular paycheck, health benefits, or a retirement. My landlord was constantly looking for me because I was behind on rent. I kept my life savings in a coffee can.

I flashed back to the night of Mark's wedding, before Ronnie appeared on my doorstep. I'd been about to say things I'd never said to Jess. Never said to anyone. Big things. Big things to me, anyway. Had Ronnie saved the day? And if she had, who really got saved—me or Jess?

But what I did for a living did mean something to me, even if it wasn't a J-O-B. It had never failed me, never betrayed me. It was freedom. It was not having to report to anyone else. It was all the things I'd have had to give up if I'd spoken the words Ronnie had interrupted.

I should've felt relieved, but all I felt was lost.

Cash wandered over and placed his head in my lap, and I instinctively petted his head.

"That dog seems to like you."

He did. And the bonus was he didn't have big expectations. Feed him, walk him, take him for a ride. About all the commitment I could handle. Funny how such a low bar was more commitment than Jess thought I was up for. I'd been crazy to think that even if I'd spoken out loud any of my crazy thoughts, she'd melt in my arms and agree to forever. Jess wanted more than I could ever offer. She deserved more.

"Look at me."

I waited a long time, and I thought she might refuse, but finally, she turned her head and we locked eyes. If I'd known this morning was the last time, I would have…I don't know what I would've done differently, but surely it would've been something. Probably something stupid, like say some of those words. Words she wouldn't believe, words she wouldn't say back. Hours after the haze of sex, I was smart enough to know exactly what to say.

"I have to see this through."

She didn't flinch. She didn't ask questions. She didn't react at all. I now knew all I needed to know. I stood and motioned to Cash. He followed me to the door and sat with his tail thumping on the floor as I tried to think of some parting words that didn't sound trite and stupid. In her usual way, Jess saved me by speaking our last words.

"Take care of yourself."

What choice did I have?

CHAPTER THIRTEEN

R onnie was waiting on my doorstep when I got home.
"Go away. I'm off duty for the night."

"I'm sorry."

She meant it. I could tell. But she wasn't sorry enough to back off, to leave me alone, and find someone else to help her brother out of his mess.

"I can't deal with you right now."

"I didn't realize you were in love with her."

"Fuck off."

"You should've told me no. When I asked you for help. You should've told me no."

"Pretty sure I did."

"Maybe you should've said it harder."

"Like that would've done any good. You're kind of hard to run off." I smiled. She hadn't meant to cause me so much trouble. Any other time, I might have admired her fighting so hard for her family, but right now I just wanted to be alone and not deal with her drama. While I tried to think of a way to get rid of her for the night, I heard a loud voice call out.

"Luca Bennett, you think you can stop entertaining long enough to talk to me about when you're going to pay your rent?"

Old Man Withers had finally caught me. I glanced at Ronnie who grinned at my predicament, and then back to Withers. "Do I break up your dates to ask you to fix my toilet?"

He took his time looking Ronnie up and down, even licked his lips. She placed a hand on her hip and pushed her chest out a little, as if giving him a show. If she'd really been my date, I would've clocked him. As it was, I enjoyed watching their silent challenge. He looked back at me and said, "I'll never understand how you get so many pretty ladies to go out with you."

"Not for you to understand." I opened the door, walked to the kitchen, and fished out my coffee can. For the first time ever, I handed over the entire rent for this month and next to Withers, too worn out to enjoy the look of shock on his face.

"What about the dog?" He pointed at Cash. "I don't allow dogs."

I motioned toward the couch and Cash ran over, hopped on the cushions, and said his version of thanks. "You do now."

He knew better than to pick this battle with me, but he left grumbling.

I shut the door and turned to face Ronnie. "Haven't we seen enough of each other for a while?"

"You look like you need one of these." She hefted a six-pack of Blue Moon, condensation dripping from the bottles.

I did and I wasn't too proud to hold out my hand. I took the icy cold bottle to the couch and joined my dog. Ronnie stayed in the kitchen searching the cabinets. "You won't find any clean glasses," I called out.

"Like that's surprising. I'm perfectly capable of washing a glass myself."

I watched while she did just that, enjoying the contrast of her impeccable attire in my sloppy kitchen. When she walked into the living room with a tall glass of amber beer, I told Cash to get down and then patted the space beside me on the couch. She flinched only a little bit before sliding in next to me.

She clinked her glass against mine. "See, it's not so bad having me around."

"Are you back for good or just until you're sure your little brother is out of trouble?"

"Would it matter either way to you?"

I should've never asked the question. I didn't think I cared either way, and I sure didn't want to send her the wrong signals. But since when did I care about signals? A pretty woman was here in my house wanting favors from me. That was signal enough. I needed to stop letting other stuff get in the way. Whatever I'd been feeling for Jess had been an illusion, my imagination on overload. She made that clear when she'd asked me to compromise who I was for her security, for her goals. If she loved me, she would know that had been too much to ask. She would know my cabinet was full of dirty glasses and she wouldn't care.

I answered Ronnie's question in the best way I knew how. With hungry lips and searching hands, I closed my eyes and dove full in. She spilled some beer before I heard the glass thud on the table, and then her hands were on me, tugging at my shirt, raking my chest. Her lips were fuller than I remembered, her fingers softer, longer, more insistent. Within moments, my shirt was on the floor, my jeans unbuttoned. Cool air and warm lips skimmed my chest. Her hand found me wet and ready and she wasted no time, stroking, pushing, pulling. Eyes still closed, I let the sensations wash over me, around me until she was done.

When I finally opened my eyes, she was perched on the edge of the couch, sipping her beer. A slight flush in her cheeks the only sign that anything had happened between us. Perhaps sensing I'd come back to life, she looked my way, a flash of smug in her eye.

She'd been a tiger and I was her prey. Her willing, submissive prey. If I'd thought about it, I guess I could justify sex with her. Other than the first kiss, I hadn't been the aggressor. I'd just lain there and taken whatever she'd had to offer, my only offering was an orgasm that hadn't reached further than the nerve endings she touched.

"You okay?" I asked as I pulled on my shirt and buttoned my jeans. I wasn't the best host in the world, but leaving a woman unsatisfied wasn't normally my style.

"I'm good." She set her beer down and reached for her bag. "Let's talk about the case." She spent the next thirty minutes going over her notes and asking me questions. I tried to focus, but my mind had shut down and I couldn't process anything she had to say. Finally, she packed up her purse and stood to leave. I walked her to the door and she kissed me again without all the animal hunger. A nice kiss. A see you later kiss.

"I'll call you tomorrow. See where things stand," she said. And then she was gone.

I stood in the doorway, the warmth of her kiss still lingering on my lips, realizing she'd never answered my question about whether she was back for good and wondering if I cared.

❖

I woke to the sound of my ringing phone and I fumbled to answer it. "Hello?"

"Luca, it's Nancy. You asleep?"

I held the phone away from my ear and checked the time. It was only nine p.m., but I was asleep. Hard asleep. The experience with Ronnie had left me drained. Having someone ravish your body is tough work.

"I'm awake. What do you need?"

"You still want to come over? Everyone's gone now." She gave me her address. "Don't bring anyone other than Jess, okay?"

I let her hang up without explaining that Jess wasn't likely to be going anywhere with me for the foreseeable future. I took a quick shower to wash off the Ronnie, and then Cash and I headed to the car with the rest of the six-pack Ronnie had brought over.

When I pulled up to Nancy's street, I glanced around, looking for other cars, fully expecting there to be some kind of a surveillance on a cop who'd just been shot. Nancy lived in suburbia, cars with garages, and every garage door on the street was closed up tight. Not a car in sight. Odd. Still, on the off chance some of her cop buddies might drive by, I parked on the next block and walked Cash to her door.

She answered before I knocked and pulled the now four-pack from my hand. "I could so use one of these."

I followed her to the kitchen where she opened a bottle for each of us and poured a bowl of water and set it on the floor for Cash. We both sat at the table. I'd never been to her place before. It was bigger than Jess's small house. Bigger than I expected, prompting me to say, "Nice place. You live here long?"

"A while. Thanks. I like it."

I bet. The kitchen was enormous. One of those gourmet kinds with double ovens, a fancy built-in fridge, and pots hanging from the ceiling. Reminded me of the kitchen Ronnie had when she'd lived in the snooty University Park neighborhood of Dallas. I caught Nancy staring at me, her brow kinda furrowed as she watched me assess her place. I kept my tone casual. "Guess, unlike me, you like to cook?"

"Maybe I'll cook for you someday." She smiled and I saw a glimpse of flirting Nancy, the one I always avoided. Time to change the subject. I pointed at the sling on her arm. "You okay?"

"Yeah. It was a little more serious than a graze, but the bullet went through and through. Hurt like hell at the time, but they gave me great meds." She pointed to a burnt orange prescription bottle on the table, "And I'm feeling no pain right now. They say with physical therapy it'll heal just fine."

I didn't bother telling her that they lie. She might be able to use her arm exactly the way she had before, but it would always hurt a little, especially when it was cold outside. And she'd always be a little more leery about engaging. Getting shot left more than surface scars.

"Jess couldn't make it?"

"She's got other stuff going on."

"Perez got to her."

"Perez is an ass. No one gets to Jess. She just needs to focus. She doesn't need to spend time dealing with my shit."

"Sounds like trouble in paradise."

"Shut up, Walters. You want to tell me why you think you got shot?"

Her response was immediate. "I think I got shot because I was meeting with you."

"Oh, really? Then I guess it wasn't really a good idea to have me come over tonight."

"I mean meeting with you and Jackson. I think someone didn't like the fact I'd taken you to meet him."

"If someone didn't want me to talk to Jackson, seems like it would've made more sense to shoot him before he talked to me instead of after."

"Maybe. Maybe they figure if he's dead, it'll just be your word as to what he said to you."

"And you were just collateral damage?"

"Maybe."

"You got a whole lot of maybes."

"What did Jackson tell you, anyway?"

I studied her face. The question seemed honestly curious, but something felt off. Jackson had made sure Nancy didn't hear what he had to say. Was that because he didn't trust her? And who else besides Nancy knew I was meeting Jackson that night? I hadn't told anyone. Sure, Nancy had gotten shot, but like she said, she'd been lucky—a comparatively minor injury. Jackson was the one who took the hard hit and, but for Cash, who knows what would have happened to me?

Jackson hadn't given me any concrete information that pointed toward Nancy or anyone really. The overall impression I got from him was that he didn't know all that much, only that the CI was bad news and maybe Jorge was set up to take a fall.

Nancy's face told me nothing, but my instincts told me to trust no one. "He didn't seem to know much. I'm not even sure why he agreed to meet me."

"Maybe he's dirty and he wanted to see what information you have. Size you up." She sounded genuinely curious, but I still wasn't convinced.

"And he couldn't have gotten that from you?"

She shrugged. "I guess he would rather assess the situation himself than trust a wet-behind-the-ears detective."

"Did you know he beat his wife?" I dropped the bomb and waited for the fallout. Nancy's eyes widened a bit, but not enough to convey real surprise.

"I heard a rumor."

"It's true."

"And you know this because?"

"Because I talked to the right people." I let that sit a moment, but she didn't have a response. "Talk to me about how Jackson reacted when you told him I wanted to meet with him."

Nancy shifted in her chair. The action was subtle enough that she could've blamed it on her arm if she hadn't already told me how well the painkillers worked. I called her on it. "You want to move somewhere more comfortable?" I pointed at the armless chair she was sitting in. "Where you can rest your arm?"

Again with the sly smile. "I can think of only one comfortable place I'd like to be with you, but"—she pointed at her sling—"you may have to do most of the work."

I'd always written Nancy's flirting off to harmless fun, thinking both of us knew it wasn't going anywhere. I wasn't above sleeping with inappropriate women, but I'd always drawn that line at Jess's cop friends, and as much as Nancy pretended she didn't know Jess and I were really a thing, I wasn't stupid enough to believe it was a secret. And I didn't think Nancy was stupid enough to follow through. Nope. Her proposition was designed to get me off the subject of Greg Jackson, and although I desperately wanted to know why, I knew pushing her wasn't going to net any answers.

I stood up. "As much as I'd love to help you start your physical therapy, I'm bushed. Spending all night at the police station answering questions robbed me of my beauty sleep. Maybe another time?"

"Sure, Luca. I'll count on it." Back was the confident smile, and I couldn't get away from her fast enough.

Cash and I stopped at Whataburger on the way home and loaded up on cheeseburgers and fries. When we got home, we wolfed down our food. After dinner, all I wanted to do was go to bed, but my brain wouldn't shut down. I started pulling open drawers, looking for something to write on, but the best I could do was a stack of napkins from various fast food dives. Figuring that would have to do, I started making notes.

Greg Jackson was connected to Jorge and to Teresa Perez.

Jorge didn't know Perez, but Jackson had been his partner.

Teresa Perez was connected, in a bad way, to Ronnie, Jorge, and me. She was also connected to Jackson, but in a good way. Good for her, anyway.

The CI, Roberto Garcia, was connected to Jackson who admitted to having used him in the past and to Jorge who he said paid him off to do illegal deals.

Nancy was connected to Jackson and Jorge since they all worked in vice. Come to think of it, she was also connected to Perez since they all worked for DPD and they both played on Jess's softball team. Or did, since I didn't think Jess would be asking Perez back after today's events.

Focus. I added Nancy's name to Perez's napkin. Now I had a bunch of scrawled-on napkins and not a clue as to what to do with all the information I'd compiled. But I knew who would. I reached for my phone and started dialing out of habit. Halfway through, memory kicked in and I cancelled the call. Jess might answer, but she wasn't going to help me figure out this case.

Back to the napkins. I shuffled them around and finally settled on the one that seemed central. Confidential informant, Roberto Garcia. He wasn't going to be easy to find, and he probably wasn't stupid enough to talk to me, but my gut said he was the key to everything. I pulled out my laptop and started searching. After about a half hour of wishing the guy didn't have such a common name, I shut it down. Finding a guy like Garcia was going to require good old-fashioned street work. I'd get started in the morning.

CHAPTER FOURTEEN

M y phone rang in the few minutes before I planned to get out of bed. You know that time, when you think you have a few more sweet moments of sleep, but whatever it is that's interrupting you is going to last too long for you to be able to return to slumber. Ruins my day every time.

Maggie's voice was way too loud for morning. "Luca, do you want us to pick you up?"

"What?" I yawned and rubbed my eyes while I tried to figure out what she was talking about and why it couldn't wait until a time when normal people started conducting business.

"We got donuts. We can swing by and get you."

Mark's. That's right. I'd stupidly promised to help Maggie and Dad decorate the newlywed nest this morning. The very last thing in the world I wanted to do was be stuck in a car with them. The second to last thing was having them show up on my doorstep. "I've got an errand to run on the way," I lied. "Give me the address and I'll meet you there."

I used one of my spare napkins to jot down the location, hung up the phone, and took Cash outside to do his business. Old Man Withers was out front, and I could tell he wanted to give me a lecture about his alleged no pet policy. Whatever. I'd spent countless nights cursing my former next-door neighbor's mutt for barking at every damn noise he heard. At least my dog knew how to behave. To taunt Withers, I walked Cash around the entire perimeter of the apartment complex before heading back to our place. Once we were back inside, Cash sat at my feet staring up with hungry eyes. I poured some food in his bowl. "Eat up, but save some room for donuts," I told him.

A quick shower later, I grabbed my notes and Cash and left for the day. I figured I'd put in an hour with Maggie and my dad, and then Cash and I would figure out a way to find Garcia.

Mark and Linda had moved to Texas from Boston just before the wedding. They'd purchased a bungalow in the coveted M Streets in East Dallas, an investment made possible by a generous gift from Linda's uber wealthy parents. The house was tiny, but probably cost more than a couple of apartment complexes in my part of town. I pulled into the driveway and parked behind Dad's beat-up Oldsmobile. Cash and I walked up onto the porch, and I peered into the big window. Maggie and Dad were sitting in the living room with a dozen Krispy Kremes between them. I rapped on the glass and Maggie appeared at the door.

"Luca, come in. We've been waiting for you."

I pointed at the half-empty box. "I see you found a way to kill the time."

Dad stood up and wrapped me in a hug. "Hey, how's my girl?"

Last time I'd seen him we'd both been pretty wasted, which was usually the only time Dad was this affectionate. I sniffed the air. No scent of morning beer. Maybe he was glad to see me. Maggie broke up our father daughter moment.

"You brought your dog?"

Cash was sitting at my side. He couldn't have been better behaved, which was quite an accomplishment considering a tiny white fur ball was hissing in his direction. "Sure. Why not? He's way better behaved than that dust bunny."

"That's Snowball."

I'd always been the butch one, but the fact that Mark had a cat named Snowball made him even more tease-worthy than ever. "Cash, try not to eat the marshmallow." Cash responded with a few yips that sounded like he was sad to be denied the tiny snack. I reached into the donut box, fished out a glazed, and split it with him to make up for his loss.

Maggie shook her head. "Guess that dog really is yours."

I wiped the glaze from my fingers and said, "Let's get this show on the road. I have to be somewhere."

Maggie held up a bag from Party City and started pulling out streamers, confetti, string, and a bunch of foil letters that spelled Just Married. I gathered the object was to trash their place so they'd be sorry they ever left. I could do that better than most, but I listened to Maggie's instructions anyway because not to do so would've kept me there twice as long.

I was sent to the master bedroom to scatter fake rose petals all over the bed. Maggie supplied me with four good-sized bags of the things. They'd probably still be finding these things on their fiftieth wedding anniversary. As if. I didn't know anyone who'd been with anyone that long, married or not.

The master bedroom wasn't any bigger than the only other bedroom in the place. The only reason I knew it was the love nest was the amount of couple pictures scattered on every available surface. Mark and Linda at the beach. Mark and Linda at a picnic. Mark and Linda at a cocktail party. There were lots more. A bit much, but it got me thinking. I didn't have a single picture of Jess, let alone a picture of Jess and me. I'm sure someone did. We'd had our pictures taken at softball games and after parties. In large groups of friends. But never as a couple, and I'd never handed a camera, even the camera on my phone, to anyone and said, "get one for me."

I didn't know what that meant, or even if it meant anything, but the absence of any photographic evidence of an "us" left me feeling a little empty.

❖

When Cash and I finally escaped, my first thought was lunch. Can't live on donuts alone. Fortunately, this part of town was known for its many patio restaurants. We settled on Snuffer's and Cash waited patiently while I went inside and ordered cheeseburgers and fries for us to share.

While we ate, I scrolled through the list of numbers on my phone, trying to decide who would be the most likely candidate to help me find Garcia. Jess was out and so was Nancy. I couldn't ask Jess's partner, John. I knew a few other cops, but after the way Jess and I had parted, I didn't want to go that route. Besides, most of them would immediately know what case I was working on when I mentioned Garcia's name, and my chances of getting help were slim to none.

This whole exercise was feeling a lot like shuffling through the napkins. And then my scrolling stopped on a familiar name. Diamond Collier. I don't know why I didn't think of her sooner. I'd seen her just a few weeks ago. When she coaxed me into finding a couple of mobsters. The work had gone to hell and I wound up plowing into more than I bargained for, and getting Jess shot along the way. Hard to believe it had been less than a month and my life was already a mess again.

I didn't want to call Diamond. She was complicated, like Ronnie. I didn't need to add to the level of complications in my life, and the last time I'd seen Diamond, she'd kinda asked me out on a date, which was pretty weird since we'd seen each other naked on numerous occasions. When the mobster case was over, she'd left a note on my door. All it said was "I owe you" and her phone number. I'd plugged it in my phone just in case, but I'd never intended to use it.

I rolled the options over in my head for all of two minutes before I decided I didn't really have a choice. Because she was a federal agent, Diamond had access to all kinds of information I'd never get on my own. And she owed me. I dialed the numbers before I could talk myself out of calling her.

"Luca?"

"Is that how you always answer the phone?"

Her voice was still as sexy as ever. I did my best to tune out the tone and focus. The last thing I needed was another female distraction. "I need some info and you owe me. Meet me in an hour at Maggie's." I hung up before she could reply.

Early afternoon at Maggie's was slow and, as I suspected, Maggie was absent. Probably she and Dad were still hovering at

Mark's house waiting for the happy couple to return home. Ah, wedded bliss. I sat at the bar and ordered a beer from Harry. He poured me a draft, his eyes on Cash the whole time.

"Come on, Harry. Maggie doesn't have a problem with him." I reached down and rubbed Cash's fur to demonstrate what a nice thing a dog was to have around. Harry shook his head. "Maggie doesn't have a problem with a lot of things as far as you're concerned."

That wasn't how I saw it, but I decided against arguing. I drank my beer while watching the door. Diamond strolled through the door exactly an hour from when I'd hung up with her. Still a brunette and still sleek and sexy, every head in the bar turned her way as she walked toward me. She took the seat on my right and ordered "whatever she's having." Harry handed her the beer and shook his head again at me. Next time I saw Maggie, I was going to get another lecture about bringing women other than Jess to her place. Little did Maggie know, my days of hanging out with Jess might well be over.

Diamond waited until Harry left to wait on some other customers before asking any questions. Her first one was, "This your dog?"

"Yes. His name's Cash."

"Suits you. He's a handsome guy." She rubbed behind his ears and he pressed against her leg. Bonding. I recognized it even if I didn't do it much.

"He's a good dog."

"I can tell." She gave his head one last pat and then faced me. "You're right. I owe you. What do you need?"

I hadn't expected it to be this easy, and I still wasn't sure it was going to be, so I launched right in. "You familiar with the Jorge Moreno case? Local DA's handling it. Fake drug deals. Lot of bad arrests, deportations?"

"Heard about it. There's a big civil suit."

"Right. In federal court."

"But not involving any of our agencies," she was quick to add.

"I know, but I just figured you guys might know something about it."

She laughed. "'You guys'? Like we're a little club? Tell me what you want, Luca. If I can help you, I will."

"I need to find Roberto Garcia."

"Who's that?" She was good, but it's not just lying perps that have a tell. When Diamond lied, while she lied, she kept her fingers busy. Sometimes doing fun things, things I liked, but right now they were shredding a napkin into tiny bits of confetti. When she was undercover, the guys she tried to fool probably thought it was cute. But I knew better. I reached over and scooped up the debris and pressed it into a ball. She watched with a fixed expression of nonchalance until I threw the napkin at her face.

She frowned. "What the hell did you do that for?"

"Didn't you agree that you owe me? You don't have to take me to meet the guy. Just give me his last known and I'll find him myself."

I watched her face and could read the train of emotions. "Luca, you don't want to get more involved in this case."

More involved. She'd only had an hour since I called her. I guess that was enough time for her to have made some calls and found out what I was working on, but it seemed unlikely. No, she'd already known before I'd called. But why?

Diamond had spent a good portion of her career working undercover. Lying came too easy, so I wasn't big on asking her direct questions. I decided to use some lies of my own to flesh out some answers. "I'm already involved. Local cops think I set up a couple of cops who got shot. I need to talk to Garcia. I think he's got info that can clear me."

"I wish I could help you." She didn't have a napkin to fiddle with, but her hands were twitchy. She definitely knew more than she was letting on. I pushed harder.

"DPS booked me in last night on assault charges. One of the cops is in a coma. He dies and I'm toast." I took a drink of my beer and waited. Only a completely heartless person wouldn't help me now. If Diamond knew anything about this case, she knew I'd only given her half-truths. Would she admit she knew more, or persist with the "I don't know anything" line and walk away?

She glanced around. No one was sitting anywhere near us, and Harry had disappeared to the back. Cash's ears were perked up, but I trusted him, and apparently, Diamond did too. "Luca, I know there've been too many times I wasn't straight with you, but I've always had your back. You need to walk away from this case. Don't try and contact Garcia. Walk away from Moreno. Walk away from every Dallas cop you meet. This isn't your battle and nothing good can come from getting in the middle of it." She reached for my hand, an oddly romantic gesture. "If you keep pushing, I don't think you'll live to tell about it." She squeezed my hand to emphasize the point.

I lifted my hand and stared at the spot she'd touched. We'd never exchanged anything beyond physical interaction, but the touch had emotion behind it, and I felt like I'd just betrayed something by letting her touch me like that. *But you let Ronnie fuck you and you felt no guilt.* The fucking was release. This touch? It was tender, caring. Ronnie didn't care about me. She only cared about keeping me satisfied so I'd help her brother. Our whole relationship had started with her fucking me to get me to help her on a case. She'd deny it, but I knew that's all there was. No, Diamond's touch had felt like something else. Someone else. Jess.

Jess wanted me off this case too. Maybe I should take it as a sign that the only people who cared about me wanted me to stop helping Jorge Moreno. I could sort out my time, do a bill, and give Ronnie back whatever money was left. Walk away from Ronnie's mess and back into Jess's arms.

The pull was strong. But so was the nagging suspicion that if I did, there'd always be a chink in the metal of our relationship. I'd never cared before about righting a wrong, choosing instead to take the easy way out. I'd only ever had a list of people to bring in. I spent my time catching them, turning them in. It wasn't my job to stick around to make sure they were really good for their crimes. If justice was served by anything I did, it was by accident, not because I went looking for it. If I walked away now, someone was going to get away with something, and I sensed it was someone big. And for the first time, I cared.

"If you want me to live, you'll tell me how to find him. Because I'm going to find him, and the easier it is, the less chance I'll die trying."

CHAPTER FIFTEEN

I sat on my couch and waited for the phone to ring with a call or buzz with a text message. I'd parted ways with Diamond two hours ago and she'd promised to get in touch this evening with information about Roberto Garcia. My natural impatience caused me to define evening loosely. It was barely six p.m., but I'd already walked and fed Cash and eaten an entire pizza from i Fratelli's. I didn't have anything else to occupy my time and that started an itch that I only knew three ways to scratch: sex, alcohol, or gambling.

I considered my options. If I started drinking, I wasn't likely to stop and I wanted to be alert for her call. My sex options appeared to have multiplied over the past few days, but appearances aren't everything. I'd come when Ronnie touched me, but the orgasm was a reflex, a well-honed one. She knew where to touch, and my body was programmed to offer up the same reaction every single time. Didn't change the fact my head wasn't in the game.

And my heart? Well, I wasn't in the habit of associating feelings with sex, but I wasn't above comparing. What Jess and I had shared, earlier that day in her bed, felt exponentially more satisfying than the quick and dirty finger fuck Ronnie had delivered.

And then there was Diamond. Every time we'd fooled around had been great. Except the last one. I flashed back to the scene at a casino hotel just weeks ago. We'd fucked like usual, but instead of feeling sated, I'd woken up the next morning feeling used and not in a good way. Jess and I had used each other off and on during the years we'd known each other, but I'd never felt like something had been taken from me, only given.

I shook my head. Jess wasn't an option for me now and she might never be again. The loss of a sure thing made me distrust my instincts, robbed me of the will to gamble. I'd gone full circle on my options and there was nothing left to do but wait for Diamond's call.

When the phone finally rang, it wasn't Diamond. I stared at the familiar number and debated answering. I would've thought Nancy would steer clear from me after I'd tried to pump her for information the night before, but either she really did want my body or this was just a friendly call. I was curious enough to answer.

"Hey, Walters, guess you're feeling well enough to dial the phone."

"I'm doing better, but I'm still up for some physical therapy if you're still offering."

I started to argue that I'd never offered, but I bit my tongue. I'd never considered Nancy for sex, and I wasn't going to start now. I wasn't even sure why we'd never done it. She was attractive enough and definitely willing, but it was too easy. I may be lazy about most things, but challenge was arousing. Nancy wasn't.

"I appreciate the offer, but I've got a busy day. Rain check?"

She laughed, a nervous laugh. I couldn't tell if she was hiding embarrassment about the rejection or if it was something else. "Definitely a rain check. That's not really why I called anyway."

I waited for her to go on, finally offering an, "oh, really?"

"Yeah. I checked into that story you mentioned about Jackson and I think there's something to it. Perez was involved somehow. I think she helped cover up Jackson's arrest. Maybe they're a thing."

"Interesting." I slowly digested the information, trying to decide if I was being played. What she said tracked with what Sally had told me—Perez had investigated the case, but when Nancy added in the "maybe they're a thing," my antennae went up. I'd always assumed Perez was a lesbian. She'd leered at girls enough on the softball field, but I'd never actually seen her with anyone of either sex. Maybe she was bi. I shook my head, wanting to clear all images of Perez with anyone at all. Was Nancy screwing with me, or was she actually feeding me good intel?

"I thought she was gay." I wished I could see Nancy's face through the phone to judge her reaction.

"She's whatever she needs to be. She's been married before. Years ago. Definitely not a gold star."

I didn't bother pointing out that lots of lesbians had been with men before they discovered the fairer sex. Didn't mean they went back to men. "Interesting." I figured if I kept repeating the one-word response, she'd keep spilling details in an attempt to get me to engage. It worked.

"So, obviously, she's tied to Jackson somehow. Might be worth looking into."

I mustered up enthusiasm I didn't feel and said, "I think you might be on to something. Thanks for the tip. I totally owe you." I added lots of innuendo to the last phrase to cover any trace of disbelief. Nancy Walters was lying about something, but I wasn't going to call her on it until I knew exactly what and why.

Diamond didn't call and she didn't text until the next morning when Cash and I were standing outside the corner convenience store eating a second hotdog each. Even then, her message was cryptic: *Still looking. Hold tight. Be in touch.*

I'm not big on "holding tight," and I had a strong feeling Diamond was stalling until she could divert my attention. She wasn't ever going to lead me to Garcia. Time to stop waiting and start doing. I'd spent the night thinking about how to find the CI, and I'd latched on to a possibility. Garcia had to be a key component of the case against the city. I didn't know a ton about lawsuits, but I figured one of the plaintiff attorneys must have him on a witness list, maybe they'd even deposed him. I fired up the computer and started searching for the players involved. In federal cases, all the records filed in the case were online, easily accessible for pennies a page. Didn't take long to get a list of the lawyers in the case and see what had been filed. Lead lawyer for the plaintiffs was Ryan Foster. I recognized the name, but couldn't place it until Google filled in the blanks. She'd been a big deal at the DA's office a few years back, but left in the wake of a scandal. According to the papers, she hadn't been directly involved, but now she spent her time going after the powers that be on behalf of the little guy. Definitely not a law and order type. I liked her already.

Foster had filed a bunch of discovery requests, including a deposition notice for Roberto Garcia. The city had responded, saying Garcia didn't work for them now and to the extent he ever did, he was a contractor of sorts, so they weren't responsible for getting him to show up for a civil suit interrogation. Foster then requested every record the police department had regarding his confidential informant status and every deal he'd ever transacted on behalf of DPD. She was a shark, and because she'd worked on their side in the past, she knew exactly what to ask for, but the other side wasn't rolling over. They'd filed motions to quash every single one of Foster's requests. I read through two pages of legal mumbo jumbo, and I still had no clue who was getting what information from whom or if they were getting anything at all. I signed off Pacer and dialed Foster's office number, hoping she would just explain what was going on, in simple English.

I'd expected to leave a message, but was surprised when a woman answered.

"Foster here."

"I hear you want to talk to Roberto Garcia. So do I. Any chance you want to pool our resources?"

"Who is this?"

"Just someone with similar interests. You interested or not?" No way was I going to tell her I was a) a bounty hunter, or b) a PI working for the cop she thought had set up her clients. Defense attorneys have no love for the people who go hunting their bond-jumping clients, and the second reason was completely obvious.

"What do you have in mind?"

"How about we start by talking. You free now?"

After a few seconds of silence, Foster answered, "I have some time if you can get here in the next hour. I'm at Brett Logan's office." She gave me the address. Another napkin down.

After we hung up, I Googled the address. Brett Logan was a lawyer, like Foster, but Foster's name wasn't listed in conjunction with the address. I grabbed Cash's leash and motioned for him to head to the door. Based on everyone's reaction so far, he was a surefire icebreaker, and I'd need every tool I had to crack this case.

The law office was just blocks away from the courthouse. The brown stone courthouse was located in front of the towers of the Dallas County Jail where I'd turned in Susie Kemper less than a week ago. And run into Jess for the first time since our fight after Mark's wedding. Kind of hard to believe so much had happened in so little time. Now I wasn't entirely sure that if I ran into Jess she'd acknowledge me in front of her cop pals.

That wasn't true. Jessica Chance would never be disloyal, but with her loyalty divided, I didn't know where I stood. Maybe when this case was over, when Ronnie returned to DC, when I went back to the mindless art of catching fugitives, maybe then we could pick up where we left off. If I could figure out where that was. In the meantime, I needed to stay focused.

The office was in a small building that housed suites for several law firms. The woman who answered the door was wearing faded jeans and a Harvard sweatshirt. She was tall, thin, and her hair was long and kind of wild. If this was the lawyer, I was impressed with the way she rolled. She held the door partly open and waited. I realized I hadn't told her my name.

"Ryan Foster? I'm Luca Bennett. I called you earlier. Can we talk now?"

She gave me another up and down examination, shot a look at Cash, smiled, and then invited me in. I followed her to a messy conference room. Boxes lined the walls and file folders lay open all over the large table. "Looks like you've been working hard."

She motioned for me to take a seat. "David vs. Goliath. The underdog always has to work harder." She reached into a fridge tucked in the corner of the room. "You want something to drink?"

"Sure. Whatever you're having."

She handed me a bottle of water and then poured the contents of another into a bowl she pulled from a cabinet next to the fridge. I watched while she placed the bowl on the floor and then stroked Cash's head while he lapped at the cool water. Apparently satisfied her guests were refreshed, she took a seat at the conference table directly across from me. "You want to tell me what it is you want?"

"I want to talk to Roberto Garcia."

"I can't really help you, but you already knew that before you got here. Am I right?"

"I know you filed a deposition notice and the City of Dallas tried to quash it."

"We're still waiting on a hearing date for that along with a bunch of other discovery requests they haven't responded to."

"I'd like to talk to Garcia in a less formal setting than a deposition."

"I may fight the establishment on a regular basis, but I'm not going to help you do something illegal. Before we go any further, you need to tell why you're so interested in Garcia."

"Same reason you are. He's the key to these fake drug cases you're working so hard on."

"If you were working for any of the plaintiffs, I'd know about it."

"Why don't you have your own office?"

"Excuse me?"

"Just seems odd to me that you don't have your own office, that you're working here in some other guy's firm. You're not even listed in the phone book."

She stood up. "I think you should go."

I stayed in my chair. "Look, I didn't mean to piss you off. It's just that you seem like you could use some help. You've got boxes scattered everywhere, a key witness is avoiding you, and you don't even have your own office space."

"For your information, the some other guy who owns this office happens to be my wife, Brett Logan. I'm not a big fan of offices since…since I left my last one. I work where I want, when I want, and for whom I want. The only reason I'm at an office at all is because I don't want all this"—she waved her arm toward the stacks of boxes—"scattered all over our house."

I liked her. If I needed an attorney, she was the kind I would want, the kind who bucked the system and didn't get caught up with the trappings of the job. No, this chick worked where she wanted, wore what she wanted, said what she wanted. I made a snap decision to trust her.

"I'm working for Detective Jorge Moreno."

She laughed. "Well, if you hadn't already insulted me, now it's definitely time for you to leave. If you know anything about the case, you know he's the reason I've got clients to represent."

"But what if he isn't?"

"Come again?"

"What if he isn't the reason your clients were arrested? What if Garcia's been lying all along? I mean, you'd seriously believe a CI you can't even find over an officer of the law?" I would, but I'd be willing to bet she, a former badge-carrying ADA, had been bothered by that very fact.

She shook her head. "Doesn't make any sense. Why would the department throw one of their own under the bus if the reason for all the arrests rested solely with a bad CI?"

"I don't know, but something else is going on." I hadn't brought the napkins, but I had memorized the details. I gave her a thumbnail sketch of what I'd learned about Jackson and I detailed the shooting.

"Holy shit. Is your friend okay?" Took me a minute to realize she was talking about Nancy.

"She's fine. Barely scraped." A slight exaggeration, but not much. The minor injury still bothered me. If someone was out to get Jackson and whoever he was talking to that night, how did they wind up putting him in a coma, but Nancy and I walked away with scratches? Were the shooters just amateurs, or had they known exactly what they were doing? I didn't want to go there, and I wasn't ready to talk to anyone else about my vague suspicions, so I changed the subject. "I think Garcia has to be the key to all of this, and I plan to find him. You have any information that might help?"

She folded her arms and appeared to be deep in thought for a bit before saying, "You realize you're hunting for the guy who can nail your client? From what I hear, Roberto Garcia is the key witness the state has in Moreno's case. I'd love to find Garcia, but if he's disappeared, that's a jackpot for your guy."

I got what she meant. This wasn't really my case. I was working for Ronnie, and she should be the one to make the call when it came to making alliances, but I had a powerful feeling I could trust Ryan Foster, and I decided it would be easier to ask forgiveness than permission. "You might be right, but I'm not big on sitting around hoping things don't happen. Besides, what if DPD has him under wraps until Moreno's trial?"

"Then they lied to the court in my case."

"Wouldn't be the first time. Only one way to find out for sure and that's to find Garcia. You with me?"

Back at home, I spent an hour scouring the file Ryan had developed on Roberto Garcia. The first look only took about fifteen minutes. There just wasn't much there. Name, date of birth, no driver's license, no social. Allegedly, the guy wasn't a citizen, so the last two weren't that surprising, but I'd suspected that someone who ran with criminals would have more on paper than he did. One trip to the Dallas County Jail two years ago, a felony drug case that got dropped to a misdemeanor. I guess this was the case that got him hooked up with law enforcement and started his career as a confidential informant, but it didn't make sense to me that a guy his age—he'd just turned thirty-five—would only have one prior arrest. It also didn't make sense that this guy was supposedly so connected that the cops would've used him as a regular CI. Once again, I instinctively reached for my phone to dial Jess before I remembered where things stood.

I needed to find someone new to kick theories around with.

I looked over the criminal history report again. I didn't recognize the name of the defense attorney who'd handled the case.

Garcia had posted a cash bond, so there was no bonding company that might have additional records. The printout from the court that had an address for him was the same address where Foster had served her notice of deposition. I doubted it was good anymore, but it was all I had.

The GPS on my phone told me I wouldn't have to go far. Not surprising that a drug dealer didn't live far from me. I liked living in a sketchy neighborhood. Nobody breaks into ratty apartments hoping for a big haul. My guns and coffee can bank were safe as long as I lived here. Cash was asleep on the couch, but perked up when I opened the door. I'd planned to leave him behind since I didn't have any idea what kind of situation I was headed into, but now that I thought about it, that actually seemed like a good reason to take him along. I picked up his leash, and he leapt off the couch and ran to my side.

I found a house at the listed address. Small, run-down, with weeds as high as my waist. That and the pile of junk mail bulging out of the rusted mailbox told me no one lived here anymore. Good. That meant no one would care if I had a look around. The front door was locked, so Cash and I went around back where I found a locked back door as well. I turned over a trashcan and climbed up to the one window along the rear wall and, using my pocketknife, I managed to jimmy it open. I ordered Cash to stay put while I crawled inside. It was dark and I heard a bunch of tiny feet scraping along the floor, which totally creeped me out. I used the flashlight thing on my phone to scare the rats away and I resolved to make this quick. I opened the back door and let Cash in, hoping he had special rat chasing skills.

The place was tiny. One bedroom, one bath. The only piece of furniture in the bedroom was a stained mattress, and the bathroom was a petri dish of mold spores. Neither room had any clothes, towels, or paper goods. Whoever had lived here had either purposefully moved out, or the place had been looted.

I scoured the miniature kitchen and den but found nothing. The fridge and cabinets were bare—not like I could judge—and there wasn't a shred of paper anywhere in the place. I opened the front door and scooped up the mail. All junk: insurance offers, coupons, notices from the new dental clinic down the road. Most of them were addressed simply to "occupant," but a few were slightly more specific: Samuel Landon or current resident. Nothing was personal or important. If Garcia had lived here, he'd probably rented the place and Landon was the property owner. I chose a single envelope from a local insurance agent soliciting business that was addressed to Landon and stuck it in my pocket, confident no jury would give me time for stealing junk mail.

I relocked the back door, closed the window, and Cash and I walked out the front. The disarray of the house fit in with the rest of the neighborhood. City inspectors would have a field day on this street, but I had a feeling none of these folks would actually pay the tickets they received, so it was likely a waste of city resources to even try to enforce code violations in this part of town. Besides, if most of the houses were rentals, like this one, then the folks living in them had even less motive to keep up the properties.

I drove home because I couldn't think of anywhere else to go right now. It was Saturday afternoon, and I was sick of working. I had money to spend. I was free as a bird. I should head north to the casino or I should go out to the bars. But the only thing I wanted to do was call Jess. See if she wanted to grab something to eat, have sex, or any one of the casual things we used to do. If we were still casual, I could still work on this case, right? Isn't that what had changed? We'd morphed into something different, something hard to define, and it had made things between us fuzzy. It had blurred the lines I hadn't ever considered we had. But now the lines were stark and very real, and I doubted either one of us was going to cross them without the risk of changing us both.

I should stop even thinking about it.

I wondered if she had.

I hoped she hadn't.

CHAPTER SIXTEEN

Taking off Saturday night and all day Sunday had seemed like a good idea, but by Monday morning, I was sick of my own company.

My cell phone had gotten lots of attention. Mark had called. Maggie had called. Ronnie had called three times. Mark probably wanted to tell me all about his honeymoon. Maggie probably wanted to tell me all about Mark's honeymoon. And Ronnie probably wanted another report I wasn't prepared to give. I didn't want to talk to any of them, so I'd let it ring.

An hour later, when the phone rang again, I almost let it go to voice mail, but the desire to hear another human voice gave way to the annoyance of being bossed around or told details about exotic vacations, the kind of which I would never take.

It was Diamond. I punched answer before she could leave a message. "Hey, about time you called."

"Sorry. Took me a while to get any information. Looks like he's blown town. No one seems to have a clue where to find him. He may have gone back to Mexico until your guy goes to trial, or the state prosecutors have him under lock-down and they aren't sharing."

"I thought you feds kept tabs on everyone. Can't you point one of your little NSA satellites down there and figure out where he is?"

She laughed, but I could tell she wasn't really amused. I imagine the news stories lately about all the NSA spying on private citizens didn't make for comfortable conversation if you were a federal agent. I changed the subject. "I found where he used to live. At least according to his record. Shack of a place. Not far from me."

"Oh, really?"

There was more than disbelief behind her question, but I couldn't put a finger on it. "Yep. I think he was only renting. Place was deserted."

"That's rough, but I think it's probably better this way. I've heard this guy's bad news."

She was lying, and I had to make a decision: call her on it or act like I went along with her story and figure things out on my own. I chose the option that would create some action. "That's funny, because when I pulled his record, the only thing on it was a minor drug arrest. He did some county time. That's it."

"Hey, Luca, I'm sorry about this, but I'm getting another call and I have to take it. Call you later?"

"Sure." I clicked off the line and yanked open my laptop. She didn't have another call and she knew I knew that. I had to be faster at finding Roberto Garcia than she was at covering up his location, which didn't leave me any time to figure out why she was hiding him and why she knew where he was in the first place.

I pulled up the Dallas County tax rolls and typed in Garcia's address. As I suspected, despite the pile of junk mail at the abandoned house, the owner had a completely different address than the shit hole I'd visited. The owner, Samuel Landon, had an address on Greenville Ave, a popular strip in Dallas, but pretty much all commercial property. Google maps told me the location was one of those mail stores, where you rent a box and act like you have a real street address. The "suite" number on the address I had was likely a post office box number. Time to get moving and find out since Diamond was a step ahead of me. I pulled on my boots and smiled when I saw Cash already waiting at the door. In less than a week, the dog already knew me. Why couldn't women be like that?

The mail store was in a strip with a yoga studio, an ice cream store, a dry cleaner, and a resale clothing store. I parked close enough for a good view of the big open windows and debated my next move. If Diamond was setting someone into action, chances were good they would show up here, but I wouldn't have a clue who to look for, and I didn't have any idea about what they would do to keep me from getting information. More likely, whatever information I might find here would be destroyed or hidden with a few simple phone calls.

My natural hatred of waiting around won out. I took Cash with me because I'd already discovered people are nicer to people with cute dogs. The twelve-year-old at the counter whose nametag read "Mike" was no exception to the rule.

"Man, that's a gorgeous dog. What's his name?"

I knelt down and nuzzled Cash and encouraged the guy to join in. He looked around, but the place was deserted. I urged him on. "His name's Cash. Go ahead, pet him. He loves it." Seconds later, he was out from behind the counter, goofing with my dog. I waited until he was totally in love before I eased in with my questions.

"I'm thinking about getting a box. Can you tell me a little about how that works?"

"Sure. You just fill out some forms and pay the fee. You can pay by the month or the year—it's cheaper by the year."

"Any kind of waiting period?"

"Nope. We can get you set up today." He giggled as Cash licked his ear.

"I'm sorry. He's a licker."

"It's okay. I used to have a dog, but my parents gave her away to my cousins who live out in the country."

He obviously never recovered. "And if I rent a box, how private is my information?"

He cocked his head. "What do you mean?"

"I mean if someone came in and wanted to know if I had a box here, would you tell them?"

"Oh, I get you. Well, we wouldn't tell just anyone, but we would have to tell government people. You know, because of nine eleven and the Patriot Act stuff. That's on part of the forms you have to fill out."

"Gotcha, that makes sense." I glossed over it to keep him from dwelling on my questions. "If I wanted a particular box number would that be cool?"

"If it's available. You want me to check?"

"That would be great."

He reluctantly untangled himself from Cash, went back behind the counter, and started typing into his computer. "Okay, what number do you want me to check out?"

"Two twenty nine."

He looked up from the keyboard. "For real?"

"For real."

He didn't type anything else, which told me all I needed to know. He knew something about that box and now he was trying to figure out how to get rid of me. I urged him along. "Is it available?"

"Uh, no. I mean not really. Not right now, anyway. You want me to check on another one?"

"I have a special thing for that number. I'll check back. Unless you think maybe I can ask whoever has the box now if they'd consider giving it up."

"What? No, you can't do that. I can't tell you who has the box." He looked like he was going to pass out and I felt a little bit bad about messing with him. A little.

"But if I come back with my friend, who has a badge, you can. Right?" I didn't wait for his answer. My mission had been to stir up some shit, and I was certain I'd succeeded. Time to leave and wait for the fallout. When Cash and I got back in the Bronco, I made sure the ringer on my phone was turned up all the way. Diamond should be calling any minute.

Diamond didn't call, but Ronnie did. She wanted to come over, talk to me about what she'd learned so far. At the sound of her voice, I flashed back to the scene in my apartment. Me half-naked, her hot and hungry. I'd purposely not thought about it since then, and now I realized I felt something I'd never felt when it came to sex. Embarrassed. I wished I'd kept my pants on. Wished I told her I wasn't in the mood or I didn't want to have sex with the woman who was paying my bills. Things I'd never wished before, and I didn't want to think about why I was wishing them now. I told her to meet me at Maggie's.

Cash and I beat her there and, while we waited, Maggie regaled us with stories about Mark's honeymoon. As much as I hadn't wanted to hear the stories, I gave her my full attention. Other people's happily ever afters distracted me from whatever I was missing.

Ronnie arrived right in the middle of Maggie telling me how Linda had been stung by a jellyfish while they were snorkeling in whatever island paradise they'd run off to after the wedding.

"Who's Linda?"

Maggie ignored Ronnie's question and shot daggers my way before she stomped off. I was glad I'd already had one good beer, since I was about to get served shit the rest of the night.

"My brother's wife."

"Your sister-in-law."

"I guess. I don't know her well enough to call her that yet."

"Did your brother get married recently?"

"Uh, yeah." I waited for her to make the connection.

"Oh, right! Last Friday, the tux. You were headed to the wedding. How was it?"

I bit my tongue, but I wanted to ask how she thought it was when she—the hot ex—had shown up minutes before my date and I were ready to head out the door. "Let's talk about something else. You have anything new to tell me?"

"Matter of fact, I do. I found out where Greg Jackson's wife lives, and"—she pushed an envelope toward me—"I have copies of the pleadings in their divorce case. It was nastier than most."

"And what am I supposed to do with this?"

"Talk to her. Looks like she went after him for support and punitive damages for beating her. Maybe Jackson needed money so he cooked up this scheme with the CI.

"The guy's in a coma. You get that, right?"

"And that makes him less of a suspect?"

I shrugged. "I don't know, but it just seems chicken shit to go after him right now." I couldn't put my finger on it, but something about her eagerness was bugging me.

"The only thing funny about this is your reluctance. When did you develop such highbrow ethics?"

I'd never been accused of having ethics, highbrow or not, but the question, coming from her, pissed me off. My anger led to clarity. If she was right and Jackson had set Jorge up, then why was Jackson the one in a coma? Wouldn't Jorge be the one most likely to have wanted Jackson out of the picture?

But he'd acted so surprised when I told him about Jackson, and how would he have known about the meeting anyway?

I searched my memory for every detail about that night. Nancy had picked me up. It had never occurred to me anyone might have followed us. But someone had followed me earlier that day. Ronnie. She'd mentioned seeing me talking to Nancy at lunch. And she'd been at my apartment not long before Nancy picked me up that evening. Could she have arranged the shooting? Maybe tipped her brother off? If Jackson was working with IAD, then Jorge had a strong motive to get him out of the picture. And with Garcia nowhere to be found, the evidence against Jorge seemed to be slipping away.

Maybe Nancy had been only collateral damage. If Jorge was behind the shooting, it would explain why I hadn't been caught up in the crossfire. Why shoot your own employee?

If Jackson was out of the picture and Garcia truly vanished, then the last link between Jorge and the case was Perez. Was she in danger? Would I care if she was? All I really cared about was whether I was being used.

I stared at the woman across the table from me and considered whether to confront her with my suspicions. She'd lied to me before. I thought I'd be able to tell if she did it again, but now I wasn't so sure. I decided to play along with her until I could figure out what was real and what wasn't. I opened the envelope she'd given me and pretended to be engrossed with the papers inside. Took a lot of paper to break up a marriage.

"Okay, I'll go talk to the former Mrs. Jackson." I kept my eyes on the papers as I made the concession.

"Great. I really think this will lead to something. Have you managed to find out anything else?"

"Not yet." No way was I going to tell her about my hunt for Garcia. If her little brother was into eliminating witnesses, I wasn't going to lead him to any more. "But I'll go see Jackson's ex and let you know what I find out." I stood and motioned to Cash. "I'm supposed to meet up with my brother. See you later?"

She looked surprised at my obvious dismissal. "Uh, sure. Tell him congratulations on the wedding."

That would have been sweet, had she known my brother, or even ever met him. As it was, her attempt to get close to me by talking about personal stuff creeped me out, especially in light of all the crazy notions going through my head. All I wanted to do right now was get far enough away from her to process what was going on.

Cash and I walked back to my apartment, and I took the time to consider what to do next. I'd already decided I would try to talk to Jackson's ex-wife. She probably wouldn't have a clue if he had snitched on Jorge, but I'd take any information I could get at this point, and if Ronnie was watching me, acting normal seemed like the best thing to do until I figured out where things stood.

We passed Withers on the way into the apartment complex, and he actually waved at me, all friendly-like. Guess paying my rent a month in advance meant I was his new favorite tenant. At least he'd stopped hassling me about Cash. Good, since the way things were going, this dog was probably the only friend I had left.

I had my key in the lock, when I heard footsteps behind me. Cash started talking, and I turned to see who had gotten his attention.

Jess.

She bent down and used both hands to rub Cash's ears. He leaned into her and growled his pleasure with every touch. Traitorous dog.

I wished I was him.

When the dog became a puddle of mush on the sidewalk, Jess looked up at me with soulful blues of her own. "Luca, we need to talk."

CHAPTER SEVENTEEN

Talking was the last thing I wanted to do. I put my key back in my pocket and dropped my hand from the doorknob. Jess wore dark jeans, a tight white T-shirt, and a sleek black leather jacket. The dark circles under her eyes didn't detract from how hot she looked or how much I wanted her.

"Aren't you going to invite me inside?"

I was scared that if I opened the door, invited her inside, all my self-control would slip away. I'd abandon this case, promise anything, do anything, to feel Jess's body against mine. To keep her in my life. To recapture what we'd had before.

And that scared me to death. I stalled. "Do you think it's a good idea to be seen here?"

"Probably not, but it's a little late now."

She didn't offer anything else, and I was torn between being pissed that she was making me pull information out of her and being glad to see her. "What about all the 'I can't see you while you're working on this case' bullshit?"

"Seriously, Luca, are you going to open the door? I need to talk to you, and I'm not doing it out here." She glanced around and not in a casual way. Something was going on. Had to be or she wouldn't have shown up here. I looked down at Cash, who stood at full attention, like he'd picked up on her cautious mood. Neither of them wanted to be sitting ducks, but if danger lurked nearby, being in my apartment wasn't going to protect us. I tentatively put a hand on Jess's arm, and when she didn't pull away, I held her more tightly and started walking to the parking lot. When we reached the Bronco, I led her to the passenger door and whispered, "Get in."

I saw the rise of a protest in her eyes, and I shook my head. She remained silent as she climbed into the car. Once Cash and I were in as well, she waited at least ten seconds before asking, "What the hell are we doing?"

"We're going for a drive. You have something better to do?"

If she did, she didn't say it. I was glad she hadn't fought me on this and wasn't asking any more questions, because I didn't have any answers. All I knew was she'd shown up at my door when I'd least expected her to, and whatever had prompted her visit had both of us a little spooked. But I didn't care about that as much as I cared about her being here with me.

My car was on autopilot, and we hit a ton of traffic on I-35. I didn't usually visit the casino on Monday afternoons, and I'd never taken Jess with me. My gambling wasn't something we talked about much, but I knew she didn't approve. At least today it would be legal, unlike all the games I'd played at Bingo's place. She waited until we pulled into the parking lot of the Winstar World Casino before she finally brought up something besides the weather and how the Mavericks were doing.

"I'm worried about you."

Way to change the subject. Wasn't like I didn't know Jess thought I was one step away from disaster most of the time, but I couldn't remember her ever saying it out loud. I kept my eyes straight ahead and tried a little levity. "Good thing someone is."

"I mean it, Luca. It's not my place to tell you who to sleep with, but if you want to go around playing detective, you may want to know more about what you're getting into."

I started to say a bunch of things in protest, but they all died on my lips as I realized Jess thought I was sleeping with Ronnie. She wasn't entirely wrong, but where there once was a time I would have admitted it like a badge of honor, now I only wanted to hide in shame. Instead, I stuck to what I thought would be safe ground—the case. "What do you know that I don't?"

"Diamond Collier called me today."

"What?" Now I wasn't sure if the "who to sleep with" comment had to do with Ronnie or Diamond, since Jess knew I'd been with both. Either way, I was more unsettled Diamond had called Jess than I was that Jess was giving me a hard time about sleeping around. "What did she want?"

"Apparently, she thinks I have some influence over you. She wanted me to warn you off Roberto Garcia, the CI in the Moreno case. She wouldn't tell me much, but she made it very clear you might be putting yourself in danger if you keep snooping around for him." She paused. "You want to tell me how Diamond's wrapped up with what's going on with Jorge Moreno?"

I did. Very much. I'd been desperate to talk to Jess about the case, but she was the one who'd cut ties. I told her so.

"Luca, my job is all I have. I've gone out on a limb for you before, but if I take a risk again and things go south…What am I supposed to do then?"

"Yet, here you are."

She looked out the window and I followed her gaze. The casino did indeed represent the "world" with cheesy facades featuring landmarks like the Coliseum and Big Ben. As corny as it was, it was the closest legalized gambling place to Dallas, and it was huge. I'd gotten lucky here in more ways than one.

Not today. I wasn't sure why I'd driven here, except I couldn't think of another place where Jess and I could talk without the risk of being seen together. I'd paid close attention on the drive up and was certain we hadn't been followed. Now that we were here, we could get lost in the crowd. I paused to wonder why I cared so much about protecting Jess when she'd shown up on my doorstep in broad daylight. "I don't have a clue why Diamond is so hell-bent on keeping me off the trail of a witness, but it bothers me a whole hell of a lot that she's so worked up about it that she came to you." I left unsaid the part about why Diamond would think Jess would have any influence over me.

"Don't look at me. She didn't share her motivation with me."

"But you thought it was important enough to show up on my doorstep."

"It wasn't a hard decision. I wanted to see you." She delivered the simple statement and then looked out her window, seemingly transfixed on something in the distance. She didn't fool me. I decided to cave first.

"I'm glad you did."

She looked back my way. One look and I didn't care about Diamond or Nancy or Jorge or Ronnie. All I cared about was the want in her eyes, the craving she inspired. My clothes were too tight, the air in the car was too thin. I opened my mouth to gasp for air, but better than oxygen, Jess pulled me to her and kissed me. Long. Hard.

I kissed her back, imprinting every trace of her tongue, every brush of her lips. Unlike when we'd parted on Saturday, I was determined that if this was the last time, I would remember it always. Breathing seemed so not important anymore.

When she finally broke the embrace, I sank back against the seat and basked in the glow of it. I felt a slight pressure on my shoulder and looked up to see Cash's head resting there. The expression in his eyes was questioning.

"He's either hungry or he needs to go," Jess said.

"Probably both."

"What do you want to do?"

"What do you want to do?" It was like we were two teenagers on our first date. We'd made out in the car and now neither one of us was sure how the rest of the evening should go. I decided to step up.

"How about we take Cash for a walk over there?" I pointed at the picnic area to the side of the casino. "And then we go inside and take a look around."

"Hundred dollar limit. First one who loses that, we're out of here."

She'd offered way more than I expected. "Deal."

❖

We called it quits at eleven o'clock even though neither one of us had lost a dime. Instead of driving back, we booked a room with our winnings and ordered a bottle of champagne. Jess's choice, not mine. I figured I could concede my usual beer since she'd spent the evening indulging my other vice.

"I can't believe they let Cash in without giving you more flack," she said.

"Good-looking people, good-looking dogs. It's all the same. If you're cute, you get better treatment."

"Is that right?"

"Why do you think the room service guy threw in these snacks? It wasn't because you're ugly."

"Whatever." She poured us each a glass of bubbly and joined me on the bed. "I think we should talk."

"That's what you get for thinking." I drank half my glass and tried to ignore the fizz up my nose. Maybe if we got drunk really fast, we could avoid "the talk."

Didn't work.

"I know you don't want to."

I put my glass down. "Okay, so here's the deal. You say that so I'll say 'you don't know that' and then you say 'well, if that's true, then why don't we talk?' and then I say 'why don't we' and then we wind up talking just like you wanted, and I didn't, in the first place."

She stared at me like I had three heads. "Are you done?"

"Yeah, I guess so."

"You really think I'd set you up like that?"

I considered more champagne, but it wasn't helping and I had a feeling I was going to have a colossal headache tomorrow. "I don't know. Maybe."

"You don't know me at all."

We sat in silence for a few minutes, her pronouncement hanging in the air. It might be true.

"I know you well enough."

"Well enough to call when you need help. Well enough to fuck. But what else do you know?"

"I know how you like your coffee."

"Not funny, Luca."

"I wasn't trying to be funny." The edge in her voice was getting on my nerves. It was almost like she was accusing me of something, and I couldn't help but feel like I was coming up short. "You're mad at me because I don't know your favorite color or—"

I fished around in my brain for trivial things girlfriends share, but I didn't have a good reference point so I made it up on the fly. "Or the make of the first car you ever drove."

"Don't be a jerk."

"What's gotten into you?"

"You. You've gotten into me. Something changed between us. Tell me you don't feel it."

Oh, I felt it all right, but saying it out loud was completely different. I looked at the champagne bucket, the bedspread, the nightstand, and Cash, who lay at the foot of the bed in a deep sleep—absolutely no help at all. No matter where I tried to focus my attention, I couldn't deny that Jess was here in the room, wanting something from me, something I wasn't sure I knew how to give. I was scared to death.

"Luca, look at me."

I buckled down and did what she asked. When our eyes met, I felt it in my gut. I'd expected to see her wanting, but she was giving. Offering anyway.

"Tell me what you're thinking," she said.

"I don't know."

"Then tell me what you're feeling."

I didn't think she wanted to hear my stomach was in knots, my heart was about to beat out of my chest, and I was a second away from needing a paper bag to breath. "I, uh, I…"

Jess's eyes dropped, and I experienced a second of shame at the relief I felt when I was no longer the object of her laser focus. My relief was brief.

"I love you."

Holy shit. My head shot up on the second word, and I saw her lips moving, but I couldn't process. "What?"

"I said I love you. Now you say something stupid that'll make me sorry for it."

Well, I guess she was scared too. Except suddenly, I wasn't scared anymore. Hearing her say it first had a strange effect. It made me bold. Like I could say it now without risk. And I wanted to say it. My lips even started to form the words.

I love you, Jessica Chance. I think I've always loved you. When I heard the words in my head, they sounded right, but not for right now, because if I said it now, it would be like I was just saying it because she had. Right? I mean, shouldn't I wait and say it without being prompted? Like it was my own idea.

Okay, so I wasn't going to say it, but I wasn't going to say something stupid either. I had no idea how much time had passed with Jess waiting while her words hung in the air, waiting to see if they would find their mark or land with a thud. I may not be ready to say it back, but I could show her how she made me feel.

I kissed her. Gently. I took my time, enjoying the way she melted into my embrace. It wasn't dramatic. It wasn't rushed. We had all night. We had longer even. If what she'd said was true, we had a very long time. I undressed her and did it slowly, taking time to look at her, feel every inch of her. The scar on her shoulder, the soft skin and the strong muscles just beneath. Her blue eyes were midnight, her gaze hazy. I knew her, I wanted her, I…

Three little words. Should be nothing to say them out loud, but I couldn't. Not right now.

Just because I didn't say it doesn't mean I didn't feel it. I hoped she knew me well enough to know that was true.

❖

I woke up the next morning curled around Jess. I would have stayed that way, but for the insistent paw at my back. I motioned to Cash to be quiet and eased out of bed and into my clothes, wishing we'd gotten a room on the ground floor of the hotel.

Turned out I was grateful for the time spent walking the dog. Away from Jess's willing body, I had a chance to think, literally in the light of day. I felt like a different person. I should've wanted to run away after last night. A few weeks ago, after any kind of discussion about feelings, I would have lit out at the first chance, but here I was, anxious to get back to bed. Back to Jess. She'd told me she loved me. I knew she hadn't meant the platonic crap she was supposed to feel for a close friend. But even knowing that, I'd stuck around. I amazed myself and I let the new me think about what would happen next. And I made a big decision.

I whistled for Cash who'd found a potential rabbit hole, and he reluctantly joined me to return to the hotel. When we got back to the room, Jess was still in bed, but awake now. She looked a little surprised to see me walk through the door. "You didn't think I was coming back."

She grinned. "Maybe. Maybe I just hoped you'd bring coffee."

I wasn't great at this having someone around the morning after thing. Even Jess had a habit of taking off while I was still catching z's. "I'm sorry. I can get some and be right back."

She patted the bed. "I was kidding. Room service is on the way. I optimistically ordered enough for two."

I stayed dressed until the guy came and unloaded his tray. Jess had ordered eggs, bacon, and pancakes with an extra side of eggs for Cash. Those two loved each other for sure.

I watched her eat, paying close attention to her tiny quirks like the way she had to have a taste of everything in each bite or how she doctored her coffee. I'd known all this stuff, but I'd never thought it was so damn adorable before. I had it bad.

"Aren't you hungry?" She pointed at my still full plate.

"Sure, but you look like you might stab me with your fork if I try to eat any of this."

"Ha. Eat. You're making me feel like a pig."

I ate for diversion mostly, but the food was good. Everything about this morning was good.

When her plate was empty, Jess tossed her fork down and leaned back on the bed. "I can't remember ever being that hungry. So, what's your plan for today?"

An innocent question any other day, but the morning after she'd said she loved me, the simple inquiry was loaded with innuendo. Luckily, I'd prepared.

"I want to spend the day with you…"

"I hear a big 'but.'"

I nodded. "But there's something I need to do first. Before we can…you know…" I'd decided I was going to cut ties with Ronnie. I'd give her my notes—after I transferred them from napkins to regular paper, and I'd add up my time and give her the balance of her money back. Jess wasn't asking me to, but I knew it was the right thing to do. Curiosity wasn't a good enough reason to risk what could be, and the way Nancy had been acting didn't inspire me to stick with it for her sake. I prayed Jess would accept my vague explanation about today and know I'd be back when I took care of business, but I didn't want to have to spell it out.

Her hand tugged at my shirt and she pulled me back into the bed, then rolled over to top me. I lay on my back while she loomed over. "Okay, but tonight"—she reached down and gave me a maple syrup kiss—"you'll come over tonight."

I could see it in her eyes. She was still hungry and not for pancakes. "Fuck yes."

CHAPTER EIGHTEEN

No one was answering their phone. Figured that when I'd finally made up my mind to take some action, no one was around to help out.

Diamond, I understood. She rarely ever answered when I called, preferring instead to call back and catch me unaware. Ronnie, on the other hand, I would've expected to be waiting by the phone to see if I'd found out anything from Jackson's ex. When my call to her went to voice mail, I left a cryptic message designed to get her to call me back right away. The sooner I was off this case, the sooner I could figure out what was next between Jess and me.

Thirty minutes later, I heard a knock at the door. Typical of Ronnie to decide to show up in person in response to a phone message. Probably for the best. Our professional breakup would be more challenging this way, but I was up for it. I threw open the door and started in before she had a chance to speak.

Except it wasn't her.

It wasn't anyone. I looked around, but there was no sign of whoever had committed the knock and run. I started to shut the door when I saw a plain brown envelope leaning against the doorframe. The last envelope delivered to my door had a big fat check in it so I didn't hesitate to open this one, hoping for a second win.

No such luck. Whoever had written this message had a flair for the dramatic, but it had nothing to do with finances. The note, spelled out with letters clipped from magazines, was only two lines:

Stop asking questions and stay away from your cop girlfriend if you want her to live.

I would've laughed at the crazy threat, but something about the crooked, uneven letters spooked me. It was all so very serial killer. I'd expected reactions like Perez's—typical protests from the loyal brotherhood, but this? This note came from someone with a screw loose. Normal folks don't cut out letters from magazines and spend time arranging them into ominous warnings. *Cop girlfriend.* Had to mean Jess.

Before I could give it any more thought, my phone rang. Ronnie. She started talking before I could get in a "hello."

"Luca, I need you. It's Jorge. It's bad." She spat out an address, said come quickly. She was off the line before I could process what had happened. I stared at the note in my hand. I wasn't about to stay away from Jess, but the stop asking questions part? I was all for that, but I needed a few answers before I could stand down.

I poured some food for Cash and made sure he had fresh water. He wove in and out of my legs while I tended to him, no doubt sensing something was up, but I wasn't taking him this time. For all I knew, I was walking into another trap like the meet with Jackson. I checked out the Colt, put a twenty-two in my boot, and grabbed a shotgun to put in the special compartment in the Bronco.

I recognized the address. It wasn't far from where Ronnie's parents lived, and I guessed it was Jorge's house. That seemed like a good sign. If someone had gunned him down, like they had Jackson, he'd probably be at the hospital or the morgue, not his own place. If the creepy note hadn't come within minutes of Ronnie's call, I probably would've blown her off, but my gut told me they were related. I hoped I was wrong and that this field trip would just be a good way for me to see Ronnie and quit the case.

A few minutes later, I pulled up in front of a modest bungalow with a detached garage. There were several cars in the drive, so I parked on the street. I was barely out of the car before Ronnie came running over. She grabbed me by the arm and started dragging me toward the house. I dug in and yanked her back. "What's going on?"

"Jorge is inside. The ambulance was just here. Mama went with them. We called the cops and they sent some jerk-off who stayed all of fifteen minutes before deciding it was just a kid's prank. You've got to do something."

I shook her, but it still took a minute for her eyes to lose their wild and crazy and focus on mine. "Ronnie, you're not making any sense. Who was in the ambulance?"

"Esmeralda, Jorge's wife." She took a deep breath. "Someone threw a brick through the window, and she was cut by a piece of flying glass."

It did sound like a kid's prank. "Did anyone see who did it?"

"No, but they heard a car speed away. Mama was here, but she went to the hospital with Esmeralda, and she took the baby with her. Jorge wanted to go, but I wanted him here so he could talk to you."

This wasn't my territory, but I didn't want to say it straight out for fear of upsetting her more. "He called the police?"

"For all the good that did. They sent a patrol cop, a mere child. This was probably the first call of his career. He didn't even take the note with him when he left."

"Note? What are you talking about?"

"Oh, damn. That's the most important thing." She pulled on my arm again. "Come on."

Once inside the house, she led me to the kitchen where Jorge sat at a small table, his head in his arms. He looked up as we entered and shook his head. "This has got to stop."

Ronnie took the seat next to him and motioned for me to sit across from them. I watched her pat him on the arm and heard him moan about his troubles. I didn't want to be here. Jorge should buck up and use his cop training to figure a way out of his own mess. The only thing that kept me sitting was the mention of a note and the fact I'd gotten one myself less than an hour ago. "Let me see the note."

Jorge pulled a folded piece of paper out of his pocket. Dumbass had probably put his hands all over it. How the hell had he ever made detective? He started to hand it to me, but I motioned for him to put it down in front of me.

When I saw the uneven cutout letters, I gripped the side of the table. *Accept your punishment or people you care about will get hurt.*

"What's wrong?" Ronnie asked.

"Tell me everything that happened. Every detail."

Jorge walked me through it. He'd been sitting in the living room watching TV. Esmeralda came in the room to tell him something, and the brick came flying through the window. It hadn't hit anyone, but a large shard of glass had struck her in the head. Jorge looked out the window, but all he saw was the back of a dark sedan flying down the street. He called 911 and gave a statement to the responding officer. The officer glanced at the note, but hadn't asked any questions about motive, and when Jorge tried to talk to him, he said he had all he needed and if there was anything else, a detective would follow up. The paramedics told Esmeralda she'd need stitches, so Mrs. Moreno had gone with her to the emergency room.

Based on his timeline, he'd gotten his ominous warning about the same time I'd gotten mine, the only real difference was method of delivery. It wasn't a coincidence, and I was sufficiently spooked. I spent the next half hour grilling Jorge, but he didn't waver. He professed to have no clue about who would have set him up, and he insisted he had no idea why he'd been singled out. I was convinced there was more to it than random selection, and I was determined to find out the common denominator.

I pointed at the note. "Don't touch that again. Use a glove, something, and put it in a plastic bag and give it to me."

"What are you going to do with it?" Ronnie asked.

"I'm not sure yet."

"Shouldn't we keep it in case a detective calls?"

Damn, she was persistent. I drew Jorge into the conversation. "No detective is going to call, right, Jorge?"

He looked up at me, but I couldn't read his expression. Lost, angry, scared. The mixture didn't translate. "Jorge, if you know what this note means, you need to tell me, right now. Other people are at risk, not just your family."

He shook his head. "I don't have a clue, other than whoever did this wants me to take the rap and do it quietly. What makes you think I know more?"

"Because no one threatened to hurt you, which means keeping you alive is valuable." Maybe it was as simple as keeping him around to take the heat, but wouldn't it be just as easy to blame the fake drug fiasco on a dead guy? I didn't care so much about Jorge's safety, but my resolution to walk away from this case was fading in the face of the threat to Jess. The note I'd received had threatened her if I didn't cut ties, stop asking questions. If I did what he wanted, how could I be sure that whatever whackjob was behind these threats would keep his end of the bargain?

I couldn't, but I was determined to find out.

❖

I sent enough texts to blow up Diamond's phone and then curled up with Cash to wait. When she finally called, she started talking before I could say hello.

"Luca, what the hell?"

"We need to talk."

"So talk."

"In person. I'm fairly certain my place is being watched. Use your super secret undercover skills to figure out how you can talk to me, face-to-face without anyone knowing. You owe me, remember?"

I heard a heavy sigh. "Are you at home?"

"Yes."

"Stay there and give me thirty minutes. I'll send you a text with the location."

It was afternoon, way past lunchtime, but for the first time in forever, I wasn't hungry. Judging by the amount of food left in Cash's bowl, he wasn't either. Since the phone had rung, he kept moving from the door back to the couch and nudging me with his long nose. He wanted me to know he was going with next time.

How was it this dog and I had gotten to know each other so well in less than two weeks, but it had taken Jess and me forever to figure out we were in love?

The text from Diamond was short. *451 Riverfront. In back. Leave now.*

Not so long ago, Riverfront Drive used to be called Industrial Avenue. That was before the city decided the nearby swampy Trinity River was going to become a world-class playground with parks and shops and restaurants. Didn't matter what the city's plans were, changing the name of a street didn't change the fact that it was bordered by the huge county jail, dozens of bail bond agencies, liquor stores, and grimy warehouses. The address Diamond had given me was for one of those warehouses.

I drove by a couple of times. There were no cars out front, but since she'd told me to meet her out back, I didn't think it was a big deal. Still, I was hesitant, the recent shooting still fresh in my mind. "What do you think, Cash? Should we check it out?"

He mumbled a reply, and I decided it amounted to a reluctant yes. I pulled to the side of the building and turned the car off. The car didn't have time to cool before Diamond knocked on the passenger side window. I unlocked the door and she slid into the front seat.

"Drive around back. There's a place you can pull in and we can talk in private."

"I don't think I was followed."

"You weren't."

Her hard look told me not to ask, but now I knew I hadn't been smart enough to spot the tail she must've had on me. I wanted to know why she'd had me followed, but it wasn't as important as the reason I'd called her in the first place. Once I parked in back, I launched into the spiel I'd planned on the drive over. "I think you're lying when you say you don't know where Roberto Garcia is." I voiced an idea that had been eating at me. "I think he may even be working for your side."

She didn't blink, so I kept going. "I also think you're lying when you act like you don't know anything about Jorge Moreno's case."

She started to interject, but I held up a hand and kept talking. "I don't care about either of those things right now." I shoved both of the whacko notes at her. "All I need to know right now is whether these are real threats."

She stared at both pieces of paper for a long time, starting and finishing with the one I'd received. The one threatening Jess. Finally, she looked at me, her expression both serious and sympathetic. "Yes, they're real."

"So if I keep looking into Jorge Moreno's case, if I don't stay away from her, Jess could be in danger."

"Yes."

I needed to hear her say it, but it didn't stop my gut from twisting when she delivered the bad news. "Do you know who's behind this?"

"I have a theory."

"And I guess you don't plan to share your theory with me?"

"Luca..."

"Just say it."

"No. I can't talk to you about an *ongoing* investigation."

The inflection was slight, and maybe I was grasping at straws, but I was desperate for clues. Desperate for some sign telling me what to do. Maybe Diamond couldn't tell me anything directly, but maybe her reactions would give me some sense as to whether I was hot or cold. I held my hand out for the notes, but she held them just out of my reach.

"I need those back."

"What are you going to do with them?" she asked.

"I know people on the force. Jess is a cop. They protect their own."

"That's true. And some will go to great lengths to protect their own."

Ah, I was starting to get her innuendo. That whatever threat I faced, whatever threat Jess faced, was likely to come from someone she wouldn't suspect. Was Diamond telling me cops were in on whatever was going on?

Not like I hadn't suspected, but I'd never suspected Jess could be caught in the crossfire.

Your cop girlfriend. Key word, girlfriend. Whoever had left me the note threatening Jess did it because they thought she was my girlfriend and I would care enough about her to do whatever they asked to keep her safe. I don't know how they came to that conclusion, when I'd only just figured out my feelings.

But they were right.

❖

I stood outside Jess's door, but I hadn't yet worked up the nerve to knock. I wished I could've done this over the phone, even sent a text, but I needed the show to make it really work.

After I'd left Diamond, I'd gone back to my apartment, partly to drop Cash off and partly to give whoever was up in my business a chance to catch up with me. Cash hadn't wanted to be left behind, but I figured it was good practice for next summer's hot temperatures. I wouldn't be able to take him with me everywhere then. Funny that the only long-term relationship I was certain about was between me and a dog.

Once I reached Jess's neighborhood, I'd driven around the block several times until I was certain I was followed. I didn't know where the sedan was right now, but I hoped they had a good view.

When Jess answered the door dressed in a tank top and boxers, my knees buckled.

She'd taken a nap. I could tell by the way her short blond hair was smashed against the side of her head and the sleepy haze in her eyes. The bed was probably still warm. I desperately wanted to find out. All I had to do was walk through the door, sweep her in my arms, and tell her how I felt.

And then wait. Wait for something bad to happen. I knew it would. Diamond had lied to me many times, but she wouldn't have lied about Jess being in danger, and I knew in my gut Jess would be in trouble, no matter what I did. I already decided I was staying on the case. Not for Ronnie, not for Jorge, but for me and Jess, for the possibility of a future. But I had to convince whoever was watching that I was following their instructions. To seal the deal, I was also going to let them know Jess wasn't my girlfriend anymore, so they could look elsewhere if they wanted to motivate me.

"I was hoping it was you. Come in."

Jess's hand on mine was almost my undoing. I shook it off and took a step back, hoping distance would make this easier. All that happened was I got a better eyeful of her legs. Her naked legs. Legs that could be wrapped around me in a matter of seconds, if I only did what she asked and came inside.

I shook my head. If all I cared about was sex, this would be easy. But things between us were so much more complicated. I needed to do what I'd come here for and get out. Like ripping off a bandage.

"I'm not coming in."

"Okay."

Her voice was sluggish and I guessed she was still tired. Understandable since neither of us had gotten much sleep the night before. I pushed the memory of hours of lovemaking out of my head and prepared to do the damage I'd come here to do. "I told Ronnie I quit."

She smiled. "That's great."

"No, it's not great."

"Luca, what's going on?"

She was alert now. I raised my voice, but not for her benefit. "Where do you get off thinking you can tell me what to do?"

She shook her head. I didn't blame her for being confused. Hell, I was confused. I tried again. "I only quit because of you, so I could be with you."

"You're not making any sense."

"I control my life, not you." I waved my arms for effect. I was making a total mess of this, but my heart wasn't in it. Please let her catch on quickly.

"I'm not trying to control you."

"Yes, you are. If you weren't, then why give me an ultimatum?"

"Do you want to be with me?"

"No," I lied. "Not bad enough to give up who I am." That was closer to the truth, but still off the mark. Jess hadn't asked me to be anything I wasn't. This whole case was totally outside my usual MO. Wasn't I the one who was trying to be something I wasn't? I couldn't think about that now. I had to focus on why I was here.

Whoever was watching needed to believe Jess and I were done. But more importantly, Jess needed to believe it, or she'd wander into my life and get herself killed. And if anything happened to her, we'd never have a chance and I'd never forgive myself.

I ignored the hurt in her eyes and pressed on, my voice raised. "I'm leaving now. I just wanted you to know we're done." I waved my arm between us and then gave an umpire sign for "you're out" for the benefit of anyone watching. I spun around and jogged down the sidewalk before I could register her reaction. She might be mad now, but she'd get over it. She'd probably come around to thinking she should have expected it, just not so soon.

When I reached the Bronco, I looked at her door, thinking it might be safe to risk a final look.

I was wrong. I'd expected anger, but pain? The hurt in her eyes ripped me wide open. All I wanted to do was run back to the door, sweep her in my arms, and tell her I was sorry. Instead, I drove away.

CHAPTER NINETEEN

I pulled up in front of Ryan Foster's office and glanced down at Cash. He'd slept the entire drive with his head on my thigh, like he could sense something was up. I wasn't sure how Ryan would feel about a dog in the office during business hours, but I wasn't ready to be separated from his unconditional dog love. He hadn't left my side since I'd returned home from Jess's last night.

With Jess in mind, I made a call. John answered on the first ring, and I didn't bother with small talk. "I need a favor."

"Surprise, surprise."

"Seriously, John. It's important."

"Hit me with it. I'll do what I can."

"Jess may be in trouble. Look out for her and don't tell her I called. If she's going to stay safe she needs to steer clear of me."

"It would help if I had a little more information."

"I'll tell you when I can. Promise me you'll look out for her."

"I promise, but it would sure help if—"

I hung up. Time to go see Ryan.

Unlike Saturday, today, the law office had a gatekeeper. The guy at the front desk looked at me and the dog, but I didn't register judgment for either of us. "Are you here to see Ms. Logan?"

Took me a minute, but then I remembered Ryan had said the office was actually her wife's. "Actually, I'm trying to track down Ryan Foster. Is she around today?"

He took my name and went off somewhere in the back to see if she was available. I'd had this brainstorm sometime during the sleepless night. I wanted to talk to a lawyer, but the thought of confiding in Ronnie made my gut churn. She'd left a half dozen messages, each more panicked than the other. She sounded genuinely scared about the incident at Jorge's house, but I didn't feel like sharing my ideas with her. On the other hand, I'd liked Foster, and my gut told me to trust her.

A few minutes later, the guy, who said his name was Anthony, led Cash and me to the conference room where I'd met with Foster on Saturday. Before he left, he offered both of us water. I declined, but couldn't help but appreciate the fact he acted like it was perfectly normal to bring a dog to a business office.

When he left, I looked around at the boxes. Judging by the volume, the lawyers for the police department were trying to snow Ryan's clients under. If the attorneys were willing to go to great lengths to keep from paying out, I wondered what the boys in blue would do if their scheme was being threatened. Something bad. The only way to stop them would be to figure out what the scheme was and shut it down. After talking to Diamond, I was convinced there was a bigger picture. Bigger than Jorge, bigger than Ryan's case. Maybe together we could cut through the crap.

"Did you find Garcia?"

I turned at the sound of her voice. Ryan was dressed in a suit, which threw me a little. "Where's the T-shirt and jeans?" I asked.

She looked down at her clothes as if she wasn't sure what she was wearing. "Oh, yeah. I had a hearing this morning."

"Judge give you access to the police department records you wanted?"

"Different case." She took a seat and motioned me to do the same. "Did you find Garcia?"

"Not exactly."

"I'm not following."

"Not surprising. I think Garcia might be working for the feds."

She leaned back in her chair, her fingers steepled. "I guess that could be. After getting burned on these state cases, maybe he peddled his information to the DEA."

"No, that's not what I mean. I mean I think he might be a fed." Without telling her everything I knew about Diamond, I gave her a rough sketch of my search for Garcia. "I think he was involved with DPD, not as a former criminal enlisted to help the cops, but as a federal agent investigating something way bigger than minor drug buys."

"Sounds like a bit of a leap to me."

I didn't blame her for being skeptical, but my hunch was strong. "You have any better ideas?"

"Not really. So, what do you suggest?"

"I don't think we're going to find Garcia. At least not the way we've been looking. I think we should go about it another way. Flush him out by exposing whatever's really going on with DPD."

"I don't get it. Why are you so interested? I did a little checking of my own. You're a bounty hunter, not a PI."

"Well, technically, I am a PI." I read the yeah, right expression on her face. "Let's just say I have a friend who might be in trouble if this whole thing doesn't come out."

"Cop?"

"Yes." I'd already shared more than I intended, but Ryan's sympathetic expression lured the words out. "Detective Jessica Chance. You know her?"

Ryan let out a long breath. "I always thought Chance was a solid cop. She's mixed up in all this?"

"Yes. I mean, no. What I mean is, she's likely to be a casualty if someone doesn't stop these guys."

"And she's a good *friend*?"

I ignored the emphasis. The wound was too fresh to revisit. "Yes."

"But you said yourself, you're not sure who these guys are or even what they're really up to."

"I know. And it's not like we can call the cops."

"Then I guess the someone who stops them will have to be us."

"I had a feeling you'd say that." I handed her the envelope containing Greg Jackson's divorce papers. "I think there's a clue in here, but I need a good lawyer to cipher it out. You up for the job?"

❖

I drove back to Ryan's office after lunch for our first adventure. Cash was home, sleeping off a bowl of kibble and half a hamburger. Ryan was waiting in front, wearing the suit she'd had on earlier, but without the jacket. She slid into the passenger seat of the Bronco and set the envelope I'd given her earlier on the console.

"Well?" I asked, motioning at the envelope.

"Looks like Greg Jackson's ex hates his guts. And she was inordinately focused on his finances. Strange for a woman who'd been married to a cop for that long. You think she'd realize he wasn't ever going to bring home big bucks."

"Ready to go talk to her?"

"I'm game." She looked around the car. "Where's your dog?"

"Cash. He's at home. Not sure how the former Mrs. Jackson feels about dogs."

"Who doesn't like dogs?"

"I wasn't sure I did until I had one. We never had any pets when I was growing up."

"Me neither. I lived with my aunt and she wasn't big on anything that disrupted her sense of order. I always wanted a dog, though."

I'd never brought up getting a pet to my folks. My dad would've been all about it, but my mother resented having children. A dog would have sent her over the edge. I'd known enough not to even ask.

When we pulled up in front of the apartment complex where Lily Reynolds, formerly Jackson, lived, I shut down the car and turned to Ryan. "Let's talk about how we're going to play this. Since I don't understand all the legal mumbo jumbo, why don't you take the lead?"

"Fair enough, but feel free to chime in. I told her on the phone that I wanted to talk to her about her ex-husband's career as background for a case. She acted like she was dying to give me the scoop on him, and she didn't even ask why I wanted to know. I'm sure she'll be happy to answer any questions we have."

Lily Reynolds answered the door dressed in scrubs. Maybe that was her idea of lounge attire, or maybe she was actually a nurse getting ready for a night shift, which would make sense given she was home in the middle of the day. She was petite and, even in scrubs, pretty in a made-up-to-go-somewhere kind of way. Ryan made the introductions, after which Lily gave us each a once-over and then invited us in. Ryan declined coffee so I did too even though I was feeling a post lunch coma creeping in. Lily disappeared into the kitchen and reappeared a few seconds later with a mug of her own. I smelled a hint of alcohol, but passed it off to nurse stuff. Once we were settled on the couch in the living room, she opened the discussion without any prompting from us.

"Look at this place. Can you believe I have to live like this?"

Ryan murmured sympathy, while I looked around the room, unsure about the source of her complaint. If by living like this, she meant in a clean, neat, and well-decorated apartment, I couldn't really relate. I for sure didn't live this way, but I knew people who did and liked it. I guess it could be a burden.

"As I told you on the phone, I'm working on a lawsuit against the police department and your husband's name came up," Ryan said. "We'd like to ask you some questions about his career."

"Ex-husband, may he rot in hell."

"Sorry, ex."

"You call it a career. I call it a life of crime."

"Why don't you tell me what you mean?" Ryan asked.

"Take our divorce, for instance. He fought me every step of the way. Cost us both a pretty penny."

"Now that you mention it, that's something I was curious about. It looks like you had a lot of questions about his finances and wanted his records reviewed by a forensic accountant. Did you have some reason to believe he had more money than a normal cop with his tenure on the force?"

She laughed. "You're kidding, right?"

We both stared at her as her laugh trailed off. Guess it wasn't as funny if we weren't in on the joke.

"Actually, I'm not," Ryan said. "What am I missing?"

"He was loaded." Lily nodded her head vigorously, and then to emphasize the point, said, "I'm sure of it."

Ryan and I exchanged a glance. If she was so sure of it, why hadn't she been able to prove it to the divorce court judge who'd declined to award spousal support? They didn't have any kids, so basically, Lily had walked away from the marriage with half of everything, which included a decent debt load.

"I know what you're thinking, but I'm convinced Greg had money squirreled away. He was just smart enough not to flash it around like the others."

"What others?"

"All of them. They were all in on it."

I was now convinced Lily Reynolds was a bit of a nut, but being a nut didn't mean her theory was completely wrong. I wanted to believe her. If something bigger was going on within the police department, that would explain the shooting, Diamond's reluctance to share info, and the threats against anyone who might expose the scheme. The key was to find out what "it" was. I decided to cut to the chase. "Tell us what you think they were involved in and why you think so."

"If I could prove anything, I'd be rich right now. Every one of Greg's pals on the force had expensive cars. Their wives had nice clothes, jewelry. Plush houses. I was the only one married to a tight-fisted asshole."

"If Greg wasn't flashing any money, what makes you think he had any?"

"Because no one works that much overtime and has nothing to show for it. He was never home, and when he did come home, he was always drunk. He said he was working, but I'm not stupid. He was with his pals, probably spending his share as fast as he made it."

I was getting frustrated. Her theories weren't going to get us anywhere, and it didn't sound like she had anything concrete to offer. I was about to suggest we leave, when she dropped a bomb.

"He probably spent it all on her."

"Her?"

"Teresa Perez. Those two." She twisted two fingers. "They're like this."

She'd finally hit on the connection that had bothered me from the start. Perez had covered Jackson's tracks on the charge of assaulting his wife. Perez had shown up to question me after he got shot. Perez sat with Jackson at the hospital. "What's the deal with those two? They having an affair? I thought she was gay." I added that last to let her know I knew the players so she couldn't just make stuff up.

"I don't know what she is, but she's got Greg wrapped around her little finger. She says jump and he jumps." She took a sip from her mug, which I was now sure wasn't coffee. "Why are you asking all these questions, anyway?"

I decided to let Ryan field this one and shot her a look to let her know it was time for her to use her lawyer superpowers.

"Lily, did you know Greg was shot? It happened last week. He's been in a coma ever since."

"Shit, really? I read something about a cop getting shot, but I didn't know it was him. I mean, how would I know, seeing as how we haven't talked except through lawyers in forever. I don't know how I would've known."

She was trying too hard to act like she had no idea Jackson was in a hospital bed, comatose from a gunshot wound. Could she have had something to do with the shooting?

I dismissed the idea as quickly as it came. Even if she wanted revenge for the abuse she'd gotten from Jackson, it was too much of a coincidence to believe she would've done it that night. And why have Nancy shot? The idea was silly, but I couldn't seem to let it go. I took a chance. "Lily, was Nancy Walters in on the scheme with Greg and his pals?"

"Who?" She glanced around the room as she asked the question, her eyes on everything except me.

"Nancy Walters. Young, fairly new vice detective."

"Walters…Walters…Walters…"

She drummed her fingers on the coffee table as she repeated the name, as if she were searching her memory for some sign of recognition, but I knew exactly what she was doing. She was stalling for a lie.

I urged her along. "Yeah, Walters. Nancy."

"Fairly new, you said? Probably why her name doesn't ring a bell. Is Greg expected to recover?"

I ignored the abrupt change in subject and flashed Ryan a look that said we'd probably gotten all we were going to get from Lily Reynolds. "I have no idea, but we'll keep you posted."

Back in the car, I waited until we drove out of the complex before I spoke to Ryan. "You thinking what I'm thinking?"

"That we should pay a visit to Nancy Walters?"

"Yep. And I just happen to have her address."

CHAPTER TWENTY

Three calls came in to my cell on the drive to Nancy Walter's place. I glanced at the phone each time, hoping it was someone other than Ronnie, but it was her every time.

"If you need to take that, let me know," Ryan said. "We can pull over and I can step out and give you some privacy."

"I don't think so. It's my client. Or my client's sister, anyway."

"You haven't told her you discussed the case with me?"

"Nope."

"I doubt she'd approve."

"She doesn't know it yet, but I'm not working on her dime anymore."

"I see."

Good thing she did, because I wasn't sure I understood my own motivation anymore. Part of me wanted to pack it in, go get Jess, and head out of town until whatever was going on blew over. But my gut said it wasn't going to blow over on its own. I don't think I'd ever been so twisted up about what to do. Ryan's voice cut into my internal debate.

"So how do you know Detective Chance?"

Mind reader with a loaded question. I gave her the easiest answer. "We graduated from the academy together."

"You were a cop?"

"Don't sound so surprised. Didn't you used to be a prosecutor?"

"I was. I was a good one too."

"The whole law and order thing's a little too black and white for me. I'm guessing you found that out for yourself."

"I guess you could say that. Anyway, Chance is good people. She was always an excellent witness—not overzealous. Fair and evenhanded."

"She's the best." Sorry little summary of how I felt, but it was all I could manage under the circumstances. If I started diving into how I really felt, I wasn't sure I could get the words out. And since we were pulling up in front of Nancy's house, I wouldn't have the chance.

"Someone lives in a nice neighborhood," Ryan remarked. "And she's got a whole crew installing Christmas lights. Didn't you say she got her shield not that long ago?"

I stared at the front of Nancy's house. Four guys worked between ladders, hanging lights along the roofline. As I watched them work, all the facts I'd overlooked came roaring back. The Corvette, the nice house, the fancy kitchen. Even after she'd been detective for a few years, Nancy wouldn't be able to afford all this stuff on her salary. I guessed there could be some other explanation, like family money or a lottery win, but my gut kicked in again to tell me Nancy was deep into whatever was going on with Jackson and his pals.

"She's involved in whatever's going on, but I don't know how. I think we need to go in there and bluff our way through. This time I'll take the lead."

Ryan stood to the side when we reached the porch, so when Nancy swung the door open, she thought she had me all to herself.

"Luca, what a nice surprise. Two house calls in one week. People are going to start to talk."

"Hey, Nance, I brought a friend along. Hope you don't mind." I pushed forward, and she backed into the entry to let me through. When she saw Ryan follow me in, her smile faded. I introduced them. "Ryan Foster, lawyer. Nancy Walters, cop."

Nancy cocked her head, an odd smile on her lips as she tried to sort out what Ryan was doing in her house. I helped her along. "I think you're going to need a lawyer. Ryan can't represent you, seeing as how she's suing the police department, but I bet her partner can. Do you have anything to drink?"

The non sequitur threw her off balance, and I took full advantage. "Ryan, you should see Nancy's kitchen." I started walking that direction and motioned for Ryan to join me. "I bet she has five or six different kinds of glassware for you to choose from. She definitely has room for it in all these fancy cabinets." I made a big show of pointing out the features in the kitchen and Ryan made the appropriate I'm impressed noises. Nancy, meanwhile, looked back and forth between us like we'd lost our minds.

"Luca, I think you need to tell me what you're doing here. For real."

"Happy to, but first I have a question." I paused to let her squirm for a bit longer. She was already jacked up, but I wanted her completely off guard for what I was about to ask. While she stood there waiting, I looked around the room, taking in way more than I had before she'd become suspect in my eyes. I'm no decorator, but I know high-end when I see it. From the wide-planked wood floors to the granite countertops, to the double-sized appliances, it had taken some serious cash to buy all this. I watched her watching me. Her jangling foot and shifting eyes signaled she had some hint of what I was thinking, but I waited for her to ask.

"What, Luca? What do you want?"

"I want to know who arranged the hit on Jackson."

The nervousness flooded out of her. She thought she had this one down pat. "How would I know? In case you don't remember, I got shot too."

"Barely."

"What do you think happened?"

"No, we're not playing that game. I'm the one asking the questions."

"I think you should leave."

"If I leave, I'm going to tell everyone I know that you gave up the shooters. Won't matter if you did or not. Good thing you have such a nice house, because you're not going to want to leave it."

Nancy shot a look at Ryan like she thought maybe she would bail her out. Ryan shrugged and said, "She means what she says."

Defeated, Nancy said, "Can we sit down?"

We followed her into the living room and Nancy slumped into a chair while Ryan and I took a seat on the couch across from her. We all sat there for a minute. Nancy had apparently decided that if we sat here long enough, I'd forget my original question. No such luck.

"Start talking."

"I don't know who arranged the hit."

I started to stand, but she waved me back into place. "Please, Luca, I'll tell you what I know, but I don't know that."

I settled back into my seat. "Let's hear it."

She crossed and uncrossed her legs, flicked at an invisible speck of lint on the chair, and then, having exhausted all her delay tactics, said, "It's complicated. I took you to see Jackson because Teresa Perez asked me to. Other than that, I don't know what happened."

"How did Perez know I wanted to talk to Jackson in the first place?"

"I might have mentioned it to her in passing."

"And she said 'hey, let me make the arrangements because I love Luca Bennett and want to do whatever I can to accommodate her.' Yeah, right. Try again."

"Seriously, Luca, she and Jackson are tight. I told you that. I don't have a clue who else knew about the meeting. Maybe Jackson told someone else. If he ever wakes up, we can ask him."

I took a stab in a different direction. "How much does a place like this cost?"

"What does that have to do with anything?"

I leaned forward. "Here's what I think. I think you don't make enough money as a cop to live like this. I think you have another source of income, and I think that's what got you shot."

That got her riled and she couldn't wait to fire back. "I think Ronnie Moreno has you wrapped around her little finger. And look, now you're here with another lawyer who has it in for cops." She turned to Ryan. "Yes, Foster, I know who you are. And you, Luca, I think your client comes from a long line of lawbreakers and he thought having a badge gave him a license to carry on the family tradition without consequence."

I started to reply, but Ryan spoke first. "Detective Walters, you and I both know reputation isn't everything. If you ask some people, all you'll ever hear about me is I was a ball-busting prosecutor who never came across a defendant that wasn't guilty, even if a jury said otherwise.

"The truth is nothing's ever that easy, that black and white. I think you know that very well and that you've been living in the gray for a while now, but here's what I know beyond a shadow of doubt: the truth, whatever it is, will always come out. If you tell us, maybe we can help you, but rest assured, we're not going to quit looking. If we find it elsewhere, heaven help you."

Nancy was instantly out of her chair, pointing her finger in Ryan's face. "Nice speech. Save it for your loser clients. You think they're any less guilty because they had fake drugs? You think they got ripped off? Oh yeah, they're real sad victims of the terrible justice system. They'll never see a dime from the city and neither will you."

I caught Ryan's eye and pointed to the door. Time to go. Nancy was responding like a caged animal. Time to let her out of the cage and watch to see what happened next.

I dropped Ryan at her office and we agreed to meet there again in the morning. We were close to a break, but we agreed we needed to know more about the connection between Perez and Jackson. Hard to do when we couldn't get any cops to talk to us. Ryan said she'd kick around some ideas with her wife and maybe a good night's sleep would bring clarity.

Sleep wasn't on my agenda. I wanted to check on Jess, but I needed to figure out how I was going to do that without driving the Bronco by her house every hour on the hour. I went through a Sonic drive-through and ordered four hotdogs and a Route 44 Coke and then headed home to the man in my life.

Cash was glad to see me, but I had a feeling his affection was mostly for the hotdogs. We settled onto the couch and shared the take. After we ate, I checked my phone. Ronnie had finally stopped at four voice messages, each escalating in impatience. The last one said something disparaging about my upbringing, which was true, but not for her to say. I sent her a simple text. *Working on leads. Will call you when I know more. Out of touch for now.* A text message wasn't the way to let her know that I wasn't working for her anymore, and I planned to do whatever I wanted and not report to her. I'd get around to that part later. Or never. I turned off the ringer so I could ignore her reply and leaned back on the couch intending to give my current predicament careful thought.

The knock at the door sounded like gunshots, and I sprang off the couch, nearly knocking Cash in the head in the process. The noise and the near miss started him barking his damn head off, which only added to my just woken up state of confusion. I stumbled to the kitchen counter where I'd left my gun and I grabbed it and whirled around the apartment. The knocking started again, and I realized it was someone at the door and I'd slept the rest of the afternoon away.

"Luca, I know you're in there. Open up."

No amount of confusion could cloud the memory of her voice, but I hadn't expected her to show up here now or ever again. I swung the door wide. Jess was never more beautiful than when she was angry.

"Put that damn gun away. I'm coming in." She pushed past me and shut the door. Cash ran to her and started weaving between her legs as she made her way to the couch. I vowed that when she left, he was going with her. See how many hotdogs he got then.

"What are you doing here?" I kept my voice gruff to hide my happiness. She shouldn't be here. She couldn't be here.

"Getting some answers." She pointed to the space beside her on the couch. "Sit down." She waited until I was settled before delivering her lecture. "You think you can show up on my doorstep and pick a fight and say we're done? You don't get to decide that. Not for both of us. You can be as scared as you want, but you're not running away from me. You get that?"

I pulled her into my arms and kissed her. Rough at first, angry at the risk she was taking, but then gently when I realized she didn't know. "I did it for your own good."

"I know. John called. Besides, you'd make a lousy actress."

"Then why did you wait a whole day to come around? You coulda called me, sent a text?"

"Right. After your dramatic sendoff, I was going to send you a text and everything would be all right? Besides, it took me a little while to come up with a cover."

While I sorted through her words, I noticed she was wearing a baseball cap and shades. I'd seen Jess wear a ball cap plenty of times, but only while actually playing ball. She always complained they were uncomfortable, and she always took off her hat the minute she left the field. And the shades? It was dark outside. "What's up with the disguise?"

"Just a precaution. I'm hoping that anyone who's been watching will think I'm well on my way to Ohio."

I shook my head. "Help me out here. What's going on?"

She explained the scheme she'd concocted with John. She'd notified her captain she needed a few days off for an illness in the family, purchased a ticket for Ohio where a few distant cousins lived, and had John drive her to the airport. Once he dropped her off, she'd gone through the motions of going through security, but then snuck out of the airport and caught a cab to Maggie's where she'd hidden out until it was dark to make an appearance.

"I've been thinking," she said. "Perez has to be wrapped up in all this. I think if we figure out why she and Jackson are so tight, we'll get some answers. I have some ideas we can look into."

I liked what I heard, and we'd worked well as a team before, but I was still cautious. "What's with the 'we'? I thought you were staying on your side of the thin blue line?"

"When it was a safe place to be. Now I don't know who I can trust besides John. And you. Luca, I trust you."

We both knew the words extended beyond this case, this moment. She was telling me she'd take my side even when it might cost her everything she knew, everything she believed in. What she offered came without conditions. She was all in, no matter what.

She should've questioned my loyalty first. Quizzed me about what I had to offer in return. Tested whether I was trustworthy. But she didn't, and because she didn't, I knew with complete certainty exactly what I felt. Exactly what I wanted to say back to her.

"I love you, Jessica Chance."

Chapter Twenty-one

When I woke up the next morning, Jess lay on her stomach beside me. She'd pushed the sheet down or it had slipped, leaving her body bare except for her legs tangled in the sheets. The sun streamed in, and shadowed lines from the window shade crisscrossed her naked back. I didn't recall ever taking the time to watch her like this, completely relaxed. Completely mine.

I'd lost count of how many times we'd made love the night before, but each time had been different. Deeper, closer. As tired as I was, watching her now, I felt even more aroused, and I wondered if we could get closer still.

Cash started to rouse from his pallet on the floor. He raised his head slightly, but then shut his eyes as if to say, do what you need to do, I'll wait.

I started with light, soft kisses along her side. I kept my hands to myself and trailed my tongue from the side of her breast down to the small of her back. She opened her mouth and groaned in response to each touch. I groaned back. Not loud enough to wake her up, but the intensity left me wet and writhing for more.

I slipped my right hand between her legs, and she drew them apart, welcoming, wanting. She was awake now. I could tell by the way she rocked in place, hungry for my touch. With her back to me, I could fuck her any way I chose, enjoying nothing more than the way her body felt as it reacted to mine.

Once upon a time, that would have been perfect, preferable even, but not anymore. I wanted to see her eyes when she climaxed.

I wanted to know she was thinking of me. I wanted her to know every touch from my hands, from my mouth, was meant just for her. I moved my hand away and gently rolled her over.

"Good morning," she mumbled. Her barely open eyes were dark and sultry.

"Good morning."

"Don't stop. Okay?"

"I don't plan on it." I propped her up on pillows and then slid between her legs. I massaged her breasts while I drew soft, slow circles around her clit with my tongue. She bucked in place, but our eyes were locked and the message passing between us was clear. We belonged together.

I took Cash down the block while Jess showered. After a night full of the best kind of exercise, I didn't need my morning run. Cash would have to do with a day off.

The corner store didn't have the fancy coffee Jess liked. I bought a pint of half-and-half to make up for the lack of foamy topping Jess was used to, and added half a dozen donuts for good measure. There were four of them left when we got back to the apartment.

She was still in the bathroom, naked and wet from the shower. Going to Ryan's office suddenly seemed like torture. I handed her the coffee and left the room to keep from forgetting the more pressing business. From the bedroom, I called out the morning plans. "We need to leave in fifteen minutes. Cash and I'll head to the car first and make sure no one's around. I'll text you and then we'll pick you up on the other side of the complex. If I think anyone's watching, we'll drive on by and make another plan."

"You plan on telling me where we're going?"

She walked into the room, wearing only a towel, and I struggled to stay on track. "We're meeting with Ryan Foster." I watched to see if she was going to back out, but all I got was a nod. She'd said she trusted me, and she must've meant it. Now I felt bad for not trusting her. Again.

An hour later, we met Ryan in the reception area of her office. If Ryan was surprised I'd brought Jess along, she didn't show it.

"Nice to see you, Detective Chance."

"Call me Jess."

I watched the simple exchange, aware it was a huge step for both of them. Lots of trust going around.

Ryan led us back to the conference room and invited us to take a seat. "I'm not sure where to start. It seems like we have a lot of connections, but none of them really lead anywhere."

"I think Perez and Jackson are the key," I said. "I just don't know how we prove it."

Ryan nodded. "It would help if we had some idea about how they got so tight in the first place."

Jess reached into her pocket and pulled out a flash drive. "I think I can help with that. Before I left work yesterday, I pulled a report cross-referencing all the cases they ever worked together or that had witnesses in common." She set the drive on the conference table. "Everything's on here."

"Holy shit, Jess. When were you going to tell me about this?" I couldn't help my reaction, but the sly smile she gave me in return told me I should've kept my mouth shut unless I wanted Ryan to know I'd chosen sex over work the night before. "Uh, what I meant to say is wow, that's great."

Jess looked at Ryan. "What do you say, Counselor? Got a couple of extra computers around here so we can all chip in?"

A few minutes later, Tony appeared with a couple of laptops to go with the one already in the room. Jess copied the files from the drive onto the computers and the three of us started searching. After an hour of pecking away, I wanted to gouge my eyes out. I hated work like this, but Jess acted like we were on a treasure hunt. I glanced over at Ryan who seemed totally in her element. Whatever.

"Restless?" Jess asked with a knowing smile.

"A little. Maybe I should get us some lunch."

"It's ten a.m."

"If you're hungry, I can get Tony to order some food," Ryan offered.

"She's not really hungry. She's bored."

"I'm not bored. It's just I feel like I should actually be doing something."

Jess turned to Ryan. "Don't worry. She's not insulting us or the work we're doing. She doesn't think it's a full day's work unless she gets to use a gun or handcuffs."

I opened my mouth to respond, but my phone rang. Ronnie. For the thousandth time. Jess raised her eyebrows and I showed her the display.

"You should probably get that."

"No need."

"You're going to have to talk to her sometime."

"I guess."

"Now's as good a time as any. Answer the phone, Luca."

I stared hard at Jess, trying to penetrate any hidden meaning, any trick behind her words. Nothing. She was right. It was time to act like an adult, face the other woman, and tell her to buzz off. I answered the call. "Bennett."

"Where have you been? I've left a dozen messages. We can't work together if you won't communicate with me."

"About that." I fumbled for what to say. Jess was staring straight into her computer screen, but I knew she was listening. "We need to talk."

"You bet we do. Did you know Jackson's out of his coma? That he's on his way home right now?"

"What?"

"I called the hospital this morning. Pretended to be Detective Perez and the nurse was more than happy to tell me he'd been discharged. Apparently, his injury wasn't as severe as they first thought. She was a little confused, since she thought I, make that Perez, had been the one to take him home."

"You're insane. What were you thinking?"

Ryan and Jess were both staring at me now, neither pretending to continue looking up files in favor of eavesdropping on my conversation. I didn't blame them. I could hardly believe what

Ronnie was telling me, but I was already thinking of how to take advantage of the information. "When did you call the hospital?"

"About eight this morning."

"And you're sure they said he left with her?"

"The nurse said he was going home with me, I mean Perez. Luca, what are you going to do? What have you been doing? Jorge's been a mess ever since his wife got back from the hospital. They're staying at my mom's, which only makes me worried about her."

I tuned her out in favor of the train of thought chugging through my brain. "I have to look into something. I'll call you back when I know more."

So much for telling Ronnie to get lost. I hung up and turned to face Jess, while Ryan kept her gaze focused on the computer screen in front of her.

"Yes?" Jess asked.

"Jackson left the hospital with Perez this morning. He's out of his coma."

"That seems sudden."

"I guess. I'd just assumed he was done for. Anyway, I'm thinking I should go over there and see what I can find out."

Jess shook her head. "Are you crazy?"

I assumed it was a rhetorical question. "We're trying to find the connection, aren't we? Why not show up where I know they're both going to be and settle this once and for all?"

"Down, girl. You're not going to settle anything by going over there. Perez'll shoot you before she lets you through the door. Sit down and let's think this through."

"Maybe you should both sit down," Ryan said. "I think I've found something."

Jess and I crowded around Ryan's computer and watched while she brought up several reports on a split screen. "See here." She pointed. "This looks like the first time Perez and Jackson crossed paths in an investigation, back when they both worked in vice. And here, look at this one. The defendant in this case, Jose Calderon, is listed as a CI in this one." She pointed to another section of the screen. "And here he is again. And again."

"Okay, so what's that mean?"

"By itself, it means nothing, but I just happen to recognize the name. It's come up at least a dozen times on the police reports from when my clients were arrested. Supposedly, he's a fairly big-time dealer vice and the feds have been investigating. Word is he's the one who supplied the drugs that were the source of all these busts. Of course, all the drugs in the Dallas County cases turned out to be fake, so he may be a big bunch of nothing, but I think it's a little odd that someone who used to be a CI and did extensive work for Jackson and Perez is now a wanted man."

"Maybe it's just a case of once a criminal, always a criminal," Jess said as she reviewed the reports on Ryan's computer screen. "Looks like he was never arrested again after this first time, but he turned into Perez's go-to witness. She must've cut a deal with him." She rocked back in her chair, and I recognized her thinking look.

"When's the last time you show him listed as a CI on these reports?" Jess asked.

"Let me check." Ryan punched a few buttons on the keyboard and pages started whirring by. "Interesting. Looks like the last time Jackson used him as a CI was about a month before the first documented fake drug case. Of course, Perez was in homicide at the time, so she wasn't involved in that case, so I don't know what this means."

I didn't know what any of it meant, but I had an idea. "I think it's time I paid her a visit and got some answers." I was tired of trying to figure things out in the abstract. Perez was up to no good, and I was convinced I could persuade her to talk.

Jess stood up. "Actually, I think that's not a bad idea, but you're not going. I am."

"The hell you are."

"Ryan, can you give us a minute?"

Ryan shot me a look that said "you're in for it now" and left the room. I took the time to square up for a fight. "You're not going over there. It's insane. Besides, aren't you supposed to be in Ohio?"

"Maybe I can use that to our advantage. If Perez acts like I shouldn't be there because I'm supposed to be out of town, we'll know she's been the one watching us. But I don't think Perez was the one who sent you that note. It's not her style. If she has something to say, she just comes out and says it. Face it. She's way more likely to talk to me than you. I'll record whatever she has to say and get out as fast as I can. I know what I'm doing."

She did know what she was doing, but it didn't stop me from worrying. Hell, I'd been ready to throw away a chance at a future with her to keep her safe. Looking into her eyes now, I realized I could never keep her completely safe. She was a cop, a good one. She took risks and put herself in danger on a regular basis. It was who she was. If we were going to be together, I had to accept that she wasn't going to change and I had to love her for exactly who she was.

But I didn't have to like it.

CHAPTER TWENTY-TWO

I'm going to go get Ryan so we can fill her in," I said.
"Wait. Not yet."

"What's up?" I asked.

"She can't be part of recording someone without their permission."

"I know the law. You only need one person's permission to record a conversation, and that would be you in this situation."

"Sure, unless you're a lawyer, and then you can't record anyone without their knowledge. It's an attorney rule."

"Sucks to have high standards." I was serious, but Jess just grinned. "How're we going to do this?"

"I'll see if Ryan will let me borrow her car in case yours is being watched. As for the recording, give me your phone." She held out her hand and I handed over my iPhone, trying not to act too superior that at least in the technology department, I had her beat. Jess still had a department-issued Blackberry and an ancient flip phone for personal calls. Never mind I didn't use half the features available on the phone because I couldn't really figure the damn thing out.

Jess scrolled through the screens on my phone. "There's this app, it'll let me record the conversation, but show something else on the screen to keep anyone from seeing what I'm doing."

"Jess, I need to be able to hear what's going on. I know you don't think Perez was behind the shooting, but you don't know that. I don't trust her."

She ignored me and kept scrolling. "Here it is. This one will let me record and use other functions at the same time."

"English, please."

"I can keep the phone line open while I'm recording and hide what I'm doing with a fake screen. I'll take your phone and leave mine with you. You can listen in, but you've got to promise you're not going to go busting down Perez's door just because you think she's being an ass."

"Pretty much a given she's going to be an ass. How about you come up with a safe word? Something you wouldn't normally say. If I hear the word, all bets are off."

"Sure, great idea. How about rabbit?"

"Rabbit? How are you going to work that into conversation?"

"Easy. You know, like falling down a rabbit hole, or scared like a rabbit?" She put an arm around me and shoved a piece of paper into my hand. "Here's Perez's address. She lives in Oak Cliff, not far from here. I promise, I'll be fine, but if you hear me talking bunnies, rush in like the badass you are."

I knew she was teasing, but I'm not immune to flattery. I ducked to hide the blush I could feel creeping across my face. "Yeah, okay. I'll be there if you need me."

Now that we'd exhausted any reason for delay, I felt awkward. If I was such a badass, why was I staying behind while the woman I loved took care of business? We'd agreed I shouldn't follow her in case my tail had figured out where I was. If something did go wrong, I wouldn't be close enough to do a damn thing about it. Jess's voice interrupted my thoughts.

"I can handle this."

"I know." Knowing didn't make me feel any better.

"I'll be back soon."

"You better be."

"Count on it."

Jess opened the door of the conference room. She had her back to me. Coming or going, she was beautiful, but I couldn't let her go like we'd just had one of our usual casual encounters. "Jess?"

She stopped and turned. A flash of a smile in her eyes, like she knew I'd have one more thing to say. "Yes?"

"I love you."

"I know. I've known longer than you have. Now, take some time and get used to it, Bennett, because I'm not going anywhere."

Seconds later, she was gone and I started worrying.

"Everything okay in here?" Ryan entered the room with another woman. "Mind if we wait with you? Luca, this is Brett Logan, my wife."

"Nice to meet you. I hear we're about to be part of a clandestine operation," Brett said.

"Actually, I think I'm supposed to keep you two out of it. Something about lawyers being held to a higher standard."

Brett sat down and Ryan took the seat next to her, saying, "Let me guess. She's going to meet with Perez and record their conversation."

I'm sure my expression confirmed she was right and she had more to say on the subject. "We've talked it over and decided to deal with any fallout when it comes, if it comes. Technically, we're not doing the recording, and we think it's important to be here with you while Detective Chance is off taking a risk."

"You should probably start calling her Jess. That's what her friends call her. Detective is kinda like ma'am."

We chatted about inane stuff for a few minutes until Jess's phone, which was sitting in the middle of conference room table, buzzed wildly. I lunged for it and flipped it open. "Jess?"

"Hey, Luca. I'm about a mile away. I'm going to get set up to record in a minute. Go ahead and put the phone on mute so they can't hear anything you might inadvertently say."

"I'm going to put you on speaker. Ryan and Brett are listening in. They feel like living on the edge."

"Good. I'm glad you have people with you. Oh, and I guess I should tell you I love you now, so they can wonder why you're blushing."

I squelched a grin. "Putting you on speaker now."

I put the phone on speaker, hit the mute button, and set it in the middle of the table. Brett reached over and put her hand on my arm and squeezed. Normally, I would've been put off by the invasion of my personal space by someone I didn't know, but the touch felt kind of, I don't know, nice.

Jess's voice came through the phone. "I'm pulling onto her street. Next sound you hear should be me getting Perez to talk."

We sat silently through the slam of the car door and her footsteps striking the pavement. Her stride sounded strong and sure. Good for her—I was coming out of my skin. I held my breath when she stopped walking. I imagined her pressing the doorbell, taking a deep breath, preparing for Perez's surprise when she found her standing there.

"What are you doing here?"

"Hey, Teresa. I came to check on Jackson." Jess's voice sounded calm and friendly.

"He's fine. I'll tell him you came by." A creaking sound, like Perez was closing the door.

Jess. "Actually, I'd like to talk to you if you have some time."

"I'm pretty busy. Another time." More creaking, followed by a loud smack. Jess's hand against the door?

"It's urgent." Steps and then the thud of the door closing. "We need to talk about Jose Calderon."

"You need to leave," Perez said.

"Come on. I did what you said."

"What's that?"

"Bennett. I figured out she's bad news. You were right about her. You've always been right."

I winced at the words. Jess was acting a part and she had to say that stuff, but it stung just the same. I steeled myself for whatever else she had to say.

Jess kept talking, faster now. "Problem is she's on to you. However much of a fuckup she might be, she's not stupid, and if you're not careful, you're going to get caught."

"Is that right? I think you're blowing smoke." Perez.

"I think you're in way too deep with one of your own CIs and you're covering for him. Maybe even working with him. What's Calderon got on you that would make you cross sides? Did he figure out you and Jackson were an item while Jackson was still married? Did he threaten to tell Jackson's wife? Or maybe better, he threatened to tell the department that Jackson's a wife beater?"

Jess was fishing, but maybe one of her crazy theories would get Perez talking.

"You don't know what you're talking about."

"Did you bring Jackson here to keep him from talking to anyone else, or is he in this with you?"

"Seriously, Chance, you don't know what you're talking about. You need to leave."

"What I can't figure out is why you decided to point the finger at Jorge Moreno. You know his family, especially his sister. Did you really think she wouldn't turn over every possibility to find out who framed him?"

"Who says he was framed?"

"I'm not stupid. He's the newbie. It was easy for Jackson and others to set him up."

"You think the fresh-faced boy is so innocent? Guess that shows what a lousy cop you are. I thought I trained you better, Chance."

Jess wouldn't be baited. She kept punching. "Come on, Teresa, what are you getting out of this? Is Jackson so good in bed that you'd risk a distinguished career just to stand by your man?"

Silence. Then Jess again. "Did I strike a nerve?"

"You act so high and mighty. You have no clue what I've had to go through."

"Next you're going to tell me he beats you like he beat his wife."

"Have you met that woman? If you had to spend any time with her, you'd beat her too. She's a conniving bitch who threatened Greg when she didn't get what she thought she was owed."

"What she was owed? What's that supposed to mean?"

Teresa stuttered for a moment and then finally said, "Nothing."

"Come on. You can tell me. If he's threatening you I can help you." Jess lowered her voice to a whisper. "If it's just a good business deal, maybe you can help me."

We waited through the beats of silence, and I thought we'd been disconnected until I heard one of them clear her throat. Had Jess wedged into what sounded like a crack in Perez's resolve?

No such luck. Perez growled her next words. "Leave now or I'll call the cops. You know, the real cops, the ones that stick together."

We heard the sound of a door slamming shut, footsteps, and then a car engine starting. Finally, Jess spoke again, this time directly to us.

"Sorry, guys, I guess that was a bust."

"Not so sure about that," I said. "You got her riled and probably set something in motion. All we have to do now is keep a close eye on them and watch for their next move."

"I guess I'd hoped for something a little more immediate."

I took the phone off speaker. "Come back and we'll figure out something." I wanted her here, by my side.

"Deal. I'm going to make one quick stop to pick up a few things since I guess I'm going to be staying with you until things blow over."

Anxiety rose in my throat, but I managed to choke out, "Wait a minute. You're not going by your house. What if someone's watching it?"

"Chill. I'm going to run by the store. Get a toothbrush and a couple of other things. I'll be there in thirty minutes, tops."

"Hurry. I miss you." Wasn't until I hung up the phone, I realized Ryan and Brett were still in the room. Of course they were. It was their office, after all. "When Jess gets here, we'll head back to my place and give you guys your space."

"Tell you what," Brett said. "I'll have Tony order lunch. We can brainstorm together when she gets here. I'd like to meet Jess, if that's okay with you."

"Sounds great." I kinda meant it, although for once, food wasn't one of the top things on my mind. All I wanted was for Jess to be back here, by my side, and for this case to be solved so we could move on to the next step in our lives—whatever that was and however scary it might be.

❖

An hour and a half later, scary thoughts about love and relationships took a backseat to another kind of fear. Lunch had come and gone with no sign of Jess. By the time the hour stretched into two, I'd called my phone twenty times, but every call went straight to voice mail and every text went unanswered. I called John, but he hadn't heard from her. Ryan and Brett kept telling me she'd probably gotten caught in traffic. Maybe the store was understaffed or out of stock. I nodded at each of their suggestions, but all I really heard was *thirty minutes, tops*. The words echoed in my head, taunting me. Probabilities and possibilities aside, I knew Jess kept her word. She was reliable. She was considerate. She wouldn't keep us waiting. Not on purpose and not without letting us know.

I was just about to head out to find her on my own when the phone in the middle of the conference table, Jess's phone, rang. Relief flooded through me and I lunged for it. "Jess, where the hell have you been?"

"She's right here with me. Would you like to talk to her?" A male voice. Not John. Not anyone I knew.

"Who is this?"

"Not important."

"Let me talk to her." I tried to match his calm, easy tone, but my voice shook. I couldn't help it. Ryan and Brett moved close to me and I held the phone in a death grip. My only connection to Jess.

I heard a scuffle and then another voice. This time it was Jess. "Luca?"

"It's me. Are you okay?"

"I'm good. Luca, I told them you have the recording." She emphasized each word as if she was talking to a two-year-old. "The recording of Perez and Jackson telling us everything. I'm sorry. I *had* to tell them."

All I could process was that she was alive, but in danger. *Them*. The guy who'd called wasn't alone. Remain calm. Don't let her hear your fear. "It's okay. Everything's going to be okay. I promise. Trust me, okay?"

The male voice was back on the line. "She may trust you, but I don't. I want that recording or you'll never see her again. You understand?"

"Yes." I agreed just to keep the peace, but I was confused. I didn't have a recording, Jess did. She must've told them she didn't have it on her, and they must not have figured out it was on the iPhone. I glanced at the caller ID. This guy hadn't called from my iPhone. Maybe she'd managed to hide it from them, but now wasn't the time to ask questions. Something about the way Jess had been talking told me to go along.

"I'll text you the instructions. I'd say don't call the cops, but I think you know better by now than to trust cops." He laughed. "Follow my instructions to the letter. I'll be in touch."

The call ended and with it, my connection to Jess. I sat down and put my head in my hands, gripping the phone with both hands. Stupid. Stupid. I'd been so stupid. It hadn't occurred to me that whoever had been watching me would also be watching Perez and Jackson. Hell, I'd thought they were the bad guys. They probably were, but whoever had Jess was way worse, and I wouldn't rest until I found him.

CHAPTER TWENTY-THREE

S omeone's got Jess. I gotta go." I shouted the words as I ran to the door of the conference room, Cash at my side. Before I could cross the threshold, a strong hand grabbed my arm. Ryan.

"Luca, wait."

"Can't. She's in trouble."

Her eyes were calm. Mine couldn't stay focused. I had to get out of here, find Jess, get her back. I repeated my words, but this time I sounded more desperate than determined. "She's in trouble."

"Let us help you."

I looked between Ryan and Brett. They meant well, I could see it in their eyes, but they couldn't do what I had to. Instinctively, I felt for the Colt against my side. "I'll call you later."

"What if we could figure out where she is? Right now."

Brett sounded so sure. "What do you mean?" I asked.

"Your phone. She has your phone. It has GPS. Do you know if you have Find My iPhone? It's an app that allows you to find your phone."

"I don't have a clue. The guy at the store set everything up for me." All the times I'd shrugged off learning about technology flooded back to haunt me. I didn't use the damn phone to its full capacity because I took pride in doing things the old-fashioned way. Pride wouldn't do me any good now.

"Give me your password and I'll check it out."

I supplied Brett with the information, and while she pounded the keyboard, I filled them in on the contents of the phone call. Just as I finished, a map filled her computer screen. She pointed at a green dot. "See that? That's your phone."

I thought hard. "There's a Walgreens at that intersection. Jess said she was going to stop and get some stuff. Toothbrush, stuff like that. You think she's there?"

"It's the best bet."

"Thanks." I scrawled Jess's phone number on a pad sitting on the table. "I've got to go, but call me at that number if the phone moves."

Ryan met me at the door. "I'm coming with you."

"No."

"Luca, you have no idea what you're walking into."

"Neither do you. But I do know this. I'll do whatever I have to do to get Jess back. Are you prepared to break the law to help two people you barely know?"

"I know what it means to love someone so much you'd risk everything, if that's what you're asking."

Ryan looked at Brett and I did too. Brett broke the standoff. "Go, both of you. I'll call if anything changes. Be careful."

We were at my car in seconds. Ryan held the door while Cash jumped in back. "You want me to drive?" she asked.

"No, thanks. I'm good." I was glad for the company, but letting her come along had probably been a stupid idea. In any case, I would be the one in control. I had to be. Too much was at stake.

On the way, I talked to keep from freaking out. "I don't get it. Jess made a point of saying that she had the recording of Perez and Jackson telling her 'everything.' But they didn't. She only talked to Perez, and she didn't tell her shit."

"Maybe she was just trying to get the guys she was with to believe she had more evidence than she did."

"And they would only care if they thought Perez and Jackson had ratted them out. If we don't find Jess, Perez's place is my next stop."

"Not without me."

I started to argue, but her face was set in stone. Fine. She could watch Cash while I went inside and did whatever was necessary to get Perez to talk. Besides, I might need a lawyer. Hopefully, all this planning would be completely unnecessary. We'd show up at Walgreens and find Jess buying a toothbrush. Nice thought, but then I remembered the voice on the phone.

The drugstore wasn't far, a fact that stung as I realized how close Jess had been when she'd run into trouble. When we got there, it only took a minute to find Ryan's car, parked a couple of rows from the front of the building. We parked a few spaces down. I told Cash to wait for us and ignored his protests as we shut the doors and left him behind.

"Let's try inside first."

Ryan followed me in and we split up, meeting back at the front after we'd walked every aisle. I stated the obvious. "This isn't good."

"Don't give up yet. There's still the car."

Store wasn't that big. No way Jess could've been in the store and made it back out to the car without us seeing her, but I held onto a shred of hope. When we reached the parking lot, I signaled Ryan to stay back as I crept closer to the big SUV, then circled the entire vehicle to verify no one was inside. I tried the door. It was locked.

"I have an extra key." Ryan clicked her remote and I opened the driver's door and peered inside. Nothing. I walked around to the rear and opened the back hatch and held my breath.

Nothing.

Part relieved and part frustrated, I shut the rear door and stated the obvious. "She's not here."

"Is the phone in the car?" Ryan asked.

Duh. I hadn't even looked. I ran back to the driver's side door, crawled in, and started combing through the interior. Ryan took the back. A few minutes later, we met at the rear bumper.

"Nothing, you?" I asked.

"Me neither."

"It has to be here somewhere, right?"

"Unless she's not here anymore. I'll call Brett and see if the phone is still showing up here."

"I'll go back inside and ask around. Maybe one of the employees saw her."

Like magic, a wiry kid with a Walgreens nametag, wandered up. "You gals need help?"

I looked back at Ryan's SUV. All the doors were still open. We did look kind of lost. I decided to pretend like I hadn't heard the "gals" part, but I wanted him to take off so we could finish brainstorming. I started to say that we were fine, but Ryan said, "Any chance you found an iPhone in the store or out here in the parking lot?"

He crossed his arms and rocked back on his heels. "Maybe. It's possible."

I stood up. His cagey response didn't fool me. He had the phone and I'd strangle him if I had to. "Where is it?"

"If there is one, you'll have to present ID and a full description."

Again, I struggled with the desire to choke him. The desire to see Jess alive won out. "Fine, but if you don't take me to it right now, your own ID won't be good for anything other than identifying your body. Understood?"

❖

"Let's go back to the office and figure out what to do from there," Ryan said. "I'll drive. I can get someone to get my car later."

I was torn. We had the phone and the recording. The entire conversation between Jess and Perez was exactly as I remembered, random implications, but nothing overtly incriminating. I wanted to go charging into Perez's house and choke her until she told me everything she knew. I was convinced she'd warned Calderon that Jess was on his tail. She'd gotten Jess kidnapped.

I might never see Jess again, and the very idea made me want to curl up in a ball and die. So my options boiled down to letting fear paralyze me, killing Perez, or thinking things through. I'd never tried that last one, but I was game.

"Okay." I handed Ryan the keys. Cash sat in my lap instead of the backseat. He didn't say anything, but he rested his head on my shoulder and hugged me the length of the trip. I hugged him back because I knew he missed her too.

Brett was waiting for us when we got back. Ryan started to tell her what happened, when my phone rang—the iPhone. I nearly had a stroke trying to get it out of my pocket, hoping desperately it was Jess.

Ronnie. She was the last person I wanted to talk to, but a nagging feeling propelled me to answer. I stepped away to take the call. "Bennett."

"Luca, are you okay? I've left you a million messages, but I haven't heard anything from you. What's happening with Jorge's case? Have you found out who threatened him?"

I started to tell her I couldn't care less about Jorge or the threats against him, but a memory surfaced. Something Perez had said to Jess. About Jorge. *Who said he was threatened? You think the fresh-faced boy is so innocent?* At the time, I'd figured Perez was saying those things because she'd been the one to turn Jorge in and she was just sticking by her story, but maybe there was more to it. "I need to see Jorge. Now." I put my hand over the phone and asked Ryan if I could use her conference room. She nodded. "Ronnie, here's the address. Tell him to get here now."

I hung up and paced the reception area. It would be dark outside soon, and somehow that seemed symbolic. Lights out for Jess. Lights out for both of us. I couldn't lose her. Not ever, but especially not now.

"Luca, why don't you go on in the conference room? When your guest arrives, I'll show him back." Brett's voice was soft, soothing. I bet Ryan couldn't deny her anything. I followed her back into the conference room. Ryan was sitting at the table, several open files in front of her. I sank into a chair.

"I'm sorry about all this," I said.

Ryan looked up. "All this?"

I waved an arm. "You know, descending on your office, demanding your help, and taking over your space."

"I figure we're all after the same thing here, right? I want to find out who set my clients up. You want to find out if your client did what he's accused of. We may not like the answers we get, but we're more likely to find them if we work together."

"You sure you worked for the DA's office? Maybe you didn't get the memo about convictions are more important than truth."

"Oh, I got it, and you may notice I don't work there anymore. Actually, most of the prosecutors there are more interested in justice than an easy conviction, but there is a bias in favor of cutting corners. I trust you're more interested in finding out what really happened, than covering for your client or I wouldn't be helping you."

I trust you. Ryan's words made me think of Jess. She trusted me too, and she'd been taken, was being held. All because she'd helped me. She trusted me, and I had to earn that trust by getting her back. I glanced at her phone as I'd done about a thousand times in the last hour. No text from whoever had Jess.

"Any word?" Ryan asked.

"Nothing. I thought we'd hear something by now."

Brett poked her head in the door. "There's a Jorge Moreno here to see you. And—" She didn't get a chance to finish before Ronnie barged through the door, Jorge tailing behind. Ronnie ran over to my side and swept me into a hug.

"Are you okay? I was worried when I hadn't heard from you. I left so many messages. After Jorge was threatened, I thought maybe…"

Her words trailed off. I was surprised. She did seem to be genuinely concerned about me. I caught Brett and Ryan looking between us, trying to figure out the connection, and I pushed Ronnie away. "Sit down. We need to talk. Jorge, you sit down too."

Ryan stood up. "We'll give you the room."

"No, stay. Please. Ryan Foster, Brett Logan, meet Ronnie and Jorge Moreno."

"Luca, I know who Ryan Foster is. I can't believe you asked us here." Ronnie's eyes flashed as her temper flared. I used to think that was sexy.

"Sit down, Ronnie. Jorge, you too." I waited until they obeyed. "Okay, here's the deal. Ryan and Brett are helping me." I pointed at Jorge. "If you've been telling me the truth, that means they've been helping you too. If you've been lying to me, then no one can help you. Only you know the answer, so you can leave, but if you do, you're on your own. Don't have your sister come to me begging to save you. But whatever decision you make, you will tell me everything you know about Jose Calderon because the woman I love is in danger, and if anything happens to her, I will hold you personally responsible. Do you understand?"

While I stared him down, his eyes shifted in Ronnie's direction. I couldn't help it. I looked too. She looked faded, a little lost. Had she been so misguided as to think she and I were a thing? Had I misled her?

Time to set the record straight. I spoke directly to Ronnie this time. "I love Jessica Chance and she's in trouble. If you care about me at all, you will help me find her."

She didn't say a word, but Jorge piped in. "I know who Calderon is. He's registered with the department as a CI, but I've never used him. I tried to make contact with him, but Jackson told me to steer clear."

"He give you a reason?"

"Told me to develop my own relationships. That Calderon required special handling and only worked with certain cops."

"And that wasn't a red flag?" I couldn't believe this guy had ever made detective.

"Not especially. Hell, Luca, I'm still trying to figure out how all this works. My partner who's been on the job way longer gives me advice, I follow it."

Jorge looked me straight in the eye. Not a twitch of body language. He was telling the truth. Damn. I'd hoped he would know more, be able to lead me to Calderon's door, talk his way in, get me to Jess. I gave it one last try. "So you have absolutely no idea how we can find him?"

"I don't, but I know who might. She joined vice not too long before I did. Nancy Walters. Didn't you say she's a friend of yours?"

CHAPTER TWENTY-FOUR

I didn't want to believe him, but my gut told me it was true. Whatever was going on, Nancy was in it up to her eyeballs. I leaned across the table until I was right in Jorge's face. To his credit, he didn't back up. "Tell me everything you know."

"Not much other than she was using Calderon on a regular basis when I joined the unit."

"I don't get it," Ryan said. "I've got a stack of police reports that list him as a dealer. If he's a registered CI, wouldn't the entire department know?"

Jorge hitched a shoulder. "I don't know what to tell you. I can't explain it."

I let him stew for a minute, but he didn't squirm. A beep broke the silence and the display on Jess's phone lit up. I read the text out loud. "Reverchon Park. Basketball court. Midnight. Alone." The clock on the wall read eight o'clock. I didn't know what I wished more—that we had more time to figure things out or that we could get this over with.

"Well, you may not be able to explain things, but I know who can. I think it's time we go back by Nancy's place and sort this out." I pointed at Jorge. "You're coming with me. You have your gun with you?"

Ronnie came out of her chair. "Wait a minute. You think she's dangerous?"

"Settle down. All I know about Walters is she's a conniving opportunist. I figure a little show of force will get her talking."

"I'm armed and I'm ready to find out who framed me," Jorge said. "Let's go."

He looked eager to get started. Good. He may not be the brightest, but having him show up on her doorstep might spook Nancy enough to get her talking. "Great. C'mon."

Ryan shot a look at Brett before saying, "I'm going with you. I don't have a gun, but I can talk a good game."

I paused. Alone was my preferred M.O. I was only bringing Jorge along for shock value. Adding Ryan made it a posse. I took a moment to get used to the idea. Jess would like that I had a posse, damn team player that she was. I nodded at Ryan, snapped my fingers at Cash, and headed for the door.

As I started to climb in the Bronco, I felt a tap on my shoulder. Ronnie. "What?"

"You're going to leave without saying good-bye? What if something happens to you?"

She sounded genuinely concerned and a little hurt. The concerned part was nice, but the hurt part I could do without. "I can take care of myself."

"I don't have a shot here, do I?"

"You should be a detective."

"Am I wrong, or did we have a good time together?"

"Past tense." I tapped my hand against the doorframe. I had better places to be.

"Can't blame a girl for trying. Will you at least watch out for my brother?"

Her eyes watered. Damn woman was about to cry. I softened my tone, just a little bit. "That I can promise you."

Nancy's house was blazing with Christmas lights. Ill-gotten gains sure did shine bright. Cash and I stood on the front doorsteps while Jorge and Ryan stood off to the side. Nancy answered the door with a smile, but when she saw me, she took a step back. I pushed through the door. "Expecting someone else?"

"You were supposed to be Chinese food." Her smile was starting to fade.

"Happy coincidence. I like Chinese food. So do my friends."

On cue, Jorge and Ryan followed me through the door. I pushed Nancy toward her plush living room. "Have a seat, Nance. We've got some talking to do."

She stood in place. "Get out, Luca. Take your mutt and your *friend*s with you."

"No can do, Walters. Your pals have Jess, and they're going to kill her if you don't help us stop them." I pulled out my Colt and Cash growled. Come to think of it, he hadn't liked her from the start—should've been a clue. "Start talking."

Nancy backed up and raised her hands. "Whoa, what's with the firepower? What happened to Chance?"

"Your little buddy, Calderon, snatched her this afternoon. I don't know how to get in touch with him, but I hear you're his regular sidekick. You're going to tell us how to find him or I'm going to play Russian roulette with this." I held up the gun. "Won't take long since it's fully loaded."

Nancy backed up, but she kept up a tough front. "Put the gun away, Luca. I'm sure your attorney friend here can tell you how long you'll go away for shooting a cop."

"Longer than you'll go away for being an accessory to kidnapping one? I don't think so." I pointed the gun at the couch. "Sit down and start talking."

Nancy looked between Jorge and Ryan, like they were going to help her find a way out, but all they gave her were stony faces. Without an ally in the room, she had no choice. She sat down.

"No one was supposed to get hurt."

"Too late," I said. "Tell me how I can find Calderon."

"He used to be a CI."

"And now?"

"Now he's just a drug dealer."

"Okay, tell me something I don't know."

She glanced at Jorge and then ducked her head. "I can tell you who his suppliers are."

"Quit stalling. I'm not interested in how Calderon does his business. I want to know where I can find him."

"Perez and Jackson are two of his suppliers."

She was feeding me the information in small bites, but I still had trouble digesting where she was headed. "Wait a minute. You're telling me Perez and Jackson are running a drug ring out of the police department?"

She nodded. "All those fake drugs? Pool chalk that vice cops turned into evidence after they confiscated the real drugs. Perez and Jackson managed the stock and gave it to Calderon. He sold it through his distributors and kicked back a cut to them. Since he was working with cops, he was untouchable. The guy could get away with murder." She had the decency to blush after she realized what she'd just said. "I'm sorry, Luca, I didn't mean—"

"Save it. Let me guess, you helped acquire Calderon's drug stock? You were one of his suppliers?"

"I didn't have a choice. Perez forced me into it. She said if I didn't—"

I held up a hand to stop her. "I bet I know the answer to this one too. If you didn't help you wouldn't get to drive a Corvette or live in such a nice house?" I shook my head in disgust. I had so many questions, but only one that had to be answered right now. "Just tell me where I can find him."

"I don't know. I swear. We always met at Reverchon Park."

I raised the Colt. She started talking again. Fast. "All the deals were arranged through Jackson. All I ever did was show up, make the arrest, and switch the drugs."

"Well, as luck would have it, we can ask Jackson." I motioned for her to stand up. "Let's go."

"What?"

"You didn't hear? He's out of his coma and staying at your pal Perez's place. You and I are going there now. She won't open the door to me, but she should welcome her little protégé with open arms."

❖

Unlike Nancy's holiday palace, Perez's modest brick house was dark except for one dim light, probably coming from a back bedroom. She must spend her money on something other than real estate and holiday decorations.

I drove my car past once and then parked on a side street about ten houses from Perez's place. Cash, Ryan, and Jorge all sat forward, keyed up and waiting to see what I had planned next. Nancy looked like she wanted to melt into her seat.

"What's the plan?" Jorge asked.

"You and I are taking Walters to see her pals. Ryan will wait here." I pulled out my phone and composed a text: *At Perez's house to get some answers. Chance kidnapped. If something happens to me, find her. Attorney Ryan Foster can fill you in. You owe me.*

I hit send and handed the phone to Ryan. "If someone calls, answer. If it's Calderon, buy me some time. If it's someone named Diamond, tell her everything." I slipped Jess's phone into my pocket and looked over at Cash, who was dancing in place on the console. He clearly didn't realize he wasn't coming with. Ryan followed my gaze and rubbed his neck.

"I'll take care of him. Until you get back."

I nodded, got out of the car, and I motioned for Nancy to lead the way. She started walking, and I pulled Jorge back. "Stay outside and keep an eye on things. I don't anticipate any trouble, but if any shows up, go back to the car and call the number I just texted on my phone."

His excitement faded, but I didn't care. Perez would be agitated enough at the sight of me with a gun trained on Nancy. She didn't need to see Jorge's mug too.

When we reached Perez's door, Jorge and I ducked out of sight while I whispered instructions to Nancy. "Ring the bell and get her to invite you in. If I get a hint that you're warning her, you're both dead. Nod your head if you understand."

She nodded and pushed the bell. It echoed three times before Perez cracked the door.

"Walters? What are you doing here?"

"We need to talk."

"Not now. Go away. I'll call you later."

Nancy took a step forward, her hand on the door. "It won't wait. Can I come inside? It'll only take a minute, but it's important."

"Later."

Perez's tone was firm. Time to intervene. Two big steps and I was standing directly behind Nancy. I shoved her through the door like a human shield, my gun trained over her shoulder.

"Hi, Perez. Long time no see."

"What the hell are you doing here? And what's with your little sidekick?" She spat the words.

"Looking for answers. You seem to know all the wrong people, and I'm looking for one of them. Tell me where I can find Jose Calderon and I'm out of here." I cocked my gun and held it up to Nancy's head. "You have five seconds. One, two—"

"You should leave now. You have no idea what you're doing." She sputtered a nervous laugh. "You think I care if you shoot Walters?"

I turned the gun on Perez. "Silly me, I should've known better. But you might care if I shoot you, right? Three, four—"

A deep voice cut into my countdown. "Put the gun down."

I instantly recognized the voice and it totally blindsided me.

"Calderon?"

"Well, aren't you smart."

His voice came from behind Perez. I scanned the shadows, but couldn't make out a shape. In my mind, Calderon was huge and hulking, and I braced for the showdown. "Where is she?"

He stepped out in the open. He wasn't huge or hulking, but he wasn't alone. He was flanked by two huge thugs with AK-47's. Like that wasn't bad enough, he had a knife in one hand and Jess in the other. He drew her up on her toes and pressed the blade against her neck. My mouth went dry and my knees buckled. Her eyes were tired and she had a goose egg on the right side of her head. As soon as she was safe, this guy was dead.

But right now, he was standing there, smug, talking like he was in charge. "As you can see, she's alive and well. I've kept my part of the bargain. Give me the tape."

I had to stall. "It's not midnight and we're not in the park. I didn't bring it with me."

"How unfortunate." He pressed the knife against Jess's throat. The drops of blood were like gas on fire. Blocking out the goons with the big guns, I took a step forward, but stopped when I saw him press harder and shout, "I wouldn't do that if I were you." When he was satisfied I wasn't coming closer, he said, in an eerily calm voice, "Put down your gun and let's talk about how to get me what I want."

"Don't do it, Luca."

Jess barely got the words out before Calderon slugged her in the jaw. I moved my gun back and forth, hell-bent on emptying every bullet I had into his brain, but I couldn't get a clear shot since he'd stepped back behind her. I could feel Walters and Perez inching closer, and Calderon's sidekicks raised their weapons. I never should've come in here by myself, but it hadn't even occurred to me that I'd run into Calderon, let alone Jess.

I looked around the room. My gun against two AK-47s. If I was the only one in danger, the choice would be easy, but no way would I take a shot with Jess's life in jeopardy. My only choice was to buy some time toward a way out. I took a deep breath and placed the Colt on the floor.

Calderon's smile was evil. He waved his knife at Nancy. "Search her. She has something I want."

"I told you we didn't tell her anything." Perez pointed at Jess. "She lied to you."

He barked at Perez. "Like you never lied to anyone. I'll make up my own mind about who I want to trust."

So the members of this little team weren't all on the same page. Jess had apparently told Calderon she'd gotten the goods on Perez and Jackson and driven a wedge between them. I could help that along. "You'll want the recording all right, but I'm telling you I don't have it on me. I didn't expect to run into you here."

"We'll see." He leaned back and watched while Nancy ran her hands up and down my body. She was enjoying herself way too much. I started to kick her in the crotch, but reconsidered. I still had a switchblade tucked in my boot. If I could distract her, maybe I could keep her from finding it. If I pushed her away, Calderon would probably have one of the big gun guys do the search, and they looked more interested in breaking my legs than feeling them up. I closed my eyes to keep from seeing Jess's reaction, and arched into Walter's hands. She took full advantage, and her search turned slow and thorough. It sucked beyond belief. Luckily, she wasn't big on ankles, and the knife survived the search. I glanced over at Jess, but this time her eyes were closed. I wanted to die.

"Nothing." Walters delivered the report to Calderon with a smug look.

He didn't take long to rob her of her pleasure. "You think you're in the clear? Why did you bring her here? You plan on taking me down?"

"No way!" Nancy yelled, pointing at me. "She had a gun on me. She has other people with her. They could come in here any minute."

"She's full of shit," I said. "Look outside. There's no one else. Let Chance go and I'll stay here. She can get the recording and come back."

"We didn't tell her anything."

I'd never seen Perez in pleading mode before, but I didn't have time to enjoy it. Calderon motioned to the door and told Perez, "Look out there. Tell me if you see anyone."

She opened the door and stepped outside. She was gone several very long minutes. "No one's out there," she reported when she returned.

"Take these two in the back," he said to Perez and Walters. "Tie them up while I figure out what to do."

This wasn't good. I didn't know what figuring out consisted of, but it didn't seem like it was going to go well for us. If we could keep him convinced we had incriminating evidence, we might stay alive, but if he decided we were lying, he'd probably kill us both. Either way, we didn't have a lot of time. Even if Diamond responded to my text, no way would she be able to get a team in place in time to ride to the rescue. We'd have to save ourselves.

Perez and Walters took us to what looked like a guest room. Twin bed, small chest of drawers, and a couple of chairs. After instructing us to sit in the chairs, Perez reached into one of the drawers and pulled out several lengths of rope. Who kept rope in their guest room?

Walters made a point of taking her time tying me up, and I kept up a steady stream of conversation to try to distract her.

"Hey, Nance, you think you're getting out of here alive? Sounds like Calderon thinks you're not to be trusted. And if you think Perez here is going to stick up for you, well, we know what a bitch she can be."

"Shut up, Luca," Perez said.

"Why? You have noisy neighbors? Scared one of them might call the cops? Oops, guess that's not really an option since you're all dirty."

Walters leered. "If all cops are dirty, what does that make your little girlfriend, Luca? But I guess you don't care about right and wrong as long as you're getting a piece of ass, right?"

I resisted the urge to look Jess's way. I didn't want to give Perez and Walters any more ammunition to use against us, but Jess's silence concerned me. Wasn't like her to go down without a fight. Had Calderon roughed her up worse than I could tell?

As if on cue, Calderon stuck his head in the door and spoke to Perez. "Finish up and get out here. The rest of my guys will be here soon."

When he disappeared from sight, I took advantage of the last chance I'd have to convince Perez she was on the wrong side of things. "Why are you letting that guy run the show? There's two of you, three if Jackson's up to it."

"Shows what you know," Nancy said. "Jackson's in no condition for anything and Calderon knows it. And who do you think those guys with Calderon are, his golf buddies? They're—"

"Shut up, Walters." Perez's eyes blazed anger. "You need to watch yourself."

I tried one last shot. "Sounds like you're both under the gun. Let us go. We'll help you."

She answered by slamming the door behind them as they left us alone. I listened as their footsteps faded away, and that was it.

Wherever they were talking to Calderon, they were far enough away we wouldn't be able to hear them.

"You realize that once we're out of here, you're never getting felt up by another woman the way Nancy was feeling you up. Right?"

I grinned at the sound of Jess's voice. "Nothing would make me happier. Are you okay? I was starting to get worried."

"I'm fine. Calderon's a pussy. Perez called him right after I left here and he nabbed me when I stopped at Walgreens on the way back to Ryan's office. How did you know I was here?"

"Long story, but it ends with I didn't have a clue you'd be here. Walters admitted she and Perez were involved with Calderon, so I dragged her over here to try to get Perez to talk."

"Oh, so I guess there's no cavalry waiting outside."

"Not in the traditional sense. I left Jorge Moreno outside, but if he follows my instructions, he's not going to charge in to the rescue. I do have a knife in my boot though."

Her turn to grin. "Look at you, saying the most romantic things." She wiggled her hands. "Maybe if you get close enough I can reach in and get it. I was staying quiet before to keep Perez's anger focused on you. She didn't notice I was holding my hands as far apart as possible. She'll never get a gig as a kidnapper. Now get your ass over here."

The carpeted floor made it hard to move, but cushioned the sound of my attempts. Seemed like forever before I finally managed to maneuver my chair so I was sitting behind Jess, my side to her back. "It's in a holster, right inside. See if you can reach it."

I watched while she stretched her hands as far down as she could reach. She tugged on my jeans, but couldn't quite get them over the top of my boot. "Hang on a sec." I looked around. "Maybe if I tilt back against the bed, I can get my leg closer to you."

I rocked the chair and swung back against the mattress, my leg now almost parallel to the ground. I whispered encouragement, while Jess struggled against the rope to reach into my boot. As her fingers fumbled around inside, I felt my chair start to slip. "Hurry, I'm—"

Gravity struck before I could finish my sentence. I managed to turn on my side before the chair hit the ground, but damn, that was painful. My eyes went to the door. I was sure my fall had been loud enough to send Calderon and his goons running in to check on us, but no sound of footsteps headed our way.

"Are you okay?"

"I'll live. Tell me you got it."

"Damn right I did." Jess's excited whisper sounded really loud. She started sawing away at her bonds, but I was still disturbed by the intense quiet.

"I don't hear a thing. Do you think they left?"

"All I know is I want to get the hell out of here." She kept jabbing.

"Be careful with that thing."

"Ouch." Blood trickled down her hand. "Now you tell me."

I watched her hack away at the rope for the next few minutes while I strained to hear something, anything. Maybe Calderon and company had left. If so, maybe Jorge would muster up some detecting skills and spring us. I considered sharing my rambling thought process with Jess, but I didn't want to distract her from her work and I didn't want to take the chance our talking would bring anyone back in here to discover us breaking loose.

A few grunts later, she jerked her hands loose and held the knife over her head in a silent cheer. Before I could offer congratulations, a loud bang echoed through the house.

"What the hell was that?" I had no chance of assessing the situation from my vantage point on the floor.

"Not a clue." She hefted my chair back up and cut the ropes around my hands. She kissed me hard, then handed me the knife. "Let's go see what's going on."

I stood up, a little wobbly from the strain of the ropes and the fall. Jess was almost to the door before I felt steady, but before she could open the door, it flew open toward her and she jumped back. Calderon stood in the doorway. He was alone, but with a gun fixed on Jess, he didn't need backup.

He barked at Jess. "C'mon, we're getting out of here."

"She's not going anywhere with you."

He turned toward me, like he'd only just noticed I was there. "I didn't ask you."

We stared each other down. More gunfire cracked through the silence, and I looked down at the knife in my hand, realizing his gun had me beat. He raised the gun and I knew he realized it too.

"Leave her alone and I'll go with you."

"Dammit, Jess. No." I wanted to say more, but I recognized the look in her eyes. She'd made up her mind and words wouldn't change it. I started moving toward her, but stopped when he shot just to the left of my moving feet. I stopped in place, feeling the heat rise from the punctured carpet. I raised my hands in surrender.

"Drop the knife."

I wanted to needle him. Ask him if he was such a bad marksman that he was worried about a knife beating his bullets, but it wasn't just my life at stake. I shook my head in defeat and set the knife down.

"Go over there." He pointed at the bed. "Lay down. You follow us, I'll kill her. You stay, she'll live."

Jess's face was blank, like it had been when Perez was tying her up. Was she checking out or was she plotting? I knew she thought she could handle him on her own. She'd been with him all day. But no way was I going to let him walk out of here with her. Not while I could still breathe. I hung my head, like I was whipped, while I counted the steps. Three to the bed, four to Calderon. I raised my head and faced Calderon square. "Okay, you leave me no choice."

The last word was barely out of my mouth before I took a step to the bed, bent down, grabbed the knife, pivoted, and lunged toward him. I heard Jess yell, "No," but I blocked it out, focused on Calderon's stomach. The whole thing was happening in slow motion. I saw him fire the gun, even heard the bang, but I kept moving forward, fire ripping through my side. I was about to go down, when I saw him turn the gun on Jess. I channeled every ounce of pain flooding through me and turned it into enough fuel to launch the final step and drive my knife deep into his gut. I heard another shot as we hit the floor, Jess first, me on top. We both lay still for a few seconds, while I prayed he'd missed or hit me again instead.

The next thing I heard was shouts of "clear" ringing through the house. I rolled over, groaning in pain, but with one arm still pinning Jess to the floor. Calderon was lying next to us, a big red river running out of his chest. Jess struggled against me and I released my hold. She sat up and immediately began pulling at my shirt.

I pushed her hands away. "I know you want me, but is this really the time?"

She leaned down and kissed me, soft this time. "Damn, you piss me off. You could've been killed. Lie down and let me take a look at you."

"Only because you asked me nicely." I leaned back and closed my eyes. The adrenaline was starting to wear off and I was starting to drift.

"You two lovebirds want me to give you some privacy?"

I knew that voice. My eyes shot open. Sure as shit, Diamond was standing in the doorway, a gun in one hand and zip cuffs in the other.

"Guess I won't be needing these," she said.

I started to say something like thanks for finally showing up, but Jess beat me to it.

"I hope you have an ambulance on the way," she said. "Because if Luca dies, you will too."

"Guess you don't have any qualms about threatening a federal agent."

Jess put her arm around my neck, cradling me in her lap. Her touch was gentle, but her tone was protective, fierce. "Not a one."

"Hey," I called out from my spot on the floor. "Bleeding here."

"On it." Jess kissed my forehead and then practically growled at Diamond. "Ambulance. Now."

CHAPTER TWENTY-FIVE

Even with my eyes shut, I could smell the layer of Lysol barely covering the stench of illness. I hate hospitals. The food sucks, you can't get any rest, and it's expensive. I'd recover better and cheaper at a luxury hotel for less money.

"She's waking up."

Maggie. In a hotel, I'd be able to lock my door and keep pesky friends at bay. No sense delaying the inevitable. I went ahead and opened my eyes, but shut them quickly, blinded by the glow of her neon green dress. She looked like a radioactive pear.

"Don't worry about sitting up for us. We've been waiting all night and we can wait a little longer."

She continued babbling, but all I heard was the "we" part. I opened my mouth to ask for Jess, but all that came out was a hoarse cough. I cleared my throat and tried again, but Maggie put a finger over my mouth and held up a cup.

"Don't try to talk. Try these ice chips."

I listened while she rustled around. If there was anyone else there, they weren't saying anything. Maggie placed one hand against the back of my neck and the cup against my lips. Who knew ice chips could be so amazing? I felt something cold against my arm and instinctively reached for what I thought was a stray piece of ice, but instead my fingers connected with fur. The fur barked.

"Cash," I croaked.

"He's been here the whole time. He went nuts when they rolled you into surgery. We hustled up one of those damn vests so the nosy nurses would lay off. Jessica snagged the vest from the Lab who plays with the kids in the children's wing. If anyone asks, Cash's name is Banjo."

"Got it. Banjo." In response to my touch, he snuggled his head against my right side. My left side throbbed and I remembered being shot. I fought the pain and struggled to sit up. "Jess, where's Jess?"

"She'll be right back. Didn't want to leave, but those men in suits insisted on talking to her. She was scared you'd wake up while she was gone. She made me promise to call her as soon as you woke up. Guess I forgot. I'll do that right now."

She stepped out of the room, thank God. I didn't have the energy to handle her. When she left, Cash tried to tell me what had happened, but as close as we'd become, all I got out of his yips and yelps was that it had been very exciting. When he exhausted his vocabulary, I drifted off with his chin resting on my arm.

"She's asleep."

I shot up at the sound of Jess's voice. "I'm awake."

She looked like she should be in bed. Her eyes were red and circled in black, and a big bandage tried to hide the cut on her throat. Made me want to kill Calderon again. Instead, I said, "You look fantastic."

"You're a liar." She settled onto the edge of the bed and took my hand in hers. Cash strayed only long enough to lick her hand and make sure it was really her.

I struggled to sit up again. Like Cash, I wanted to touch Jess, make sure she really was okay. She'd been with Calderon for hours before I'd stumbled across her and I'd been too caught up in getting us out of the mess at Perez's house to even ask what she'd been through. I ignored the shooting pain and managed to achieve something between flat on my back and slumped against the rock that served as the hospital pillow.

Jess watched my struggle, her eyes telling me she knew I had to do this on my own. She waited until I was done to talk.

"Bullet didn't hit anything major. It'll slow you down a bit, but you'll be out of here soon."

Maggie piped in. "You'll come to your father's house and we'll take good care of you."

My turn to talk with my eyes. I held back the "hell no" that rose to my lips and willed Jess to read my mind. She turned to Maggie and said, "Hey, Maggie, would you mind getting me something to drink? Coffee, Coke, something with caffeine."

"Sure, Jess. Whatever you need. I'll be right back." She was out the door in a flash.

"Like you're going to drink coffee from a machine at the hospital. Thanks for the save."

"She could use the break. She's been here since you came in."

"How long have I been here?"

"Two days. Your dad and Mark have been here the whole time too. And Mark's wife. Apparently, she's a surgeon. You're getting the royal treatment from this place."

"That would explain why I'm feeling no pain." I squeezed her hand. "And you? How are you?"

"I'm fine."

Her lips formed a tight line and her eyes were hard. I'd have to wait to hear more about what she'd gone through before I showed up at Perez's house, but I figured everything after that was fair game, so I changed the subject. "I don't remember much after Diamond showed up. Mind filling me in on what happened?"

"Happy to, but if you're up to it, there a few other folks who can help fill in the details. They're all waiting outside. You up for visitors?"

"If one of them has a cheeseburger, I'm all yours."

"You may be getting treated like royalty, but I think Jell-O is probably the best I can do. These nurses are guarding you like you're the crown jewel. Frankly, I'm a little scared of them."

I laughed. It felt good and it hurt at the same time. "Rain check on the cheeseburger. Bring in whoever and an extra helping of Jell-O."

She stood and I instinctively reached out. "Wait."

"Yes?"

"Come here." I motioned for her to bend down and waited until our heads were touching. "I was scared shitless."

"I know. Me too."

"I don't usually get scared. Pretty sure it was because I love you."

"I figured as much." She kissed me. Light, but sure, like we'd have forever to do it again. "We're both okay or we will be. I'll be right back."

She was only gone a few seconds, but I spent the whole time seeing a future I'd never even considered. When the door opened, Jess led a small army into the room. Ryan, Brett, Ronnie, and Diamond. I watched while they moved chairs into place and surrounded the bed. Diamond looked like she was bursting with news. Jess motioned to her to start talking.

"Hope you're enjoying yourself, being waited on and all, while the folks that saved your ass are still working hard to close this case." Diamond grinned as she delivered the words, and I knew she was enjoying her role as the one with all the answers.

"Whatever. If you did your job right, I wouldn't have gotten shot. And don't give me the line about how this is still an open investigation. Start spilling."

"Well, our unit's been investigating the DPD vice squad for a while now."

"Let me guess. Roberto Garcia was working undercover."

"I can neither confirm nor deny the identity of an undercover agent."

Didn't matter what Diamond said on the subject, the lack of denial was enough to confirm my initial suspicion that Garcia had been working with the feds. To further confirm my suspicion, Ryan chimed in.

"I can confirm it. I spoke with the U.S. Attorney this morning. He called to tell me they are considering joining in our suit due to new evidence that DPD's vice squad was engaged in practices designed to deprive individuals of their basic freedoms. A fancy way of saying, we knew all along what was going on and we don't want you to sue us for not helping you out."

"You knew about Calderon all along?" I asked Diamond and I didn't attempt to hide my anger.

"We knew about the cops, but we weren't entirely sure of the connection. We couldn't get close to the source. Calderon was Mexican Mafia, Cartel. He managed the operation, but didn't do the deals himself. Garcia had plenty of intel on the fake drugs, but he didn't have a direct link to how the operation worked after the drugs were traded out. He was trying to connect with one of the new officers in the unit to get them to work for us, but it didn't work out."

"Jorge?"

Diamond nodded. "Right after he made contact with Jorge, Jackson intervened. I guess Jackson and crew thought Jorge wasn't a safe bet to keep quiet about their enterprise. Seeing as how he came to your rescue, I guess they were right."

I looked over at Ronnie. "Is he okay?"

"He was shot, but he's going to be fine. Frankly, I don't think he's feeling any pain, he's so hopped up on adrenaline from being involved in taking down Calderon. All he really cares about is clearing his name."

"Damn. I told him to wait outside."

Diamond took up the story. "He waited outside for a while, but when you didn't come out or respond to any of his texts, he came in after you. Bad timing on his part. He got in the house just before we raided and he got caught in the crossfire."

"I'm sorry. He's a good guy. He'll get through this and he's going to come out of this whole thing okay. Agent Collier will make sure of it, won't you, Agent?"

Diamond nodded.

Ronnie stood, her eyes focused on me. "I should go check on Jorge. You want to send me a bill for the rest of your fee?"

Her tone was formal, and I knew this was probably the last time we would see each other. I chose my good-bye carefully. "We can call it even."

She nodded and her smile was forced. Part of me wanted to say something to make her feel better, but part of me just wanted her to go. She left before I had to choose.

Jess turned to me as the door closed. "We'll make sure Jorge comes out of this okay."

"What about the rest of them?" Now that I knew the background, I wanted to know more about what had happened after I'd blacked out.

"Two of Calderon's guys are in custody," Jess said. "Get this— one of them had teeth marks on his arm. I'm betting he was one of the guys who Cash bit a hunk out of after they gunned down Jackson and Walters at the Lucky Seven."

"Good boy." I rubbed his head and he licked my hand.

"Speaking of Jackson, he was still in bed when we arrested him," Diamond said. "We caught Walters trying to climb out a bathroom window."

"And Perez?"

Diamond looked around the room.

"What?"

"She's in the wind. I don't have a clue how she got past us, but she's gone. We found her car several miles away, parked in a church parking lot, but not a sign of her. She's not using her credit cards and the GPS on her phone led us right back to her house."

"I doubt you'll ever find her," Jess said. "If Calderon is Cartel, his people are going to either protect her or kill her to keep her from ever testifying against him. You can bet he was the one who arranged for the hit on Jackson and Walters in the first place. According to Nancy, Calderon was starting to have some trust issues with the whole team. She made a huge mistake when she set up the meeting between you and Jackson. She thought a quick meet would satisfy your curiosity, but it backfired. When Calderon caught wind of them talking to you, an outsider, he knew exactly how to send a warning."

I had no doubt she was right. "How did you get to Perez's house so fast?" I asked Diamond.

She pointed at Ryan. "Ryan called me pretty quickly after you left her in the car, but we'd been watching Perez's place for a while and we knew something was up. We had a search warrant and we were waiting for just the right time to execute it."

My turn to be pissed off. "If I find out you knew Calderon had Jess and you didn't do anything about it, I swear I'll—"

Jess pulled me close. "She didn't know. It's all good now." Her words were whispered comforts. I didn't make a move to pull out of her embrace, not caring that Ryan, Brett, and Diamond were all witnessing vulnerable me. Didn't matter. They could have all been pieces of furniture for all I knew, and as if they sensed their role had been reduced, they all slipped quietly from the room.

I wanted to ask more questions, but I guessed I could do it later. Right now, Jess was the only thing that mattered. Besides, I could make good on my threat to Diamond when I was feeling better. Which led me to my next question.

"When can I get out of here?"

"They want to keep you a few days."

"Okay." Seemed like forever until I thought of my messy apartment with the empty fridge. At least I wouldn't have to do laundry, make the bed, or scrounge for meals for a few days.

"Your dad and Mark would like to see you. Are you up for that?"

My side had started to hurt and I wasn't sure how long I could stay upright. What I really wanted to do was go back to sleep, but I knew they'd probably been waiting for a while. "Sure."

"I'll get them." She stood up and Cash wagged his tail like he was going to follow, but she told him to stay. "I'll be right back." She walked several feet to the door and then paused. "Oh, and you're not going with Maggie. You're coming home with me."

I felt better instantly.

CHAPTER TWENTY-SIX

Two weeks later

I couldn't remember the last time I'd had a Christmas tree. Probably before I learned to drive. But there it was, taking up most of Jess's living room, a seven-foot tall, pre-lit number looming large over a ton of just opened boxes, shreds of colorful wrapping paper, and a very sleepy Cash.

Mark and Linda, Dad and Maggie, and Jess and I drank one last toast of whiskey-spiked egg nog before they all put on their coats and drove off into the crisp, cool night. I followed Jess into the kitchen, each of us carrying a handful of empty glasses.

"I'll do the dishes since you did everything else." I put the glasses in the sink and picked up a dishtowel.

Jess took the towel out of my hand and tossed it onto the counter. "Not a chance. Leave all this. We have more presents to open." She grabbed me around the waist and pulled me toward her.

I stepped back and shook a finger at her. "But it's not Christmas yet. You have to wait until tomorrow."

"Not a chance." She looked at her watch. "Besides, it'll be Christmas in about thirty minutes. Are you seriously going to make me wait?"

"Who knew you were such a kid about the holidays?"

"There's a lot you don't know about me."

Her tone shifted from playful to serious. She was right. There were a ton of things I didn't know. I'd learned a few today, like that she hated cinnamon and that she had boxes of Christmas ornaments in her attic, including what had to be the gaudiest Santa tree topper ever, but I didn't have a clue what she'd done for every Christmas before this one.

But as far as I was concerned, we knew the important stuff, and I liked learning the rest piece by piece. I urged her back into playful mode. "I know enough. Do we get to pick which present we want to open?"

She grinned. "Sure, but only one tonight. The rest tomorrow. It's a rule."

I pulled her close and kissed her, savoring the spice and whiskey on her breath. She drug her hands through my hair, pulling me closer, but I needed a little space to open my present. I fumbled with the buttons on her shirt before finally giving in and yanking her shirttail from her pants. The sight of her skin got me going and I gasped. "Should we take this to the bedroom?" Now that we were all domesticated, fucking in back alleys and kitchens was a thing of the past. Right?

"You never used to be picky about where you took my clothes off."

"I'm not being picky. It's just…" I trailed off, not entirely sure what the deal was. Maybe it was because I'd officially moved in this morning and I still kinda felt like a visitor who didn't want to mess up the place. Before I could give it much thought, Jess pulled her shirt over her head and tossed it on the floor. When I saw her lacy black bra, thoughts ceased to form.

She watched me watching her. "You like your presents?"

I leaned down and ran my tongue along the lace, teasing, tasting. I circled her nipples with my thumbs and when they hardened under my touch, I was lost. To hell with the bedroom, we could have been on the front lawn for all I cared. I reached an arm around her and unfastened the bra and tugged it off, eager to lick, nip, and savor her beautiful breasts. She arched against my mouth and my knees buckled as heat surged through me.

This is why people do this in bed. Reluctantly breaking contact, I lowered her to the cool tile floor, balled up her shirt, and placed it under her head. "You good?"

"I'm great." She ran her hand down my side. "You?"

Even her lightest touch turned me on. "I'm feeling no pain. You're like the ultimate drug."

"Take all you want."

"That's the plan." I kissed her hard on the lips and then led a gentle trail with my tongue down her chest. My fingers worked their way into her pants while she unbuttoned my shirt. Chest bare, I slid along her stomach and nearly exploded at the sparks between us.

Jess writhed beneath me. "If you don't touch me soon, I might die."

I grinned. "Me too. It would be a pity to have saved you from being shot only to have you die on your kitchen floor." I slipped my hand into her pants and felt the matching lace of her panties. "More presents?" I ran a finger along the lacy edge and dipped lower. She was dripping and I couldn't wait.

Neither could she. Her hips arched and she groaned, "Luca, fuck now, tease later."

"Deal." I pulled away just long enough to take off her pants, then mine. I settled back between her legs and with my hands teasing her breasts I drank in her arousal, sure I'd never get my fill. I didn't get a chance to find out before she bucked against my lips and I gave her the fuck she'd asked for. Fingers pumping, I crawled up to face her and watched her eyes flutter while she rode me. I could've come just from watching, but when I felt her fingers enter me, I fought the urge for quick release. I wanted us to come together, share this moment. I reached down and caught a nipple between my teeth and she cried out, coming full force while calling my name. I didn't have words when I came too, only capable of uttering satisfied groans as we shook against each other, fully spent. When neither one of us could take anymore, I curled her in my arms and we spooned on the floor.

Jess sighed. "Now that was a present."

"I'll say. You think every Christmas is going to be like this?"

She turned to face me, her eyes lit with excitement. "Just wait until New Year's."

THE END

About the Author

Carsen Taite's goal as an author is to spin tales with plot lines as interesting as the cases she encountered in her career as a criminal defense lawyer. She is the author of nine previously released novels, *truelesbianlove.com*, *It Should be a Crime* (a Lambda Literary Award finalist), *Do Not Disturb*, *Nothing but the Truth*, *The Best Defense*, *Slingshot*, *Beyond Innocence*, *Battle Axe, and Rush*. She is currently working on her eleventh novel, *Courtship*, another romantic thriller. Learn more at www.carsentaite.com.

Books Available from Bold Strokes Books

Switchblade by Carsen Taite. Lines were meant to be crossed. Third in the Luca Bennett Bounty Hunter Series. (978-1-62639-058-4)

Nightingale by Andrea Bramhall. Culture, faith, and duty conspire to tear two young lovers apart, yet fate seems to have different plans for them both. (978-1-62639-059-1)

No Boundaries by Donna K. Ford. A chance meeting and a nightmare from the past threaten more than Andi Massey's solitude as she and Gwen Palmer struggle to understand the complexity of love without boundaries. (978-1-62639-060-7)

Sacred Fire by Tanai Walker. Tinsley Swann is cursed to change into a beast for seven days, every seven years. When she meets Leda, she comes face-to-face with her past. (978-1-62639-061-4)

Queerly Beloved: A Love Story Across Gender by Diane and Jacob Anderson-Minshall. How We Survived Four Weddings, One Gender Transition, and Twenty-Two Years of Marriage. (978-1-62639-062-1)

Frenemy of the People by Nora Olsen. Clarissa and Lexie have despised each other as long as they can remember, but when they both find themselves helping an unlikely contender for homecoming queen, they are catapulted into an unexpected romance. (978-1-62639-063-8)

Timeless by Rachel Spangler. When Stevie Geller returns to her hometown, will she do things differently the second time around or will she be in such a hurry to leave her past that she misses out on a better future? (978-1-62639-050-8)

Second to None by L.T. Marie. Can a physical therapist and a custom motorcycle designer conquer their pasts and build a future with one another? (978-1-62639-051-5)

Seneca Falls by Jesse Thoma. Together, two women discover love truly can conquer all evil. (978-1-62639-052-2)

A Kingdom Lost by Barbara Ann Wright. Without knowing each other's fate, Princess Katya and her consort Starbride seek to reclaim their kingdom from the magic-wielding madman who seized the throne and is murdering their people. (978-1-62639-053-9)

Uncommon Romance by Jove Belle. Sometimes sex is just sex, and sometimes it's the only way to say "I love you." (978-1-62639-057-7)

The Heat of Angels by Lisa Girolami. Fires burn in more than one place in Los Angeles. (978-1-62639-042-3)

Season of the Wolf by Robin Summers. Two women running from their pasts are thrust together by an unimaginable evil. Can they overcome the horrors that haunt them in time to save each other? (978-1-62639-043-0)

Desperate Measures by P. J. Trebelhorn. Homicide detective Kay Griffith and contractor Brenda Jansen meet amidst turmoil neither of them is aware of until murder suspect Tommy Rayne makes his move to exact revenge on Kay. (978-1-62639-044-7)

The Magic Hunt by L.L. Raand. With her Pack being hunted by human extremists and beset by enemies masquerading as friends, can Sylvan protect them and her mate, or will she succumb to the feral rage that threatens to turn her rogue, destroying them all? A Midnight Hunters novel. (978-1-62639-045-4)

Waiting for the Violins by Justine Saracen. After surviving Dunkirk, a scarred and embittered British nurse returns to Nazi-occupied Brussels to join the Resistance, and finds that nothing is fair in love and war. (978-1-62639-046-1)

Because of Her by KE Payne. When Tabby Morton is forced to move to London, she's convinced her life will never be the same again. But the beautiful and intriguing Eden Palmer is about to show her that this time, change is most definitely for the better. (978-1-62639-049-2)

Wingspan by Karis Walsh. Wildlife biologist Bailey Chase is content to live at the wild bird sanctuary she has created on Washington's Olympic Peninsula until she is lured beyond the safety of isolation by architect Kendall Pearson. (978-1-60282-983-1)

Tumbledown by Cari Hunter. After surviving their ordeal in the North Cascades, Alex and Sarah have new identities and a new home, but a chance occurrence threatens everything: their freedom and their lives. (978-1-62639-085-0)

Night Bound by Winter Pennington. Kass struggles to keep her head, her heart, and her relationships in order. She's still having a difficult time accepting being an Alpha female. But her wolf is certain of what she wants and she's intent on securing her power. (978-1-60282-984-8)

Slash and Burn by Valerie Bronwen. The murder of a roundly despised author at an LGBT writer's conference in New Orleans turns Winter Lovelace's relaxing weekend hobnobbing with her peers into a nightmare of suspense—especially when her ex turns up. (978-1-60282-986-2)

The Blush Factor by Gun Brooke. Ice-cold business tycoon Eleanor Ashcroft only cares about the three P's—Power, Profit, and

Prosperity—until young Addison Garr makes her doubt both that and the state of her frostbitten heart. (978-1-60282-985-5)

The Quickening: A Sisters of Spirits Novel by Yvonne Heidt. Ghosts, visions, and demons are all in a day's work for Tiffany. But when Kat asks for help on a serial killer case, life takes on another dimension altogether. (978-1-60282-975-6)

Windigo Thrall by Cate Culpepper. Six women trapped in a mountain cabin by a blizzard, stalked by an ancient cannibal demon bent on stealing their sanity—and their lives. (978-1-60282-950-3)

Smoke and Fire by Julie Cannon. Oil and water, passion and desire, a combustible combination. Can two women fight the fire that draws them together and threatens to keep them apart? (978-1-60282-977-0)

Asher's Fault by Elizabeth Wheeler. Fourteen-year-old Asher Price sees the world in black and white, much like the photos he takes, but when his little brother drowns at the same moment Asher experiences his first same-sex kiss, he can no longer hide behind the lens of his camera and eventually discovers he isn't the only one with a secret. (978-1-60282-982-4)

Love and Devotion by Jove Belle. KC Hall trips her way through life, stumbling into an affair with a married bombshell twice her age. Thankfully, her best friend, Emma Reynolds, is there to show her the true meaning of Love and Devotion. (978-1-60282-965-7)

Rush by Carsen Taite. Murder, secrets, and romance combine to create the ultimate rush. (978-1-60282-966-4)

The Shoal of Time by J.M. Redmann. It sounded too easy. Micky Knight is reluctant to take the case because the easy ones often turn into the hard ones, and the hard ones turn into the dangerous ones. In this one, easy turns hard without warning. (978-1-60282-967-1)

In Between by Jane Hoppen. At the age of 14, Sophie Schmidt discovers that she was born an intersexual baby and sets off on a journey to find her place in a world that denies her true existence. (978-1-60282-968-8)

Secret Lies by Amy Dunne. While fleeing from her abuser, Nicola Jackson bumps into Jenny O'Connor, and their unlikely friendship quickly develops into a blossoming romance—but when it comes down to a matter of life or death, are they both willing to face their fears? (978-1-60282-970-1)

Under Her Spell by Maggie Morton. The magic of love brought Terra and Athene together, but now a magical quest stands between them—a quest for Athene's hand in marriage. Will their passion keep them together, or will stronger magic tear them apart? (978-1-60282-973-2)

Homestead by Radclyffe. R. Clayton Sutter figures getting NorthAm Fuel's newest refinery operational on a rolling tract of land in Upstate New York should take a month or two, but then, she hadn't counted on local resistance in the form of vandalism, petitions, and one furious farmer named Tess Rogers. (978-1-60282-956-5)

Battle of Forces: Sera Toujours by Ali Vali. Kendal and Piper return to New Orleans to start the rest of eternity together, but the return of an old enemy makes their peaceful reunion short-lived, especially when they join forces with the new queen of the vampires. (978-1-60282-957-2)

How Sweet It Is by Melissa Brayden. Some things are better than chocolate. Molly O'Brien enjoys her quiet life running the bakeshop in a small town. When the beautiful Jordan Tuscana returns home, Molly can't deny the attraction—or the stirrings of something more. (978-1-60282-958-9)

The Missing Juliet: A Fisher Key Adventure by Sam Cameron. A teenage detective and her friends search for a kidnapped Hollywood star in the Florida Keys. (978-1-60282-959-6)

Amor and More: Love Everafter edited by Radclyffe and Stacia Seaman. Rediscover favorite couples as Bold Strokes Books authors reveal glimpses of life and love beyond the honeymoon in short stories featuring main characters from favorite BSB novels. (978-1-60282-963-3)

First Love by CJ Harte. Finding true love is hard enough, but for Jordan Thompson, daughter of a conservative president, it's challenging, especially when that love is a female rodeo cowgirl. (978-1-60282-949-7)

Pale Wings Protecting by Lesley Davis. Posing as a couple to investigate the abduction of infants, Special Agent Blythe Kent and Detective Daryl Chandler find themselves drawn into a battle over the innocents, with demons on one side and the unlikeliest of protectors on the other. (978-1-60282-964-0)

Mounting Danger by Karis Walsh. Sergeant Rachel Bryce, an outcast on the police force, is put in charge of the department's newly formed mounted division. Can she and polo champion Callan Lanford resist their growing attraction as they struggle to safeguard the disaster-prone unit? (978-1-60282-951-0)

Meeting Chance by Jennifer Lavoie. When man's best friend turns on Aaron Cassidy, the teen keeps his distance until fate puts Chance in his hands. (978-1-60282-952-7)

At Her Feet by Rebekah Weatherspoon. Digital marketing producer Suzanne Kim knows she has found the perfect love in her new mistress Pilar, but before they can make the ultimate commitment, Suzanne's professional life threatens to disrupt their perfectly balanced bliss. (978-1-60282-948-0)

Show of Force by AJ Quinn. A chance meeting between navy pilot Evan Kane and correspondent Tate McKenna takes them on a roller-coaster ride where the stakes are high, but the reward is higher: a chance at love. (978-1-60282-942-8)

Clean Slate by Andrea Bramhall. Can Erin and Morgan work through their individual demons to rediscover their love for each other, or are the unexplainable wounds too deep to heal? (978-1-60282-943-5)